Max Gunn's Pay Book.

MAX GUNN'S
PAY BOOK.

Press

Graham Lindsay

Published by 99% Press,

an imprint of Lasavia Publishing Ltd.

Auckland, New Zealand

www.lasaviapublishing.com

ISBN: 978-1-991083-09-8

In memory of William Lindsay (1914-1989)
for Robert Lindsay, Tracy Pilet, Giancarlo Vianello

Therefore, since he helps me on the path to Awakening, I should long for an enemy like a treasure discovered in the home, acquired without effort.

Contents

A Game of Two Halves/
The Raft of the *Medusa*

Mountain stones

Deep in the night while I lay quietly after the insects had stilled,
the clear moon rising behind the mountain
shone into my hut.

In the lightening sky I went out alone following no path,
in and out, up and down through fog and mist –
rosy mountains and jade streams in glistening profusion.

I saw pines and oaks ten spans round
and stepped on the stones with my bare feet –
the sound of the water rushing and the wind in my clothes.

If life were like this always I could be happy;
why must I be restrained by other men's fetters?
Alas my friends and colleagues can it be that in old age I will never
    return?

All those battles are as clear today as if they happened yesterday, and
talking or writing about them brings back too many memories and
night-time nightmares . . . I would rather leave the past alone and
carry on with my garden.

One

The fog lifted and the sun coming over the fence cut him off at the knees. The bit of dirty card that caught his eye earlier caught his eye again. He peered into the shallows. Now it looked like a photo, in fact it looked like one of the photos he used to carry in his Pay Book. What was it doing here! Had Liz been having a clean-out? He bent for a closer look and the ground opened its jaws. *Ah me bloody back!*

He was tuckered out, boy was he tuckered out: he was dog tucker, reeling in the wake of a flock of sparrows corkscrewing through the garden, hanging onto the shovel for dear life, a roar in his ears like the Huka Falls, his face white as a ghost.

The frost had retreated to the edge of the garden, the shadow had ebbed before he dared move a muscle when he cast round slowly, telling himself for the umpteenth time it was just as well he'd started the digging earlier than usual because at the rate he was going . . .

Alhamdulillah!

How could he have forgotten? He'd been looking forward to it all week, all year come to that: since the close shave at Ballymore; the second round at the Concord Oval where Jones split the forward packs like a thoroughbred clearing a brush fence, drew his man and fed Kirwan; Kirwan's trademark gallop, the slide on the one knee and dot down, followed by the planted-right-foot-rise-to-the-feet in the one movement!

He shook his head and a grin lifted his cheeks. Now that put a different complexion on the matter. The French were inclined to go up a gear against their arch rivals; it could well be the game of the year. He unfastened the pouch and drew out his fob-watch and holding it at arm's length tucked in his chin and squinted. *Tempus fidgets.*

He turned the blade and drew a roll of weeds behind him then another and another. By and by he was a boatman on the Canaletto or for that matter the river in the town where the game kicked off at 3.00. He'd grown up on an Avon – another river called river. He could see the day coming when it would be called the Avon River *something-or-other*. Latex brimming from the severed taproots twinkled like stars in the black earth. *Uno, due, tre, quattro, cinque, sei, sette uomini . . . Seven men under the stars . . .*

A blackbird landed on the fence beside him and gave him the once over. He winked at it and it scrabbled at the tin and launched itself cackling and squirting a line of uric acid. He tipped back his canvas hat and followed it out over the back fence rising and swooping over hollows rimmed with wispy stalks of grey grass before dropping out of sight. Slowly then he lifted his eyes to the poplar windbreak locked in frost haze on the far side of the paddock. Beyond it was an orchard that had once been his – he and Chas were up in the last of the pink winter light when he caught a movement out of the corner of his eye. Having come into the orchard to let them know it was dinnertime, that they had families waiting for them, she was going up and down the rows gathering the prunings . . .

'Eh, what's that?'

'When do you want your coffee?'

'When are you having yours?'

'I'm ready when you are.'

'Anything in the box?'

She shook her head. 'I'll try again later,' she said.

'You'll wear the drive out.'

'Don't be cheeky!'

They'd been back two months now and still there was nothing: did Ned have the pricker with them or something? It was the third time he'd flown. The first had been in the cargo bay of a Dakota – never again, he'd sworn, but at the thought of spending twelve hours in a coach seat with his back he'd given Liz the nod and she'd gone ahead and made the bookings. And he had to admit flying had come a long way since the war: no sooner were they off the ground than they were coming into land. No sooner had the flight attendant pushed the trolley up one side of the sky than she was pushing it up the other to collect the trays.

'You should do it the other way round,' he quipped.

'Believe me, we would if we could. Don't you want your grapes?'

'Prefer them in a bottle.'

She came back with two splits.

'You better have mine,' he said to Liz.

'Did she call your bluff?'

'Jesus,' breathed Ned catching sight of his father crossing the concourse, shuffling his gammy leg ahead of him; wearing his mustard-coloured suit jacket, his blue-and-white checked brushed-cotton shirt and green cords. Wings of hair like comet tails soared above his ears: it was a toss-up between Dagwood Bumstead and a yellow-eyed penguin. Liz smiling beatifically beached in his wake.

The flight attendant stopped to wish them a pleasant visit. Crouching beside their bags, removing the labels, she gave Ned a long look. He looked at his parents: they were looking at him too. What the . . .? He wasn't about to sell them short, if that's what they were thinking. As for the flight attendant, he was too appalled by the airline scarf – a blend of Isadora Duncan, a lemon meringue pie and Richard Pearse – to give her the time of day. It was a tableau by Caravaggio. Then she rose on her haunches and high heels and like a cow in a milking shed trotted after her colleagues.

'How was it?' said Ned.

'The flight?' said Max, squinting sideways up at Ned through pupils the size of BB pellets, eyes sunk deep in their sockets, the twinkle gone, 'Flying is an eerie unnatural sensation that frankly gives me the tom-tits.'

'You go,' said Max.

'No you,' said Liz.

'Can't it wait till tomorrow?'

'It'll only take a couple of minutes,' said Ned.

'So what's the hurry then?'

'I wanted to ask you something.'

'In that case . . . . Soil looks okay, what is it?'

'Loam I think.'

'How deep?'

'Couple of feet.'

'How do you know?'

'I dug a hole for the compost; even the clay looks alright.'

'I see what you mean.'

'I thought I might mix it up with the topsoil?'

'Not a bad idea . . . Let me know if there's something I can do while

I'm here, won't you?'

'Actually, there is something.'

'What?'

'Could you have a look at this tree?'

'Why, what's wrong with it?'

'The bark's splitting, that's why I took these leaders off.'

Max nodded.

'Then I had a go at pruning it.'

'I can see that.'

'I wasn't sure if I was doing the right thing or not?'

'Is it worth it? How long are you going to be here?'

'A few years, maybe; but it's not just for us is it? It would be for the tree and for whoever gets the benefit of it after us. Plus it would improve the value of the place.'

'So that's it!'

They moved on.

'What do you think of the shed?' said Ned pushing the door open. The tinplate wobble-boarded in the wind, the fig clattered against the grimy cobwebbed pane.

'Not a bad size,' said Max, withdrawing.

'Have a proper look.'

'Listen, Ned I need to put my feet up.'

'It won't take long.'

Max sighed and ran his eyes dutifully along the rolls of old carpet, up over the stacks of leftover paint pots, back along the wall: the studs, dwangs and chicken-wire-over-tarpaper. He was about to back out again when something caught his eye: a ray of sunlight between the fig's leafless branches was playing in a pool of blue enamel. Irises widening, Max found the black of the newly-minted pneumatic tyre and what little light was left in them went out. He could have done with a barrow like this; his had a mind of its own, the solid rubber wheel leaning first one way then the other. Adding insult to injury, it too had a gammy leg: the bolt holding it to the tray having rusted out. More to the point he could have done with a hand; they were doing it tough, he and Liz. He let the door bang.

At the back door he drew Ned aside.

'What's the story about smoking inside?'

'Sorry Pop, no can do.'

'Eh?'

'Boss's orders.'

'What about the toilet?'

'It's inside.'

'But what if the fanlight's open?'

'Sorry Pop, it won't work.'

'Shit!'

Two

One night it was the National Orchestra. Max surprised himself: in the interval when Liz went to find the Ladies, partly by way of acknowledging the shout and partly due to the attention his seniority seemed to be attracting, he announced it was the first time he'd been to hear the National Orchestra.

Going by the lukewarm reception however, he gathered it wasn't quite the thing to say. That said, Ned was more concerned about the woman in the sequin dress, who having calved from her pod for a nosy and having been richly rewarded by Max's candour, was on the point of reporting back when she became aware she too was being observed; in short the ball on top of the pyramid on top of the box might have toppled had she not given herself a good shake.

Another night it was a Swedish film, Ned's choice, a reprise from the recent festival. Max shuffled sideways into the row, Liz hurried after him; Jette stood back and Ned who'd overlooked the roll in the hay found himself sitting next to his mother. When the lights came up, Jette sprang to her feet and Ned, on the pretext of beating the exodus, wasn't far behind.

The cold air avalanching into the quadrangle was knocking over sandwich boards, lifting the skirts of shrubs, blowing a gale up Ned's trousers when Max wearing his summer trousers and open-necked shirt emerged.

'Aren't you cold?' said Ned.

'No,' said Max, eyeballing him and adding, when they'd gained a few yards on Liz and Jette, 'Not a bad film. I wasn't too impressed by some of the scenes though: not on my account, on your mother's.'

One day it was a drive to the coast. Eyes narrowing, Max lowered the passenger window to the same sweep-of-bay-round-to-grey-cliffs as at home, Norfolk pines batting their eyelashes: if the mountain wouldn't come to Muhammad then Muhammad would have to go to the mountain; Liz could walk the pup along this beach. Then he grunted and wound up his window: they'd have to sort it out themselves, it was out of his hands; it was their pigeon now.

Ned parked on the cliffs and Max wandered off, the flat of his palms tucked behind his belt, while Jette and Liz unloaded the picnic things. Ned offered to help but got shooed off.

'Catch up with your father,' said Liz.

Max and Ned followed the path down through the park. At the bottom Max eased himself gingerly onto a bench.

'Stay here,' said Ned, 'and I'll bring the car round.'

'What for!?'

'To save you from having to walk back up.'

'Just give me a minute to get my breath back,' said Max, 'you won't go away, will you?'

Ned looked at him.

When they started back up Max went at the steps two at a time.

'What's your hurry?' said Ned.

'No hurry,' said Max, grinning now.

Two young mothers, wheeling pushchairs down the slope, dark glasses on their crowns winking like tiaras, like alien eyes, rubber-necked Max; a tall ship ghosted the bay. He grinned again. At the top of the hill he hooked his arms over the eight-barred gate and hung there done-in, face red as a beetroot, eyes like boiled eggs. Ned returning to the car to get Max his jersey got an unconvincing wink.

Another day it was a drive to where the plain lapped the town's back doorstep.

'It'll be ready in fifteen weeks,' said the breeder.

'That'll do us,' said Max applying his moniker to the cheque with his customary calligraphic flourish.

One afternoon they had a session outside so Max could smoke, huddling in a corner of the yard in the washed-out sun every scrap of wind seemed to want to warm itself by as well. Ned got out a piece of writing he was thinking of sharing with his students about a man who planted trees so one day they would shade the farmhouse; it was written from his daughter's point of view long after the job had been done and the man had passed on.

'Not bad,' said Max, handing it to Liz.

'Not bad,' said Liz, handing it back.

The mist thickened. The sun reddened like an ember and went out.

He was having his last cigarette for the day when Ned, on his way round the house closing up, came into the kitchen. Reaching for the blind-pull he caught an eye among the reflections. Max's lips parted, a smile flickered.

'What?' Ned mouthed.

The lips closed.

'Can you lock the door when you come in?' he mouthed again and dropped the blind.

One morning Max said, 'The shower tricks you. You go to turn it off and cold water comes out.'

'You have to turn the nozzle away from you first,' said Ned, 'or turn the handle at arm's length. Sorry, I should've warned you.'

'I'm not complaining,' said Max.

All the same he'd touched a sore point. Having not long finished doing up their last house, Ned was staring down the barrel of having to go through the same process all over again with as likely as not the same outcome: not getting to enjoy the improvements. It took years to find the place where your bits and pieces fitted, to find the shop where the clothes suited you; a decent hardware store, a plant shop, a supermarket, a good dentist, a doctor, a mechanic, a lawyer, friends. Settling-in was a lifetime occupation; in the meantime life passed you by. What got his goat was it was supposed to be his holiday, yet as soon as Max and Liz departed he'd to put his head down. What rankled most was that while his old job had been pure escapism, with the new one there was no escape. The after-image of a hillside in Central deep in mauve shadow, deep in blue-green sunset nagged him like a siren.

Another morning they were waiting for Doreen to turn up. Liz was going to spend her last night with her cousin; sister practically, as they often said, having holidayed turnabout in the country with Liz's family and in town with Doreen's, each wishing the other's family was theirs. Since her divorce, Doreen had gone from one flat to another, from one daughter, one city, one country, one lover to another and while she sometimes regretted losing her husband Liz sometimes regretted not losing hers. Besides it would also be an opportunity for Max and Ned to have a session together.

'What are you going to do?' Ned asked.

'Go on the bash,' said Liz, eyes flashing, 'go on the town, let our hair down, live it up. What we don't do won't be worth doing.'

Ned looked at her uncertainly.

The sun had climbed as far into the sky as it was possible to climb and still be called morning when Doreen turned up looking as if she'd already begun to have second thoughts. No sooner were they out the door than Max proposed a trip to the pub.

'Not for a drink, let me hasten to add, to get something for later. It's a bit early even for me,' he said, rubbing his hands together.

'No need,' said Ned, 'we've got a cupboard full of grog.'

'What have you got?'

'Chardonnay, sauvignon blanc . . .'

'White wine?'

'Yeah.'

'Not my cup of tea, Ned, how about a flagon of sherry?'

Ned scratched his head.

'My shout,' said Max.

Still Ned looked doubtful.

'You'd finish it off, wouldn't you? It wouldn't be like pouring it down the sink or anything, would it?'

'We could use it for cooking.'

'I didn't mean any old plonk.'

'But that's what sherry is, isn't it?'

'Listen, there's sherry and there's sherry. Sherry can be a high class drink, I'll have you know.'

'You mean more expensive?'

'That, yes, not that price is always a measure of quality.'

'What about just getting a bottle then?'

'I was hoping to leave something with you. How about we see what they've got and if we don't like it we can always go somewhere else?'

The assistants' faces were puffy from having not long been washed. They left off their blow by blow accounts of the night's adventures to look along the aisle to where their first customers for the day were dithering before the shelves of fortified wine then bit their tongues as the seventy-five centilitre bottle of medium sweet sherry bobbled toward them on the conveyor belt.

'Pull in here,' said Max.

'No need,' said Ned. 'It's still half-full.'

'Our contribution for all the running around,' said Max, leaning back in his seat to claw a fistful of scrunched-up notes from his pocket.

'You don't have to do that.'

'Can't take it with you,' said Max. 'Don't think you're cutting us short. There's plenty here to get us back.'

'Giveaway,' said Ned, hanging a figurine on the mirror.

'Who's that supposed to be?'

'Rouge-Thomas,' said Ned, reading the plinth.

'Could've been worse, I suppose,' said Max, barely able to contain himself.

'You mean it could've been Condom?'

Ned took the long way back, ducking his head to glimpse the snow-covered mountains under a lemon-yellow nor' west arc, wishing he could keep on going to the edge of the plain, up through the tussock-covered foothills, the towering beech forests, over the pass and down the zigzag razorback to the rātā-choked gorge, across the swampy plain with its drifts of remnant kahikatea and out to the port, there get on a fishing boat and not come back. Only trouble was the Canterbury Plains took so long to cross that long before you had your folly had caught up with you like Rover in *The Prisoner*.

'Do you know someone called Vanessa?' said Jette holding the phone out to Ned.

'We've been invited to a restaurant,' said Ned handing it back.

'Who by?'

'Lao Peng You.'

'Who was that then?'

'His girlfriend, I suppose.'

'What happened to Deirdre?'

'I don't know, maybe he's turned over a new girlfriend? Pop, is it okay with you if we go to a restaurant?'

'By all means.'

'You sure?'

'It's no skin off my nose.'

'You don't mind keeping an eye on Troy?'

'I'll tell him when it's his bedtime, if that's what you mean.'

'Like hell you will!' said Troy.

'Don't speak to your grandfather like that!' said Jette.

'I'll speak to him how I like!'

'You sure you can you manage? It's just that it's an old friend.'

'Do what you have to do!'

Three

The dishes had been done; the table had been cleared except for the bottle. He sat hunched over the table, glasses on the sideboard, hair sticking up. After a number of discreet glances Ned still couldn't make out whether the bottle was empty or full – perhaps the level was disguised by the base of the neck, but that hardly seemed credible? He wished then he hadn't looked because anticipating being checked on was why the bottle had been left out?

'Everything okay, Dad?'

Max turned a card and leant over, peering at it through blurry eyes.

'How was the evening?'

'The food was okay.'

'Like that was it?'

'We got kicked out.'

'Business slow?' said Max looking up. He looked shattered.

'It was, but that's not why we got kicked out.'

'Oh?'

'It's probably not worth talking about.'

'No need to on my account.'

'It's not that. When the waiter asked if everything was alright . . .'

'As they do.'

'As they do.'

'And which can mean a number of things.'

'In this case probably because they wanted to close up. Anyway our friend said it wasn't.'

'What's his name?'

'Peng.'

'Chinese?'

'Lao Peng You.'

'He'd have to be with a name like that. What was the problem?'

'According to him the meat was green.'

'And was it?'

'Mine wasn't. Did you think it was green, Jette?'

'No,' said Jette, shaking her head.

'And what did the waiter have to say about that?'

'Not much. He said he'd tell the cook. "While you're there," said Peng, "tell him the spices have gone off, the rice was dry, the naan was stale and the roti was flat."'

'Bit of a comedian is he?'

'Roti's supposed to be flat,' said Jette, 'it's unleavened bread.'

'"I mean it lacks a certain oomph," said Peng. "And tell him to check the use-by date on the yoghurt."'

'We don't eat out much and often when we do we're disappointed – especially when you can get a week's groceries for the same price – but the food was great. What got me was him mimicking the waiter's accent.'

'Cripes, that's not on.'

'So then the waiter asked us again if everything was alright.'

'Just checking, just to be on the safe side.'

'Yeah, to give Peng a chance to change his tune.'

'And did he?'

'No, but I think he knew he'd gone out on a limb because while he was trying to carry on in the same vein he was running out of steam.'

'Oomph.'

'That's right, but it must've occurred to him he was painting himself into a corner because suddenly he stopped mid-sentence and said, "Why don't you go back where you came from?"'

'And what did the waiter have to say about that?'

'He said, he would have to speak to his manager.'

'What were you doing while all this was going on?'

'I was just staring at the table thinking what had already been a long night was about to get longer. The windows were steamed up. Cars were going by on the wet road. The only other customers, two couples, had long gone. I was expecting the cops to arrive at any moment.'

'And this Peng, did he not have anything to say for himself?'

'"Looks like I've done it now," he said, as if we were all in it together. The man who'd been sitting at the cash register for the previous half-hour turned out to be the manager. He was short, sturdily-built and he didn't look too impressed.'

'I'll bet.'

'"What's going on?" he said. Realising we weren't going to say anything, Peng set off on a ham-fisted explanation that was going nowhere and soon petered out. "You are a troublemaker," said the manager. "I couldn't agree more," Peng said.'

'And that was it?'

'Then the manager told us to finish our drinks, pay our bill and leave. I don't know about you Jette, but I felt about this high. It was like being accused of something I hadn't done and having no comeback. We got up and pushed our chairs in and got our coats and paid our bills. We were halfway across the car park when Peng caught up and suggested going somewhere for coffee. I said I thought we should probably be getting back. Perhaps he thought I was being diplomatic, I don't know, anyway he said they probably should too.'

'No need to cut your evening short on my account.'

'It wasn't that, I was glad to get out of there. Even Jette was flagging and she generally keeps her end up. Besides we can have coffee here if we want it, cheaper too.'

'And does this friend of yours make a habit of this sort of thing?'

'It's the first time I've seen him like that. I did wonder though if it was something he and a mutual friend had tried on perhaps at the same place.'

'The reason I ask is because I've known one or two blokes to behave in a similar way and what it came down to was a drink problem. How much had he had to drink, if you don't mind my asking?'

'Two bottles of wine.'

'It's a lot, but not that bad.'

'I'd have been out on my ear on one!'

'Had he been drinking beforehand, do you know?'

'Not as far as I know. He was on autopilot when he came in, till he'd had his first drink. We were there on time. Vanessa arrived about twenty minutes after us and he came in about twenty minutes after her, probably via the bottle store, which is probably what I should have done.'

'And who's this Vanessa?'

'One of his students I think, or former students.'

'Oh?'

'I know it happens, some of my old lecturers were a bit like that. In fact one of them turned up on my old girlfriend's doorstep shortly after I'd arrived. In fairness they may have had something going on before she hooked up with me. They looked a bit embarrassed, she apologised; he made himself scarce. We'd run out of small talk by the time Peng arrived, the bottles in a paper bag clamped to his chest. There were no hullos or anything, he sat down, got a corkscrew from his pocket, opened a bottle, poured himself a glass, drank it in one draught, refilled the glass. The waiter arrived with the menus, had a discussion with Peng about opening his own bottle and wanted to take the other away.'

'Corkage.'

'Without looking at the waiter or the bottle Peng reached down and placed it against the table leg. Having made the mistake of not getting anything on the way, then seeing what the house prices were like, with things being a bit tight for us from the move, I'd decided to manage without. But the wine Peng was drinking was so redolent of the French countryside – not that I've been there of course – I'd gladly have accepted a glass had it been offered. He didn't even offer Vanessa a glass and she'd have had less to come and go on than us.'

'I could've spared you a few bob.'

'Thanks, Pop, no we're fine.'

'And this Peng, what does he do for a crust?'

'Teaches cello, you might have heard him playing something on the radio?'

'I read something a few months ago, in the *Listener* perhaps, about a cello teacher who'd been tortured by the Red Guards?'

'That'll be him. They kept him in a broom cupboard for six months. He said he kept himself sane by rehearsing Bach's *Cello Suites* on a broom handle, air cello.'

'It's a wonder they didn't make him sit on it?'

'Eh?'

'It's a common enough torture sitting people on irregularly-shaped objects for long periods. How did you meet?'

'The mutual friend . . . Some friend, you're probably thinking?'

25

'Not at all, besides friends can be enemies and enemies can be friends or to put it another way if you didn't have any enemies you wouldn't have any friends and vice versa. As for this Peng, it could be just the boot up the bum the doctor ordered.'

Four

Slippers of earth fell off his gumboots as he crossed the turning-bay then turning side-on shuffled between the outside dunny and the car into the one corner of the carport with a wall on two sides. Placing a palm on the old dining table, the other on his knee he lowered himself to the packing case's cushion of folded sugar bags then forearms on thighs and breathing heavily lowered his head. After an age he roused himself and shucked off the gumboots. Liz's laddered stockings worn over Everest socks to save wear looked like busted spiders' nests; the horn of a big toe poked through the toe of each. Then he slipped his feet into his slippers and shuffled up the ramp. *Faith for Today*, reaching through the gaps in the louvers to buttonhole him, was homing in on its punchline. He shook his head from side to side and looked up at a towering cloud which had gathered over the plain. The plastic fly strips rattled like sheep-dags, the theme music for the news took up the baton, Liz took off her glasses and laying them on the open Bible looked up at him through shining eyes.

'Saved by the bell,' he said.

Liz pushed back in her chair.

'Where are you off to?'

'Where do you think?'

'Hope springs a turtle.'

He leaned over the radio stirring his coffee. When she got back in he turned it off.

'Is everything alright?' she asked.

'I've got no time for Rogernomics, the Round Table, et cetera, et cetera. I see no resemblance whatsoever between this government and that of M.J. Savage. The priorities of his government were unemployment, housing, health and education; what they should be for a Labour party. The Sabbath was made for men, not men for the Sabbath and the same applies to the economy. Enough! Anything or nothing?'

'Just some advertising.'

He grunted and looked up at the calendar, a Greenpeace calendar. The picture for the month looked like a stream of carbon dioxide. He filled the saucer, lifted it to his lips and slurped.

'Well it's alright for some,' he said, putting his hat on.

'Oh, you poor thing.'

Lining up the forefinger of one hand behind the forefinger of the other, he closed an eye and made a clucking sound out of the side of his mouth. 'You'll do me,' he said and winked.

'Don't forget you've got an appointment this Thursday.'

'What, who with?'

'Ross. I thought that's why you were looking at the calendar?'

'Alhamdulillah!'

He paused on the ramp (variously the bridge in his temple garden, a houseboat bridge or just a bloody lump of concrete). The cloud was closer, darker. Leaning his forearms on the rail he teased the tobacco fibres along the gutter, rolled them back and forth, drew the gummed edge over the tip of his moistened tongue, pinched out the nose hairs, struck a match, drew a puff, spat it out, spat out the match and flicked it into the garden. The mamaku at his foot caught his eye, its growing tip moist and black as a dog's nose, its longest frond trembling in a zephyr before switching to a metronomic dance. He considered his attempts to plug the gaps in the hedge: the sticks of kindling threaded through chicken-wire – nets for catching tidal mists or will-o-the-wisps, maquettes for sails – wouldn't have detained a hedgehog let alone a pup.

'Give up smoking or find yourself a new doctor,' was what his old doctor had said.

'Can't teach an old dog new tricks,' he'd replied, 'I've been smoking since I was twelve; tried giving up once, after the first week I was ready to throttle someone, after the second I was ready to throttle myself.'

'There's a million to one chance,' his new doctor had said.

'I've got one question and one question only: do I have to give up smoking?'

'If you want to smoke that's your business,' said his new doctor.

'You'll do me,' he'd said.

'Are you up for it then?'

'What, now?'

'No time like the present.'

'I'll try anything once.'

'Up you get then.'

He arranged Max's arms across his chest – 'Would it help if I crossed my fingers too?' – took his head between his hands and wrenched it one way then the other; put his right hand under Max's back and dropped his weight on him like a pro wrestler; did a similar thing to Max's pelvis till Max yelped. Next day he was on tenterhooks but for two days following he felt better than he had in months, till the pain returned with a vengeance. The pattern repeated itself.

Back in the carport, he sized up the torso of bluegum on the chopping block, part of a load gratis from his old workplace. Bluegum as you know is best split green, the corkscrew grain is easiest opened then. What happened in his time there of course was other work came first, leaving the rainy day work to pile up and dry out. The toughest nuts had been offloaded on the old sorcerer.

'Mahleesh,' he muttered, sidling up to it, eyeing it sidelong, the flats of his hands tucked behind his belt.

Scars like pick-up sticks crisscrossed top and bottom; it was like picking a lock. He looked at the axe. The inside shoulder of the hickory handle was chewed and splintered by overstrikes. The fog that came and went willy-nilly had rusted the head, the butt was split: to keep it on he'd chocked the eye with four-inch nails but these had skewed the head; to get a clean strike he had to add sideways arc to his delivery. He cupped his hands and spat – the throat being slender and glassy, spit helped grip – hefted the axe over his shoulder and threw it like a slingshot. The blade lodged.

'Bugger!'

Using the heel of his palm to dislodge the axe jarred his hand so he used a lump of wood wrapped in an old towel. He got the blade free but the effort took more out of him than the blow. He paused and examined the blade. It looked like a row of teeth. He'd tried sharpening it with a hand file but what he needed was an electric grinder. Perhaps he'd ask the bloke in the mower shop to have a look at it next time he was in the village? Meanwhile he was beached. He was reaching for his tobacco pouch when Liz came round the corner.

'What do you want for your lunch?'

'What are you having?'

'The usual.'

'What's that?'

'A boiled egg and a piece of toast.'

'You'll fade away.'

'Who are you kidding?'

'Got any meat?'

'There's the bit of tongue in the fridge?'

'That'll do.'

'A couple?'

'One.'

'That's not much for a working man.'

'If I want more, I'll get it.'

He sallied back to the chopping block and adjusted the torso a few compass points – all he needed was a foot in the door. He drew back the axe and threw. Bang, the head came flying straight back up at him, nearly took his head off; the handle flew from his grasp. Hands on his knees he stooped, blowing hard.

'Lunch is on the table!'

'Where are you off to?'

'I told you, shopping.'

'Bugger, I forgot.'

'Can't you leave it just this once? I'm only going to the village.'

'It won't take a minute,' he said, springing the bonnet, drawing the dipstick from the engine block like a sword from stone, pulling it through the oily rag, poking it back, drawing it out again and checking the tip.

'Clean as a whistle.'

Liz settled back while he topped up the oil then lifted her hand to the key again.

'Hold your horses! I don't want you blowing a foo-foo valve.'

Liz sat back again while he checked the radiator and topped it up too.

'Don't forget you're not Stirling Moss,' he said, dropping the bonnet and leaning on it with his forearm.

'What was that?' she said, revving the engine.

'You're not Stirling Moss!'

'I'll be home about two to make you a cup of tea.'

He guided her back, though she had already gone quite far enough, giving her the benefit of the doubt to make up for having delayed her. The car kept going back.

'That'll do you!' he said.

But the rear wheels, having mounted the border, were already rocking back and forth in the hollow made by previous indiscretions.

'Alhamdulillah!'

'Any damage?' she asked, winding the window down, smiling.

'Just a few herbs.'

'What's that?'

'Carry on!'

The car stuttered up the driveway and out onto the road. He heard the blast of a truck horn, the shudder of locked wheels jumping on the seal and braced himself. Air brakes hissing, the truck rolled past the mouth of the driveway, the driver beginning the long haul back up through the gears.

Five

He lifted a corner of the sandwich, eyed the mottled grey meat then picked up the tea. In the bedroom he eased himself onto the edge of the bed and when he could put it off no longer leant sideways, face screwed up, eyes clenched, groaning and whimpering and breathing shallow and hard and brought up his legs. After another spell he reached out an arm, switched on the lamp and picked up the small book with the photo of a kakemono on the cover – calligraphy like rain running down a windowpane plastered with acer leaves – removed the bookmark (a blade of grey card from an empty book of cigarette papers), glanced at the poem, laid the book on his chest and closed his eyes:

The moon in the window
The thief left behind.

The wind woke him: it had stopped. He counted his breaths, hoping to drop off again and might have succeeded had it not been so cold. His blanket glittered with frost. His shoulder, his hip, his thigh ached. He got up and wrapping himself in the blanket went to the window. The garden had been flattened again, the shadows of the broken stalks telling him yet again he was too old for this game. It had been his intention to light the fire but it was light enough outside to walk himself warm. The moon soared over Kugami: he was halfway up the mountainside when something made him turn back.

Nearing the hut he heard noises: a visitor, he thought, quickening his step. He was on the porch when the door burst open and somebody leapt past him and ran down the path. With a sinking heart he watched his visitor depart, the swinging bundle donging and all but throwing him to the ground. He listened to the diminishing footsteps, the grumbling of the disturbed snow monkeys. He'd lost the lot – kettle, cup, rice steamer, Han Shan, kakemonos, brushes, ink-stone, paper, lamp and begging bowl – everything except the zafu in a corner like the moon's dark twin or a wheel off a cart. He was on the point of following the thief to give it to him as well, was halfway out the door when he paused and backed up and sat on it instead. By and by the moon hopped into his lap and he looked up:

The moon in the window
The thief left behind.

'How are you feeling?'

He opened an eye.

'Did you think I was a burglar?'

'Ha, a cat burglar.'

'Sorry I'm late.'

'What time is it?'

'Two-thirty.'

'Half the day gone and nothing done.'

'What's your hurry?'

'I've got an appointment.'

'Who with?'

'The idiot box, who do you think?'

'Let me guess, the soccer? I'm good, aren't I?'

'Off you go.'

'Me bones are tired,' he said as they crossed the driveway wide as a riverbed, as the life of a man the sun takes all day to cross.

'How do you mean?' said Ned.

'Christ Almighty, do I have to spell it out!'

'Spell what out?'

'Alhamdulillah!'

'Listen, you haven't got a hope in hell of splitting this and if you put it on whole you'll burn the house down.'

'It's not like I'm pushed for time, you know.'

'Whose idea was it?'

'Whose idea was what?'

'To bring you the fag-ends?'

'It was mine.'

'Yours?'

'Yes, I told Angus to bring what they couldn't split.'

'They're rubbing your nose in it.'

'What are you talking about?'

'You don't play the game. How can they brag about their spoils if you're too high and mighty to put your snout in the trough? You turned your back on the RSA, you opted out of the Club, you vote Green; you're like a red rag to a bull. One day you'll wake up and find there is no pension.'

'So what do you call this; they don't owe me a brass razoo?'

He was at work, Liz was shopping. According to Ned their visitor (a tall man in shorts and singlet, grinning from ear to ear, carrying a side of lamb dressed like a bride in his outstretched arms) got a cool reception. Of course it's possible he didn't say who he was and that Ned didn't ask, but putting two and two together came up with: Board cancels bonuses; Board member turns up at worker's house with side of lamb. Of course it was possible Ned had tailored his account to fit the remarks he'd overheard them making over a drink or two and couldn't or wouldn't change his account as a matter of pride or principle. That the job and the house might have been due to a good word put in for him by Oldham on account of their having served in the same company wouldn't have registered either. However, as far as Liz was concerned the hue of the household's political colours was long overdue correction. As the daughter of a South Canterbury dairy farmer who'd declined the proposal on the last day of school of a boy due to inherit the family farm, who could have done very well thank you, she and Oldham were practically stable mates. In any case Ned had been riding for a fall for some time. So in a move harking back to her ultimatum of the 1950s – when the long hand of McCarthyism was casting its shadow over those with leanings toward a fairer society, when Max had resigned his CP membership – she rounded on him and Max, to keep the peace conceding she might have a point, she got on the blower.

An hour's drive following the weed-choked, virulent yellow river through skin and bone hills brought them to a grey tin letterbox on which Oldham's and his wife's initials and shared surname in red lettering somehow managed to combine personal candour with the gravity of a battle-tunic ribbon. The cattle-stop shook them from their stupor but then the meandering driveway lulled them again so that when they emerged from the tunnel of plane trees onto a large turning bay Ned was in two minds whether to sashay up to the door or be circumspect. The sight of Oldham in a director's chair, knotted white handkerchief on his head, trouser legs rolled, like Canute before the pond of grey metal settled his hash, the Morris Minor baulked like a horse at a water jump.

They abandoned the car for the drifts of pea-metal. As they drew closer they saw that Oldham was shelling peas into a white enamel basin in his lap. Behind him a heavy maroon door opened onto an entranceway chocker with oilskins and swandris and gumboots and riding boots, from a side door came the sounds of a table being set. With measured slowness Oldham inclined his slab-like face and considered them through narrowed flinty eyes. The cicadas' cacophony went up a notch, the shadow of a small plane passed over. Ned mumbled an apology and there being no further business and nothing to suggest the sounds from the dining room in any way concerned them, they turned and returned the way they had come.

Over drinks that night, Liz gave Max a blow by blow account. By then he could afford a grin. Besides, the unsavoury hint of a quid pro quo aside, a side of lamb was better than a kick up the bum. Oldham wasn't a bad bloke, whenever he came to the school for a board meeting he more often than not went looking for Max afterward, abandoning his pickup in the middle of the drive and leaving the door open. And Max, hoeing weeds would straighten, tip back his hat and grin shyly. That said a month or two passed before they caught up again, the occasion being the receipt of their copies of the War History Branch's monograph on Point 175 in which Oldham was quoted saying the sights of the German rifles he'd picked up when the dust had settled hadn't been adjusted from the range at which they would have been set at the outset of the battle when it was miles instead of football paddocks. The thing was they'd been there and now they were here; two of perhaps a dozen men in the district who woke in the night for similar reasons and who were rattled by the army's tanks firing blanks at the A & P Show.

'Have you told your doctor this?'

'No, why should I?'

'Don't you think he might be interested?'

'No.'

'Why not?'

'Well for a start he's not that sort of a doctor.'

'What sort of doctor is he?'

'He's a chiropractor.'

'I suppose he told you your spine was out of alignment?'

'Well, as a matter of fact . . .'

'He manipulates it?'

'It's called spinal decompression.'

'Does it work?'

'I'm still here aren't I?'

'Why did you change doctors?'

'The last one gave me an ultimatum?'

'Joseph?'

'Yes.'

'What did he say?'

'He told me give up smoking or find myself a new doctor.'

'Why?'

'Didn't want my blood on his hands I suppose.'

'How do you mean?'

'In his opinion I'd be dead in a couple of years if I didn't give up smoking.'

'How long ago was that?'

'Two and a half years.'

'You're showing a profit'

'Living on borrowed time more like.'

'Why didn't you go to an ordinary doctor?'

'I had an ordinary doctor. He was more concerned about the smoking than fixing the limp.'

'What limp?'

'Are you blind as well as deaf?'

'I mean, didn't it occur to you the limp might be smoking-related?'

'The new bloke reckons it's a pinched nerve.'

'There's a big difference between getting two years and being told your spine is out of alignment.'

'You're not kidding!'

'Why don't you get a third opinion?'

'Listen, I've got a touch of emphysema, I've got high blood pressure, I've got a history of heart disease . . . the list goes on. If it wasn't smoking, it'd be something else.'

'It's not cancer?'

'Not as far as I know.'

'So what is it then?'

'I thought you might be able to help me there.'

'I don't know the first thing about medicine!'

'I know that, I just thought you might know something I don't.'

'I could make an appointment.'

'Who with?'

'I'd have to have a look in the phonebook or I could ring the hospital?'

'Forget it. When your time's up, your time's up.'

'For what it's worth I'd say you had at least 10 years.'

'Would you?'

He was grasping at straws. He turned the page:

Pine needles on my doorstep:
How lonely I feel.

Six

Might have to put the acid on Ned, he thought watching fronds of steam curl round tongues of peeling enamel on the bathroom ceiling.

Sill could do with a lick too. What did he say last time he was up? 'You could manage that.' 'It's not that so much,' I said. 'What is it then?' 'It's the getting up and down the ladder.' 'We're getting on a bit, you know,' added Liz. 'But you're only in your sixties and Dad's only in his seventies. What if you hold the ladder while he gets up or he holds the ladder while you get up?' 'We won't be round forever, you know,' said Liz.

Everywhere he looked, jobs were piling up, even with Liz doing her bit: tools that needed oiling, plants that needed re-potting, citrus that needed pruning, the spare bedroom could do with a new light cord; cockroaches were freight-hopping on the wood he carried into the house . . . Had Ned been a bit closer they could have knocked them off together then had a beer and a natter and watched the footy. Liz would have been in her element with the kids around.

He looked down: the corporation had gone; the bit of old rope wouldn't have hurt a fly. He shut his eyes and slid under and came up spluttering, got out dripping and rubbed the mirror. The old man in the village he winked at thinking there but for the grace of God winked back. At the first scrape, a trickle of blood set off down his upper lip. He poked out his tongue, tasted rusty gunmetal, cupped a handful of cold water to it, dabbed it with the towel and stuck a pinch of toilet tissue on it.

'Flash as a Chow on a bike,' he said, shuffling into the kitchen, fingers tucked behind his belt.

'Adolf the White,' said Liz.

'Don't get me started.'

'Would I do a thing like that?'

'I wouldn't put it past you.'

'How's the back?'

'Holding up.'

'Do you want your sandwiches now or shall I put them away?'

'Put them away. I might have one later.'

He shuffled into the lounge and switched on the television. While it was warming up he put a match to the fire. Gouts of pearly smoke poured up the chimney, the paper erupted, the kindling caught and roared and collapsed. He built a log cabin on the flaming wreckage and straightened. For so early in the afternoon it was dark, even for winter. The Graf Spey that had been moored over the plain all afternoon was now moored overhead, everything about it said the heavens were about to open. He lifted the lace curtain and opened the fanlight, expecting to see the first fat raindrops, to smell their musk. Still it held off. Turning back to the room he came face to face with the bushy eyebrows and deep-set eyes, the craggy forehead and brushed back hair of a retired partkom official. He grunted and looked through the reflection at 'The Arrival of the Maoris in New Zealand'. It had been a while since he'd more than glanced at it, a lifetime since it had caught his eye in a second-hand furniture shop and with his allowance from his bread-delivery wage burning a hole in his pocket, had gone in. Lately, along with the Moriori and the Great Fleet, its stocks had taken a hammering: something to do with the suggestion the landfall was tinny and fair enough too because between the launching of bamboo rafts on the South China Sea and the arrival in this neck of the woods of the latest models, five thousand years of invention and fine-tuning had gone into the sail and the double-hulled canoe, into the art and science of navigation, into the domestication of plants and animals. It was a difficult and dangerous business all the same and doubtless some of migrants had been lost in conditions not too dissimilar to those depicted.

On another level it was a couple of blokes each with an eye on the main chance. On a third level it was window dressing; sleight of hand on the part of the colonists: you didn't have to go beyond the shoehorning of the one native word in the title to see what was afoot. When the place that came to be known as New Zealand appeared on the horizon – as predicted by them I might add – there were no people there by that name. 'Maori' was no more than an adjective used to distinguish between something that was commonplace as opposed to something that was unusual. Observers of the first European ship to enter Tūranga-nui thought they saw a large bird; when a rowing boat was launched from its back they thought they saw a fledgling. When variegated human-like figures transferred from one to the other and in due course stepped ashore, the word got another meaning.

There were other reasons for keeping it, for why the picture still hung on the wall: he knew what it was like to be at sea in a storm; he knew about the story behind the painting on which it was based. Goldie had made a copy of it as a student in Paris (in the same year as it happened that the census showed the Māori population at its lowest ebb). This other story (inasmuch as any story can be said to have a beginning) began with the appointment as captain of the *Medusa* of Hugues Duroy de Chaumareys. Now a couple of points about De Chaumareys: when the French Revolution was getting into its stride he took himself off to England, not that you can blame him for that of course. What did raise eyebrows was he hadn't sailed for a quarter of a century nor yet captained a vessel let alone a flotilla.

The peace settlement following Napoleon's defeat had included the return of its former colony Senegal to France and de Chaumareys's first commission was to deliver its Governor-designate to Saint Louis. His instructions warned him against placing too much store by his charts and instruments of navigation; he was to sail in convoy and to steer well clear of the vast maze of uncharted sandbanks to the north of Senegal made attractive to shipping by the onshore winds generated by convection currents rising off the Sahara.

He was out of his depth from the get-go, yet couldn't bring himself to seek advice or assistance from his officers because they'd all fought under Napoleon. The approaching storm season unnerved him, nevertheless he opted to go it alone principally in order to be the first ship into Saint Louis. Off Cape Finisterre a fifteen-year old sailor fell out a porthole while watching dolphins. The bungled rescue attempt was abandoned; the boy was last seen swimming after the frigate. When the Governor-designate's party insisted on stopping at Madeira for fresh supplies, the pilot's duties were handed to one of the passengers; for some hours the ship was in danger of drifting onto rocks. Fortunately an offshore breeze sprang up: an excuse for pushing on.

Two days later the sand hills of the Sahara appeared out of the blue. They hugged the coastline to the edge of the Arguin then turned southwest out to sea. However, having not taken their bearing from a recognised landmark they didn't go far enough before turning landward again. The sea dulled, sand then sea-grass then fish appeared in the waves: the passengers were beside themselves, the officers tore out their hair, sailors fished; the ship bumped against a sandbank, bumped twice more and grounded. Even so all need not have been lost had De Chaumareys allowed the ship's fourteen cannons, each weighing several tons, to be jettisoned or used as sea anchors to winch the ship off. His reason: they were on the inventory and he feared being held to account for their disappearance. After all attempts at refloating had failed, a raft was built for those for whom there was no room on the six lifeboats, which were for distinguished passengers and their luggage.

The 120 soldiers and their officers and the remaining thirty passengers, having transferred to the raft, found themselves waist-deep in seawater. The lifeboats and the raft, tied stern to bow, turned toward the coast, but could make no progress due to the raft acting as a sheet anchor so it was cut adrift. The 149 men and the one woman watched the six lifeboats dip below the horizon. They had six wine casks, two barrels of water and a bag of biscuit, but no oars, no instruments of navigation, no rudder. The sea got up and stayed up for two nights and two days, washing the skin off their legs; some slept standing up, some were washed off, others stepped off. The officers rigged up a mast and rallied round it. The soldiers got drunk and tried to cut the ropes that bound the raft together. After three days of running battles the 150 were reduced to sixty. After a further six days the sixty were half that number. Of those remaining, half were judged too badly wounded to survive and were despatched and pushed off or just pushed off so their rations would improve the chances of the dispatchers; the one woman was deemed obliged to follow her husband. The remaining fifteen erected a platform and an awning to keep them above the water and for protection from the sun. They tried catching one of the sharks that had been following them by bending a bayonet into a hook: the first strike straightened it. Finger-sized flying fish, caught in the sail and cooked over a fire in a barrel lit by dried gunpowder, garnished chunks of raw corpse till the barrel caught fire and in the dousing of it the fire was lost. On the thirteenth day sails were seen on the horizon and seen to disappear; the fifteen returned to their platform.

Then the *Argus* – part of the original flotilla: sent to pick up the stragglers from the beached lifeboats after the advance party had walked into Saint Louis and raised the alarm and to recover the 90,000 francs of gold from the wreck of the *Medusa* – hove to.

And that was only half the story. The other half was the cover-up. It occurred to Max that if Géricault, and Goldie and Steel for that matter, were making the point that the raft is the human condition then perhaps they weren't too far off the mark.

'Has it finished already?'

'Eh? It hasn't started yet!'
'Oh what would I know? Can I get you anything?'
'What have you got?'
'Tea, coffee . . . Beer?'
'Get me a beer.'

Seven

Construction sites like atolls, oil platforms, eyries fed by cranes surface on the screen to a confusing mix of spectator and traffic noise till a pan left explains the last as Max looks down the side of the biggest dick of the boom at the congested CBD. Cut to the plain and behind a tidemark of greasy orange smog the snow-covered Alps pull up a seat. They're getting a better day than we are thinks Max, leaning forward on the off-chance of glimpsing of Ned's house, then straightening chastened by the realisation he can't even see the suburb.

'Here's your beer,' says Liz at his elbow. 'Where's that?'
'Eh? That's the Port Hills.'
'Christchurch?'
'That's where we got out and had a stretch; where your bones had a breather.'

The camera zooming in on the park, the spurs flanking the Heathcote reach out like zombie arms, till a camera at the back of the northern stand picks up the baton and the crowd noise falls into place; this camera pans right past the elongated shadows of the northern goalposts to the deep blue shadow of the terraces on which a scaffolding tower has been mounted.

'There's not a breath of wind,' says Nisbo, oblivious to the flag billowing above him.

The next baton change brings up the becalmed, sun-trapped crowd in the East Stand, with in the bottom right hand corner like a signature, the silhouette of the camera crew on its raft of shadow. This camera pans back left following swooping gulls as Quinny reels off the names of an All Black side unchanged from the third test in Sydney; a French side including ten survivors of the inaugural World

Cup final, six of whom are survivors of the loss to the Baby Blacks the year before, plus two new caps. A clatter of studs sets up the next shot, a cystoscopy of the bowels of the main stand: Buck swivelling from the All Blacks' changing room, ball in hand, nostrils flaring, head already bandaged; Foxy looking white round the gills.

'What are we waiting for, bro?' mouths Buck.

The referee checks his watch.

Hearing himself say 'duty to country' Quinny hastens to add, 'in a rugby sense, of course'. For him the stars of the All Black line-up are Gallagher, Kirwan, Fox, Jones and McDowell, but being the good host he is he allows that viewers will have their own stars, that younger viewers will hope one day to step into their heroes' boots.

Buck gets the nod, grunts and charges into the blizzard of backlight; forty thousand whistles, cheers, jeers and claps welcome them onto the field. A tingle goes up Max's spine. A thread of bubbles rises up the side of his untouched glass.

Cut to the French side huddled round Blanco and Berbizier in a shot superimposed on a close-up of the tricolour that includes industrial chimneys in the background with spiral flanges. It's the bicentennial of the storming of the Bastille; it's Blanco's seventieth game, Berbizier's thirty-first birthday. As *La Marseillaise* grinds to a close, the French tug each other's jerseys. The sequence rounds out with a slow-motion pull-back on the French strip, yet another tricolour: blue jerseys, white shorts, red socks.

Sidetrack to the man with the steadicam loping across the park to zoom over the shoulders of the All Blacks mumbling *God of Nations* into the face of a nonplussed Diesel Deans, a direct descendant of those early settlers who paused on the Bridal Path to catch their breath, to consult the plain as if it were a crystal ball. J.K. licks his lips and squints.

Cut to the choirmaster in the middle of the park, ex Māori All Black Vance Whiley describing cartwheels with his arms in a valiant attempt to crank up the crowd.

Zoom in on the cricket block: some bumpy lens adjustment as the men in black, running into the frame, spread round like paper cut-outs in the form of a necklace shape with Buck at the Adam's apple mouthing something. The PA cranking up catches up and Max's rheumy eyes light up, the hairs on the back of his neck prickle, his cheeks fill like sails. All the recent talkback about the haka giving the All Blacks an unfair advantage, what a load of codswallop! If you're up for it, you raise your game, you rise to the challenge, call your opponents' bluff. If he had a quibble it would be with the puffing-out-of-the-chest part. To his way of thinking expanding the lungs into the puku provided more oxygen for the muscles, more cusecs for the voice, more composure.

Having had a crack at a translation he had a rough idea of what it was about. In the wee small hours of a sleepless night, with the help of a Father's Day gift, a set of miniature books in plastic covers on their own little bookshelf of inlaid native grains, he'd peered into the words till the mucous membranes of an old eye had parted briefly both on a world as cut-throat and end-game as the current one on the one hand and on the other as paradisal as the gardens of Anaura observed by Parkinson. By the time he was done, the little books were so puffed up from use he couldn't get them back on the shelf.

> *On your marks,*
> *get set,*
> *go!*
>
> *Slap your thighs!*
> *Expand your chests!*
> *Bend your knees!*
> *Lead with your hips!*
> *Stamp your feet!*
>
> Shield me, O hairy one
> me of all people
> in a food pit beneath a woman,
> the shame of it
> makes me shrivel.
>
> Oh but to see their faces
> when they realise
> they've been sucked in,
> now that would be something.

So you think you've got me
by the short and curlies, ay priest?
I don't mind admitting
you had me shitting for a while there,
but only a cry baby would let
fear get the better of him.

Hang about, old son,
don't count your chickens
or you'll have the pigs
rooting in your corpse.

Well what do you know,
they fell for it, I'm saved
thanks to the hairy one,
the sun shines out of
the place where
the sun doesn't shine.

But enough of this palaver,
I'm out of here!
Tihei mauriora!

He leaned back and squinted, light from the naked lightbulb gleaming on the ink's black rivers; that seemed to be the bare bones of it. He looked up, the clock ticked; with a bit of luck he'd get an hour's shut-eye before the alarm went.

Eight

'The traditional Maori haka,' says Quinny, 'this is the first time we've seen it here in donkey's years. It gives New Zealanders chills up their spines.'

The All Black forwards charge through their opposite numbers, brushing aside the interference to take the catcher out in mid air. The

French hit back, Deans gets thumped in a tackle. Then play breaks down and Sella is seen holding his forearm, hand dangling like a wounded paw. Set piece follows set piece.

'There may not appear to be much happening,' says Kirton, 'but you can bet your boots there's plenty going on in those scrums and mauls. Actually, I think the French have the upper hand tactically.'

Having seen the French scrum screwed, having seen the All Blacks maul the ball up then spin it wide; having seen skip passes, players doubling round each other for a second bite at the cherry, Max is bemused by this remark. But then the tour hasn't gone too well to date. Or is he praising the underdog with faint damn?

There's a squeak of hands on tightly-inflated dubbined leather as Berbizier feeds the lineout then runs into position to collect the tap-down . . . . Hullo, ref's spotted something. Foxy points to the posts, kneels and pours sand from a child's beach bucket, moulds it into a tee, lines up the posts then backs into a corner, fingers doing the ringaringa. An empathetic shimmy courses through J.K.'s body. Foxy moves in, leans back to kick and cuffs it, right leg following through like a golf iron. 'It's going to be short,' says Nisbo.

Blanco gathers and thumps the ball down the touchline then frowns and gestures to the linesman to take his flag further up. 'And I agree with him,' says Kirton.

'Who's winning?' says Liz.

'Eh, who do you think?'

'What's the score?'

'There's no score.'

'How can anyone be winning then?'

'It's battle of nerves.'

'Let me know if something happens.'

With the ball yet to arrive the scrum is set. Somehow it stays up and Berbizier feeds, but then the scrum twists like a tourniquet, cutting off the French supply and under pressure from the loosies and with the French inside-backs up offside, Deans flicks to Foxy, Foxy flicks to J.K. and J.K. drops it cold.

Foxy is due for a good one, thinks Max. His kicking game is under scrutiny, he has yet to dot down for the All Blacks, but so far he's doing alright, mixing them up: grubbers, box kicks, up-and-unders, wipers, chip kicks.

Meanwhile out on the wing J.K. gets the ball and a defender at the same time and the ball goes forward, he throws up his hands. Going back into position he runs his fingers round the inside of the waistband he wears on his waist, jersey tucked in; strip barely containing him. In Kirton's opinion – which Max takes issue with – the pass was a poor one: had Schuster doubling round been able to take the ball, albeit on the tips of his outstretched fingers, he'd have been in the clear. For a blind pass it wasn't a bad effort, it wasn't far off coming off.

J.K.'s been safe under the high ball; he's chased hard, putting Blanco under pressure. For Kirton to then call his hairstyle 'Italian' is to insinuate his game has gone downhill since he started working for Benetton, which is tantamount to an accusation of effeminacy with a touch of tall poppy thrown in.

Late in the half, Buck and J.K. are chasing a Deans' box kick. In the helter-skelter J.K. takes out his opposite number, then the ball pops up and Buck scrambles it into J.K.'s hands. At twenty yards out, level-pegging with Mesnel but with the jump on Lagisquet, J.K. passes infield. 'That's the first time I've seen J.K. stop and pass with almost a run-in,' says Kirton. 'Ordinarily, he would have backed himself.'

Does Kirton know something he's not letting on? Leaning forward to study the replay, Max thinks he sees what J.K. was thinking: that Mesnel would have slowed him down and together with Lagisquet would have bundled him into touch, whereas what happens from the ensuing ruck is the ball goes left and it's one deft pass after another till Gallagher draws Blanco and puts Wrighty away and Wrighty like a Lancaster skimming the white cliffs of Dover goes in over the tryline and there in the background is J.K. watching it all unfold. Which makes it a brace for Wright; his first having come courtesy of a Foxy grubber, a tad on the ugly side but with Blanco up in the line a fait accompli, not to mention earning Wright for his trouble a boot in the ribs from Rouge-Thomas, the second time he's bristled in a tackle.

Play sweeps the ground: mesmerizing, soporific; in fast forward it would be Chaplinesque. Half time is nigh before the French put a move together that's a patch on anything thus far put on them and for their trouble come away with a penalty. Berot strikes the upright (Max lifts his glass); the younger Whetton pouches the rebound and sets off, but on getting the call to put it out, by which time he's running hard, when he kicks the ball comes off the side of his boot, garnering a round from the crowd of good-natured raspberries. The ref blows his whistle, Berot thrusts his arms down and behind (Max replaces his glass without having taken a sip). 'This has been a most absorbing chest match,' says Quinny.

On a Hiding to Nothing

Dear Alwyn,

I shouldn't be writing this – I am living again that Sunday – that terrible Sunday – that Sunday of the glorious deeds of valour – that Sunday of slaughter – that Sunday when I prayed for a quick death. 'Oh God, please let it finish – please let me have the peace of death.'

By darkness on that Sunday, the 24th Battalion had ceased to exist – many had found the peace of death. This is the first time, after nearly 43 years, that I have referred to that day, and I find it very upsetting – I see it all, I experience it all again just as if it were yesterday. You will note that I recounted only the events of the first and the last days of the battle at Sidi Rezegh. It was very emotionally upsetting – I would never recount, and thus, relive, the full ten days in detail. After any action in the front line, there is the reaction. One is overcome with an awful weakness and trembling of the muscles, especially the leg muscles. To write about the action, even after so long, the same reaction occurs. I note your request for the full story – I doubt that it will ever be written.

One

DANCE – NURSES HOME – Saturday afternoons, two till six –
Central Park Hospital, Ohiro Road, Wellington –
ALL SOLDIERS WELCOME – Refreshments provided – No alcohol

Or something like that, it was on all the noticeboards in the camp. Not that I took much notice of it; after a week of bayonet practice, assault practice, firing from the hip, route marches, cross-country runs and what have you I was ready for something a bit stronger than a cup of tea.

We finished the Saturday morning with a game of rugby. The boss had played for Horowhenua before the First War and I imagine he saw it as a way of introducing a bit of fun to proceedings without departing from the business at hand. Then it was into the showers, into our uniforms and down to the station as fast as our little legs could carry us. Lunch was considered a waste of good drinking time.

In town we made a beeline for the nearest pub, the *Waterloo*, which was across the road from the station. We'd have a couple in there then it was onto the next watering hole and so on up the quay till it got near closing time when if we had our timing right we'd be in the *St. George* – that was the place to drink in those days – that or the *Grand*. Once you got a spot at the bar you didn't move for love or money, not even if you were busting for a leak because there'd be a crowd of jokers all wanting your spot. You'd get the barman to fill several glasses – more if he was busy, which he usually was – which you'd line up in front of you. Then as soon as you'd finished a glass you put it at the back of the line to be refilled. The barman meanwhile would be keeping an eye on the clock: if he thought you had time to drink it he refilled it, if he thought you had enough or had had enough already he told you. On the stroke of six they stopped serving; you had ten minutes to finish up and get on your way and if you weren't smart about it they threw you out, whether you were wearing a suit or a uniform.

Out on the street we'd be yakking and carrying on and looking out for our ride to whichever party was on that night where we would carry on drinking. Not me, I hasten to add, I'd had a skinful by that time; my number one priority was to get something into my belly to soak it up: if I could do that without having to shell out for it so much the better because then I had more money for beer the following week. I always made sure I kept a bit back for a feed in case there was no party of course. I kept it in a separate pocket – along with the fare for my return train journey – so I didn't spend it by accident.

It wasn't a question of having an invitation or not: hostesses competed with each other for our company: the more men in uniforms the further up the social ladder. It was a way of doing their bit for the war too of course. So we found ourselves in houses we'd never have gotten a look in otherwise. More to the point a party without food was unheard of in those days and so it was just a matter of biding your time till the grubstakes appeared. And there were some spreads I can tell you. If it was one of the flasher suburbs it might even be silver service: there'd be trays of asparagus rolls and pigs in blankets and sausage rolls and little mince pies and angels on horseback and devils on horseback . . . you name it and tea in cups you could only drink with your pinkie outstretched. Needless to say when the silverware started disappearing up tunics these parties dried up.

Sometimes there'd be a question mark over transport or the party would be so far out in the sticks by the time you got there it would be time to come back and if your transport was a bit iffy you could find yourself stranded. Not that this put some off: you found out who they were the following week because when you were getting ready to go on the bash they'd be lugging packs of sand round the parade ground or spud-bashing into tin baths outside the kitchen.

It was on one such occasion that Dougal and I found ourselves trekking back to the station kicking ourselves for not having kept enough dough back for the pie cart. Our expected ride had failed to materialize or somebody had nabbed it, possibly the latter because every time a car pulled up blokes would be diving in from all angles, including the boot. As the car pulled away you could hear the suspension bumping and grinding on the chassis. It would stop down the street and the doors would open and bodies would come flying out; the poor sods would pick themselves up and have a go at the next one till there was no one was left to pick up or the rides had stopped coming. We were halfway to the station when Dougal remembered the notices.

'If we get our skates on we might just make it,' he said.

'What time do they shut up shop?'

'Same time as the pubs, I would imagine.'

'No doubt there's a reason for that.'

It would have been after 7.00 by the time we got there, however the door was open and the lights were still on so we bowled on in. There was nobody there. We were looking round thinking what next when we heard tea trolleys then a couple of nurses appeared. They had us summed up in one glance.

'Looks like we left our run a bit late?' I said and they looked at each other.

'There are some leftovers in the kitchen, if you're interested?' said the brunette, the shorter of the two.

'That's if you don't mind washing up after yourselves?' said the taller one, who was blond.

'Very experienced at polishing plates,' said Dougal.

'Years of practice,' I added.

They looked at each other and sighed.

Winnie, the taller of the two, was from Vava'u, her father had run the Trading Post there. Iris's father worked on the railways, she was from Westport; her husband had not long left with the 1st Echelon.

'We're from Hastings,' said Dougal.

'Hastings! Did you go to the same school?'

'No, our parents were friends,' said Dougal. 'Our families shared a railway tarpaulin after the earthquake.'

'Looks like you're still reeling from it,' said Winnie.

'D.T.s,' said Dougal.

The long and the short of it was that Dougal and Winnie, having taken a shine to each other, the following weekend when I was getting ready to go on the bash I got roped into being Iris's escort (no great hardship, I might add) as she was required to chaperone Winnie.

It was an arrangement that worked out quite well, till our three months training came to an end; we then had a fortnight's leave after which we had to be ready to board at a moment's notice. It had been my intention to spend the fortnight with my parents, who were getting on and might not be around if the war dragged on as long as the first one had, however when Winnie insisted it was their turn to visit us I put it off. By the following Monday we had parties lined up for every one of those nights and in the end I only managed a few days at home. For a going-away present my parents gave me a Doxa pocket watch with my name engraved on the back.

On the bus from Petone railway station the locals treated us like royalty; the driver waived the fare (if I'd known what I was getting myself into I'd have insisted on paying). It was my first trip to the other side of the harbour and I thought it wasn't a bad spot: it might not get much morning sun but it got all the afternoon sun in winter and I'd rather that than the opposite; the hills had all the hunting and tramping you could want and then the city was just across the water. We had a liquid lunch then set off on the old track to the Heads. Part way up the first hill, while we were having a blow, I got out my box camera and Iris and Winnie got out their Nazi salutes: Winnie in Dougal's greatcoat with the collar turned up, head back, her eyes narrowed, her pursed lips simulating the Fuhrer's moustache; Iris's hair undone by the wind, suiting her I thought. I slipped it into the pocket with the linen gussets inside the back cover of my Pay Book along with one I had taken of my parents.

Dougal and Winnie kept falling behind so we left them to it. The track fell off the ridge into a valley where the wind threshing the treetops barely touched us: the litter on the floor brightened and dulled as clouds raced overhead, we were in our own little snow globe. We left the path where the path left the creek, following a trail others had evidently preferred to take too, keeping to the bank, ducking beneath webs of papery fuschia, clambering over boulders, till the way was blocked by a gigantic boulder jutting into the creek where there was a small shingly beach. The quarter of whisky I'd picked up at the pub came and went like the sun.

Here with a Loaf of Bread beneath the Bough,
A Flask of Wine, a Book of Verse –
and Thou Beside me singing in the Wilderness –
And Wilderness is Paradise enow.

Two

Frank grew up in a picture theatre, learning how to count by carrying his own little confectionary tray up and down the aisles. When he could see over the counter he sold the tickets; by the time he was in his teens he was as comfortable accompanying the silents as he was in the projectionist's box. He was going to travel the world in his own car, build his own house and plumb and wire it.

When he got to the big smoke he got a job as a chippie. On Sunday afternoons he would climb the nearby hill to a clearing from which he would look across the harbour and tell himself if things didn't work out home was just across the water and over the mountains. When the nurses from the nearby hospital wheeled their elderly patients past, a dozen things to say would run through his mind, but the lonely young man seemed to scare them.

It wasn't till he moved into the barracks at Trentham that he got a look in. He was a more than competent pianist and not half bad looking, according to Iris, the chair of the organising committee. After his first gig he could have had his pick of any number of nurses, but his heart was set on the bright-eyed, bushy-tailed daughter of a West Coast railway worker. They went to see the picture that had inspired him to enlist; it was having a rerun at a suburban picture house.

On his return from the crusades, Richard the Lion-heart is detained in Austria. In his absence the Normans are overtaxing the Saxons, demolishing their houses and torturing and killing them with the connivance of Prince John, Richard's brother. Meanwhile, spearheading the resistance, Robin Hood has caught Maid Marion's eye. His speech at Gallows Oak is straight out of the recruitment manual; the newsreel showing Hitler's invasion of Austria is the other half of the double act.

Frank was at the Drill Hall on Buckle Street first thing on the first day. The office wasn't due to open till 9.00 but opened earlier to cater for the demand; Frank was twelfth in line. Now that he had his Maid

Marion however he wished he hadn't been so hasty.

'Twelfth?' I said.

Iris drew the clipping from her handbag. There were hundreds of names beneath his.

'The only time I was twelfth in anything,' I said, 'was when I carried the drinks for the cricket team.'

'That would have been right up your alley.'

When leave for the wedding was posted, Frank was more than a little surprised to find his name missing, in fact he was mortified: a wedding without a groom was like a church without a steeple.

'It's a mistake,' said Dave, his best friend and best man. 'Go and have a word with him, he'll sort things out.'

'That's what I'm afraid of,' said Frank, 'he'll wipe the floor with me. You go, you're a sergeant: he'll listen to you.'

'Tell him to fight his own battles,' the CSM said to Dave, but Frank sent Dave back.

'If you had the balls,' said the CSM, 'you'd take his place at the altar!'

Shortly after his arrival in Egypt, Frank qualified as a chippie. Then he got his sparky's ticket. Next he was shifting trucks. The trip from Baghdad was sixteen hundred miles, a third of them over desert. His shoulders ached, his mouth bled from biting it to stay awake. He was winched out of a sand dune, lucky it wasn't a wadi. There were shorter trips from Haifa, day trips from the Mouths of the Nile, lessons in driving across desert without lights, how to spot soft sand, how to traverse ridges without busting an axle or shearing the diff off.

'Diff?' I said. 'I've heard of it of course'

'The bulge in the middle of an axle, it looks a bit like a bolt-threading tool. There's a gearbox in it that allows the wheels on either side to turn at different speeds. Trains don't have them; that's why they squeal going round bends. It's been so hot they've been having siestas, but it's too hot to sleep even. And water shortages.'

'I heard they had to truck beer in. Could have been worse, I suppose.'

'There could have been a beer shortage?'

We got onto talking about her job. It wasn't long before I put my foot in it: I referred to the hospital by a name I'd heard it called, the Home for the Incurables. Some of the patients called it that too, she said, that was what she liked about her job: their sense of humour and graciousness, their determination to put their best foot forward. It wasn't the patients who tried her patience: it was their visitors, their grown-up children going on about how their parents had never loved them, who was getting what from the estate, and so on.'

'This might be a bit off the mark,' I said, 'but it reminds me of a story one of our instructors told about a newly posted section leader trying to build-up one of his men for an upcoming patrol by telling him what a good shot he was. The bloke in question turned round and told him to eff off – excuse my French – the idea being, I took it, that praise can be a distraction: thinking you're alright at something can take your eye off the ball. So tell me Nurse Morris, when a new patient comes in what's the procedure?'

'Well some don't know they're dying; others haven't accepted it yet. They think there's a cure that they or we haven't heard about yet. We have to tell them as gently as possible they'd be no better off elsewhere. Others just want straight answers; they don't want to be pushed and they don't want to be held back. It's not all doom and gloom: we have visits from the Working Men's Club Orchestra and we have our own hospital choir.'

'Guaranteed to put anyone out of their misery.'

'I'll have you know I'm in the choir.'

'I take it back.'

'We bathe them, we dress and feed them, we give them their medications and we listen. Bath-time's the best, especially if they haven't slept well, because the water takes the weight of their bodies and being warm too of course. Some tell the most amazing stories. What you do think you'll do when you get back?'

'Haven't thought that far ahead as it happens – think I'll just wait and see when the time comes.'

'What about your family, I know you've got a sister and I assume you're not orphans?'

'No, not orphans or not yet – mind you Mum and Dad are getting on a bit – then there's four of us brothers and three sisters.'

'Your parents didn't do things by halves.'

'There would have been four sisters and five brothers had the first and the last lived. We came out the year my youngest sister died. I was six by that stage but funnily enough I don't remember her. I remember my grandfather, my father's father. I remember him going back into his house when we said goodbye. The door was off the footpath, a lot of the houses were like that: a door and a window and a wall were all that separated you from the street and the door had a slot in it for the mail; only the well-off had front gardens. My grandfather would have been close to eighty, which is not a bad age, come to think of it, for someone who'd spent his life hewing coal. He was on his own by this time, my grandmother having died before I was born. It was the last time my father saw his father, the last time my mother saw her parents, the last time they saw their brothers and sisters. Of course we kept in touch by mail, for a while anyway: we each had a relative we had to write to each Christmas. Mine was Aunt Rachel; the wife of my father's eldest brother. *Dear Aunt Rachel, How are you getting on? I hope you are well and that the weather is not too cold . . .* that sort of thing. As we got older, the letters got further and further apart till they eventually stopped altogether.'

'Was it for them partly?'

'I'd have gone to Spain if I'd had the wherewithal. A couple of mates and I were dead set on joining the International Brigade – till we toted up our savings anyway and found we didn't have enough for one passage let alone three. I was at home at the time: the outfit on the East Coast I'd been working for had run out of pine seedlings to plant. These same two blokes and I were in the Albion when Savage's death came over the radio. We barely looked at each other; we emptied our glasses and went out the door and down to the Town Hall where the recruitment office was. When the interviewing officer asked what experience I'd had with firearms I told him I'd done a bit of deer stalking.'

'We're short of snipers,' he said, 'how would you feel about training as a sniper?'

'Hunting animals is one thing,' I said, 'hunting men another.'

The letter arrived the following week; it was on the sideboard when I got in. The reason I hadn't said anything was because I knew Mum would take it hard. She took to her bed for the rest of the day.'

Three

The last of the units had fallen in and the bigwigs on the dais had settled themselves: the ADCs, the Ministers of the Crown, the Chiefs of Staff, the Consuls, the Trade Commissioners, the High Commissioners, the Justices, the Colonels, the Commanding Officers, the Director Generals, the Lieutenant Colonels, the Wing Commanders, the Governors, the Secretaries, the speakers and their wives and in the case of the Governor-General, his children as well.

The contingent of nurses sailing with us – epaulettes like rose petals on their grey shoulders, hands folded in their laps – widened their eyes for the press photographer. In the lull a locomotive could be heard shunting on the wharf, then the Governor-General coughed and the National Anthem commenced. Speech followed speech while the rain got heavier. Those without brollies or raincoats and those choosing not to use them got soaked to the skin. The rain seemed fitting, to a degree exalting; if we couldn't cope with a bit of rain we might as well pack it in and be done with it.

Fraser's speech was all Churchill and Thomas but lacking their rhyme or reason; the brogue was long gone, his voice went up and down and came and went, each sentence concluding on a downbeat. I had mixed feelings about Fraser: he'd come and gone on a number of things: supporting the October revolution in his younger days, backing the expulsion of communists from the Party later; opposing conscription in the first war, supporting it in the second. In fact, I'd had cold feet about Labour since Holland died, when it wooed the people who got us into the Depression then couldn't get us out of it. The last straw was when they got rid of Lee.

The Mayor was a sucker for the tried and tested. The Leader of the Opposition quoted Churchill: 'Nothing to offer but blood and toil, and tears and sweat'. It would be the greatest adventure of our lives, said the vice president of the R.S.A.; we'd be calling the shots on our return. I blew hot and cold, I scoffed, I bridled. With France out of the equation however, the battle that became the Battle of Britain was in progress as they spoke and so I listened: I might have balked at mention of the Motherland but I wouldn't have turned my back on my family.

Bayonets detached we set off on a route well known to us for other reasons and I don't imagine I was alone in wondering whether for the last time. It was jam-packed with well-wishers: the Territorials, the National Reserve were hard-pressed keeping them back. Again I had the queasy feeling of being paid up front.

Colours are brighter on rainy days; that's how the daffodils in parliament grounds struck me. It applied equally to the streamers fluttering from the office blocks and to the crepe paper teased from pompoms and flicked like baptismal water. The dye ran down our faces, dripped off our chins and fingertips. The sodden paper turned into pulp underfoot. We turned into Willis Street, from Willis into Mercer, from Mercer into Lower Cuba then it was back along the waterfront to the station and the discussion, some of it unhappy, about having to return our rifles and bayonets to camp before going on the town.

Back at the camp, I discovered there'd been a change of plan: friends spoilt for choice had passed their tickets to a dress cabaret onto Winnie and Dougal: the question was did Iris and I want to meet up anyway; she was keen if I was?

We did our usual thing of meeting for drinks and dinner before going onto a picture. The newsreel featured the 2nd Echelon in Palestine – Frank was in the 1st Echelon of course, but for Iris it was too close for comfort all the same, so we slipped out and went to the *French Maid* where we got back onto the earthquake, Iris wanted to hear more. So I gave her a blow by blow account of how it had taken me a minute or two to work out that what was different was the birds had stopped singing, in fact they'd taken off; it was if everything was holding its breath. The quake came through like a goods train, in a second or two the low rumble in the distance had became a roar. Then it was like riding a steer at a rodeo, the trees whipped over and touched their toes and came back up, those that could. Somehow I had managed to stay on the ladder, which I then got down off smartly. It was the second shock, coming at right-angles to the first that threw me to the ground. I picked myself up and went to see how the boss was getting on. He must've been thinking the same thing because we met halfway, then we had a look around the orchard to see what the damage was: half the pears had gone, the bottom fence was over and the packing shed had a lean to it. 'You better take the rest of the day off,' he said, 'your parents might need a hand.'

It was as if Rongokako had revived and not being happy with what he saw, had decided to give everything a good shake up. There were cracks in the road, the bridge had collapsed. I thought about trying my luck all the same before deciding I didn't want to be halfway across when an aftershock came.

Mum and Dad and Agnes were having a cup of tea in the backyard. Dad had built a fireplace with bricks from the fallen chimneys. He'd bound a gash on Mum's knee with one of his shirtsleeves. Agnes's hair was choked with dust; she'd crawled out of the building where she worked as a seamstress for a Mademoiselle Bignon, a Jersey islander who'd trained in Paris, as she was forever reminding Agnes.

'Thirteen minutes to 11.00 on a Tuesday morning!' exclaimed Agnes. 'What sort of a time is that for an earthquake and on a hot summer's day too for goodness sake!'

In the late afternoon I ventured into town with my camera, where I joined a crowd that had gathered opposite the *Grand*. It had been a five-storied brick building with balconies overlooking the main street. I used to take the papers into the lobby: one of the old blokes who lived there always had a wink and an extra halfpenny for me; the rest wouldn't have given you the time of day. It had lost its front and looked like a doll's house. There was an apartment where the paintings were still on the walls, chandeliers hanging from the ceilings, the dining table set with bone china, crystal glasses and napkins in silver rings awaiting the diners. In one of the bedrooms, a bedspread and sheet had been turned back ready for someone to get into; a Royal Doulton chamber pot beneath it in full view.

I had not long turned seventeen and it was an eye-opener to see that while some people went to sleep on empty stomachs others could afford to eat the finest cuts that money could buy and drink the finest wines. I used to see some of them in church; now I couldn't for the life of me see what they gained by going there.

By the time Dougal and Winnie had dropped out of the picture altogether (they were far too taken with each other's company to have time for mere mortals like us), we'd become quite capable of entertaining each other. In fact I'll take that a step further and say we'd taken quite a shine to each other and so as the inevitable drew nearer a degree of poignancy crept into proceedings. On our second-to-last night, after seeing her back to the hospital I got a wee peck. Till then, the only person who had kissed me was my mother. I was a late developer – something to do with the grubstakes, the shortage of them during the Depression possibly – anyway it woke me in a way I wouldn't have credited possible.

On our last night Iris was inconsolable and I had to draw on all my resources, because I had two trains to catch – one that night and the other the following morning – and a court martial to face if I missed the latter. Out of the blue I got the idea of giving her a pet name. It was a silly name, a made-up name but it did the trick: the rain stopped and the sun came out then she reciprocated in kind. That left the question of the future; the ball was in her court of course. It depended on which of us came back. Either way, she wanted babies, lots of babies, and if they were ours to give our pet names to the first of each sex.

Four

We were up in the dead of night cleaning the hut out. After that it was bacon and fried eggs and fried bread then shit, shower and shave and onto the train. The forecast gales didn't eventuate; the light grew over the Rimutakas as the train rolled and lurched down the old fault line straight out onto the wharf.

Other trains from Auckland and Hamilton were coming in. Word of our departure must have gotten out because the next thing we heard was brakes squealing and wives and girlfriends squealing as they flew at the fence; the odd semicircle forming on either side to afford best mates a last moment of privacy.

I wasn't expecting to see Iris and I wasn't disappointed and couldn't help smarting. I knew she'd be watching every spare moment she got. Looking up at the scars on the hills as they came and went through the mist, I got slapped on the face by a handful of raindrops. The signal to board couldn't come soon enough.

As I edged toward the ship I found myself being squeezed ever closer to the wharf edge till I was looking down at the peaks and troughs rollicking from pile to pile to grey cliff breathing like a living thing and getting greener and greener round the gills. With nowhere else to go I stepped onto the foot-high white wooden barrier.

Next thing I was flat on my back. A wharf attendant, seeing what was happening had evidently grabbed me and laid me on my back. When I came to he was rabbiting-on about the ship. I opened my eyes and looked up at it, it looked vaguely familiar.

'The *Queen Elizabeth*?'

'No,' he said, pointing to the bow.

No amount of battle grey could disguise the embossed name, a name I knew well from its predecessor, the first *Mauretania*. For all its modernity however I couldn't help thinking the hull plates looked like Meccano pieces.

'How fast can it go?'

'Don't worry, lad,' he said, 'it can out-run the fastest U-boat.'

I caught up with some mates and we bagged some hammocks on the main deck and went for a nosey. It was a bit of a mishmash I thought: the bridge looked like something out of a science fiction comic, while the mast rigging and the crow's nest harked back to earlier days. Aside from its speed the only defences were two six-inch guns, two Lewis guns and our rifles. The lounges were decorated with Art Deco carvings on the walls and pillars, while on one of the ceilings there were sketches reminiscent of cave-paintings of bulls and deer and people. The picture theatre was like the inside of a View-Master.

The wharf when we emerged was packed solid. The ship was backing out; the streamers between fathers and husbands and brothers and uncles at one end and wives and siblings and children and grandparents at the other were parting.

After all the palaver we got to the other side of the harbour and dropped anchor. There after the captain's talk, we were issued with lifebelts, shown how to lower and raise the lifeboats and how to find our way round the blacked-out ship's maze of lifts and stairwells and corridors and doorways. Eventually I got out on deck for a breather where I got talking to a bloke who pointed out his house.

'The kids will be watching from their bedroom window,' he said.

'Are you married?'

'She is.'

'Too bad.'

The *HMS Achilles*, refitted since the Battle of the River Plate and fresh from hunting the raider that sunk the *Turakina*, joined us after breakfast. On the other side of us was the *Empress of Japan*, its superstructure oddly suggestive of the Emperor's top hat and tails.

The submarine nets at the heads having been lowered, we left the harbour in the dead calm of a brilliant morning, a line of cars keeping abreast of us as far as the road went. The Pig Islanders were all camped on the port side, eyes glued to the snow-capped Kaikouras and the *Orcades* carrying the contingent from Burnham. The cold air cut through our drill but the rails remained packed till our island nation had slipped below the horizon and the last of the accompanying planes had turned back waving its wings.

On the fourth day it was *Achilles'* turn to turn back, its passage through the convoy appearing to double its speed, the crew on deck saluting and cheering, the compliment being returned with interest. As the cheering died, strains of *Haere Ra* floated over the water – Alexander III was Scotland's king when this language was first heard over these waters.

On the fifth day the Aussies joined us in Bass Strait – *HMAS Canberra* having relieved *Perth*, *Perth* having relieved *Achilles* – making us four troop carriers and two warships in total. Among the newcomers were *Aquitania* and *Ajax*, the latter coming also with Battle-of-the-River-Plate honours; there were no further complaints about defence.

There were no complaints about the grubstakes either. Breakfast was fried fish and potatoes. Lunch was salads and tinned fish, salami and hors d'oeuvres and pâtés and consommés for starters; for mains you could take your pick from roast beef with potato dumplings or cottage pie (both with cooked vegetables) or cold meats. I tended to go for the cold meats: lamb, ham, tongue, brawn, pressed beef. The only limit to the size and number of servings was the size of your eye or puku, because no longer was a platter empty than along came a cook or waiter with another. Desserts were fruit sponges with fruit salad and cream or cheese and crackers. If I had any room left I finished with a cracker and cheese and a coffee. Dinner was a variation on lunch with different consommés: Yorkshire pudding instead of dumplings, different cooked vegetables, different salads and desserts. Again I tended to go for the cold buffet where the variation might be turkey instead of beef or a different kind of brawn.

As for alcohol, the daily quota was a bottle of beer; you supplied the bottle and the ticket. There was a different ticket every three days; white or pink or yellow. Non-drinkers' tickets were worth their weight in gold.

To keep us in tone and out of mischief there was a daily schedule of weapons training, of PT, route marches, lectures, spud-bashing and sport; of rifle drill, cleaning duties and more spud-bashing. The route marches were in deck shoes so we didn't chew up the deck up with our hobnails. The deck shoes on the other hand harboured tinea and were slippery in the wet. Organised entertainment included tugs-of-war with the officers; being bigger men they usually won and that took some living down.

There were films: 'Charlie Chan at the Opera' had a run. Charlie was a shrewd, likeable Chinese-American detective with a penchant for turning the tables on the bigots he otherwise endured with the patience of Job. How you knew he was shrewd was in the way he squinted his eyes when he had the drop on someone. Warner Oland was the actor's name. I'd already seen others of his pictures: 'Charlie Chan at the Racetrack', 'Charlie Chan at the Circus', 'Charlie Chan in Egypt' among them.

'Charlie Chan at the Opera' came out in 1936. It begins with two attendants keeping an eye on a patient playing the piano in the recreation room of a sanatorium. The patient is the one-time famous baritone, Gravelle, who is suffering from amnesia from when a theatre he was performing in caught fire. The attendants, who don't go much for his singing or him, are forever trying to get a rise out of him. However when one of them slaps a newspaper on the piano with a photo of the soprano Lilli Rochelle on the front cover, whom he used to sing with and with whom he has a child, Gravelle recognising the photo begins his recovery. He escapes from the sanatorium and takes the place of the baritone (who replaced him in the opera 'Caravan', which has just arrived in town) just before the scene in which the baritone kills the soprano . . . . And so on and so forth.

The libretto was apparently a load of baloney; not having much or any Italian at this point however, this was lost on us. For days afterward, we were either Chop Suey or Egg Foo Young. 'Politeness golden key that opens many doors', we quoted. 'Confucious say luck happy combination of foolish accident.' 'Graceful as bamboo shoots, beautiful as water lily:' this last being the line Chan used to pick up his wife; the same line his son uses with similar success at the end of the film. If the thinking behind the choice of film was to modify our bigotry before we got to Egypt, I'd have to say it had at best mixed results.

When Eddy woke me in the middle of the night, according to him my response was 'I'll give you strange lights.' So it wasn't till the following night that I understood what all the fuss was about: our wake was a bluey-green colour. The wake of the entire convoy was a phosphorescent bluey-green: a chemical reaction set off in tiny sea creatures by the motion of passing vessels apparently. It made a nonsense of the blackout.

Some days out of Fremantle, when I thought I had my sea legs, the slow rollers of the Great Australian Bight ushered me to the rail. Between bouts of gagging, my cheek on the cool pillow of the rail, I watched the spray fly over the bridge, saw half the keel of the *Empress of Japan* pivoted on a crest. Meanwhile the old joke about seasickness was on repeat-play in my brain: first you're afraid you're going to die then that you're not . . .

We got the well-worn lectures we'd been getting several times a month since entering camp about the perils of foreign hospitality. According to the Sergeant Major, prostitutes were feeble-minded wreckers of the Allied cause and their patrons, cowards and shirkers who deprived genuine cases of the beds, the medicines and the care they deserved. Furthermore as a reprobate couldn't do his job, his mates had to do it for him as well as their own. Cases of VD would therefore be dealt with as if intentional.

The Doc's ploy was to scare the living daylights out of us: we'd become eunuchs with deformed penises, pus seeping through our trousers; we'd get heart conditions, arthritis, sterility, loss of virility, GPI, deep-seated sores; a drop of pus was enough to cause blindness (the implications of this last brought the house down). The C.O. appealed to our sense of patriotism and fair play: the world was watching us, not only would we be judged by how we behaved but so would our country. Wear your flashes with pride, he said, this is a battle between fascism and democracy, therefore see to it you are seen as the agents of the good and the right. And if you can't we'll dock your pay, we'll throw you in prison, we'll court-martial you; any honours you might be awarded will be withdrawn when you get back.

The Chaplain had the last word: in a soft and reasoning voice he pleaded with us to be mindful of what our families would think, what our friends and neighbours would say. Would we be able to hold our heads up, could we look them in the eye; what was the point of fighting for your family and your family's family if you passed on a crippling affliction?

Echelons before ours had walked the twelve miles into Perth in temperatures of one hundred degrees in the shade. Like us they'd been in deck shoes for a week and it had very nearly crippled them. For a shilling we got the bus to town. The locals turned out in droves, waving and clapping from the front lawns of comfortable-looking brick homes; expansive, well-tended gardens. We were treated like long lost cousins, which some of us were of course. They lined up in the hundreds to show us the sights, to invite us to picnics and parties. The Anzac Club on Saint Georges Road put on a non-stop free feed; there were views of the Swan through its Canary Island Palm-lined riverbank. There was a dance at the Embassy Ballroom. But the local beer, Swan Draught, tripped us up; at four point eight percent it was in fact a light lager and some of us needed assistance getting back.

A week out of Freemantle we had our first short-arm parade. In single file and nothing but our deck shoes we shuffled toward the M.O., who as we passed lifted each penis and turned it this way and that, squinted under it then told us to pull on it as if we were milking a cow. A few names got taken that day.

The further up the hotter and more humid it became. We fell asleep in a lather and woke in one. It was too hot for exercises so we played cards and wrote letters and read. It was too hot for that even but we had to do something to take our minds off the heat. It was too hot to eat other than a bowlful of rabbit food or a piece of fruit. When the others swam, I showered or washed and washed my underpants and singlet while I was about it, hanging them on the clews of my hammock and putting on the pair that had been 'drying'. The one thing we looked forward to was the evening singsong on the forward deck that the nurses sometimes accompanied us in, their company far-outweighing the loss of our usual repartee; dolphins and flying fish in the moonlight leading the way.

Bombay was chocker with troopships; some close enough to hail, to enquire after their origin, to hear their songs between or over ours. There being no blackout we could smoke on deck to our heart's content. The problem was getting ashore. Of the four days in port we got just half of one ashore and as it coincided with a thunderstorm we returned soaked to the skin, which highlighted other problems (having transferred to the *Ormonde*) such as the lack of drying rooms. Meanwhile a Congress Working Committee, in progress in Bombay at the time, was weighing up India's involvement in the war. Indian troops had been dispatched to the various theatres of war without Indian approval, bringing into focus Britain's hypocrisy: fighting fascism while stonewalling Indian self-government, the war being seen as an opportunity to bargain for independence. For Gandhi it was also an opportunity to push for a non-violent end to the war.

We had swapped ships because Italy had entered the war and the last leg would take us past its colonies on the Horn of Africa; the concern was not for us of course but for the *Mauretania*. At half the size and 10 times the age, the *Ormonde* hadn't been cleaned since its last commission, plus it had no ventilation below decks and was short of hammocks. The last straw was when the meat in the stew was found to be full of maggots, which was hardly surprising since we'd seen dock workers walking barefoot over the carcasses as they lay in the sun. Anyway some refused to parade, while others took over the bridge, which led to the arrest of the ship and our being surrounded by the Indian Navy. We didn't catch up to the convoy till the meat had been thrown overboard, till the ship had been cleaned up and consent had been given to our sleeping on deck. Near the Horn – ship and sharks zigzagging alike – we were issued with rifles and ammunition. There was no time for church but there was time for a last short arm parade. We passed the Gate of Tears without incident, the escorts left us and the convoy broke up, each ship going hell for leather up the Rea Sea.

In Suez we cleaned and polished and packed for two days solid. On the third day we were overrun by men in dirty shirtdresses (galabiehs) shinnying up ropes, grabbing our gear and throwing it overboard. Appalled, we ran to the rail only to see it fall into the flat-bottomed barges that in our turn ferried us ashore. Suez was aptly named:

the offshore whiff had already warned us. Ashore the combination of sewage, corpses, rubbish fires, sweat, hashish and garlic were a knockout. We had to breathe through something while eating.

Maadi Camp was on the other side of a hundred miles of the sort of desert I hadn't till then associated the word with. This desert was dead, it was grey, it was broken, it was the sort of landscape I imagined the Moon or Mars to have. Maadi Camp was on the outskirts of a suburb of Cairo by the same name; it was where the Aussies had been stationed in the first war. They had wanted to return to it, but had blotted their copybook the first time round.

Five

It was the sun on the tent that fooled me, I thought I was back on the Kaingaroa Plains, it was cold enough. Then when I put my feet on the floor I thought the Nile had come up in the night. The others being dead to the world I left them to it.

The sun jiggled above the escarpment. There was something not quite right about it that reminded me of a similar puzzlement I'd had as a boy seeing the sun rise over the coastal ranges when by rights it ought to have been coming up over the mountains opposite. I knew it was because we'd changed hemispheres, but that was as much as I could manage then and I'd gotten used to it.

This time round I'd heard blokes batting the issue back and forth: the best explanation went something like this ... Point number one: the sun rises in the east and sets in the west no matter which hemisphere you're in. Point number two: in the southern hemisphere, the sun describes an arc in the northern sky; in the northern hemisphere, it describes an arc in the southern sky. Point number three: like plants we orient ourselves toward the sun wherever it is; this being the case in the southern hemisphere we think of the sun rising on our right and setting on our left, whereas in the northern hemisphere we think of it rising on our left and setting on our right. Point number four: when we go from one hemisphere to the other we tend to overlook the fact we've turned around. Clear as mud?

I followed the rim of the escarpment to where it hung like a wave about to break over the Citadel. This was the escarpment from which blocks for the pyramids had been cut . . . I'd been saving them up (when we marched in from the Digla siding the previous night they had glowed a pinkish-grey), now I turned and it struck me that if you didn't know about them and someone told you such a thing existed, you'd have thought they'd been reading too much Jules Verne. Reveille sounded. I returned to the tent for my shaving gear then hurried to join the queue before the horde descended. The ablutions block – leftover from the first war – with its benches and galvanised metal tubs and scrim-walled urinals was a concrete raft on the sand.

After breakfast we pitched our own tents. They had to be so many yards apart and dug in so that in the event of an air raid shrapnel flew harmlessly overhead (direct hits aside of course). My group had been issued a bell tent; these had the floor sewn-in so we used that as the pattern for the pit. Then we set the tent up, stretching the eave over the ramparts and packing the diggings round the perimeter for additional protection; also against the Nile flooding. Inside we hooked up a rope as a dado to hang our tunics from, our lemon squeezers and photos and other bits and pieces. Then we sorted out who was sleeping where and tried our camp beds for size. I knew I was in trouble before I lay down: it might have been the rump end of summer but I was so badly burnt I missed my first leave in Cairo.

Bab-el-Louk Station was fifteen minutes from the Digla siding; pretty good going considering the distance was about the same as from here to Napier. The fare was an acker (a small coin, a piaster; the equivalent of tuppence-halfpenny) which sounds like chickenfeed and was, but since we were only getting seventy-five piastres a week and a bottle of beer cost six we avoided paying if we could. The gharry drivers and the peddlers, the shoeshine boys and the beggars crying *baksheesh* didn't get much change out of us either.

Everything on the map outside an area the shape of an arrowhead was out of bounds and that included the City of the Dead. Why anyone would want to visit a place with a name like that your guess is as good as mine, however in spite of the stories of soldiers getting beaten up and robbed of their Pay Books men did: Cairo was full of refugees from Europe and a Pay Book was as good as a passport.

The most popular of the local beers had a yellow label with a blue star and a quote from Nietzsche to the effect that what doesn't kill you makes you stronger. It was like drinking water; you could almost afford to drink it like water and may well have done so if like the so-called Swan Draught of Perth it didn't have a way of sneaking up on you, because the Military Police would arrest you as soon as look at you if they thought you'd had one too many.

We got back into our old routine of having a beer in one establishment then moving on to the next and the next and so on till it was time to return to the station. Occasionally we'd pop into a museum or the Mousky to get a present to send home: a tapestry of the Sphinx or the Great Pyramid to be sewn into a cushion cover; a picture of a beautiful woman in a veil, another of the same woman minus the veil. The theatres were popular because you could have a drink in them and if the picture wasn't much cop you could star-gaze because they had no roofs and the Egyptian night sky was something else.

At Agnes's suggestion I saw 'Gone with the Wind.' According to her I was a dead ringer for Ashley; apart from the hair colour however, I couldn't see the resemblance. Nor was I sure what to make of a character who appeared to have been made both stronger and weaker by war and who was described as being the joke of the story because he couldn't be mentally faithful to his wife on the one hand and on the other he couldn't be physically unfaithful to her.

The Birka, which took its name from a lake that used to be where the Ezbekiah Gardens now are, was another of the mostly out-of-bounds areas. On the footpath outside the wrought-iron fence you could buy erotic postcards and magazines. Only one of its fifty brothels was deemed worthy of the sons of the Commonwealth. It was on the Sharia Wagh el-Birket, 'the street on the shore of the lake'. On one side of this street there were arcades of peep shows and cabarets not-for-the-faint-hearted; on the other, three and four storey buildings with balconies of women in diaphanous get-ups fanning themselves and making ribald remarks to the window-shoppers below: ten piastres for the works, darling, that sort of thing.

The route marches were getting longer, they'd gone from eight to ten to a dozen to fifteen to twenty-one miles; some by moonlight and compass that took us over the vast subterranean reservoirs the Bedouin used or used to use before we (I mean the Allies, not us personally) spiked them with salt. The pace had picked up too: now it was four miles to the hour with a ten minute break for a sip of water. Singing ribald songs took our minds off the tedium.

They might have missed by miles, but after the Italians had a go at bombing us a consignment of fifty Bren guns turned up. Headquarters Company got fourteen, leaving three for each of the twelve platoons. The Bren is a Czech gun modified to take the same .303 round as our rifles; the name coming from the initial letters of the towns where the factories were: Brno and Enfield. It was accurate, easy to set up and break down, easy to slot in a magazine or refit a barrel, nor did it give you the thump on the shoulder you got from your rifle. On the downside it weighed twenty-three pounds, plus a further six for the spare barrel and three more for each loaded magazine, but then carrying a deer or pig out of the bush wasn't much fun either. Above all what the bosses wanted was someone who could get off 120 rounds a minute *and* put most of them on target; which meant five magazine changes in all, because while a magazine held thirty rounds you had to leave a few out to reduce the chances of jamming; all it took was a grain of sand. And guess who got the nod?

After a couple of months in Maadi it was down the road to Helwan: the Italians were pouring in from the desert by the thousands and someone had to keep an eye on them. The camp had a single strand of barbed wire along the top of a wooden fence: that's how keen they were to get back to the firing line. They occupied themselves sculpting borders for the tiny front yards of their tents and playing board games and soccer. We got a team together – they ran circles round us. We shipped them off to camps in South Africa.

When the battalion left for Greece, I was in the Infectious Diseases Unit. I'd patronised a spy disguised as a prostitute: that was one of the stories I had to put up with (it wasn't unheard of, Gerry wanted to know where we were going; only the head sharang knew that and by all accounts he wasn't too pleased). When they couldn't find out what was wrong with me I was discharged to Base Headquarters to be re-equipped then sent to the Training Battalion to be brought up to full fitness. By the time the battalion got back I'd been reassigned to a different platoon, so it was a while before I heard that Eddy had been captured, that Henry had been killed.

Six

The train stopped. We looked out the window at a mud hut fifty yards away.

'That'll be the Box,' said Alf.

After eating, breathing and passing sand for a year, a beach full of white-bottomed men galloping through the wheeling shelves to plunge head-first into the turquoise sea was as natural as a nudist colony. With my fair skin however I was happy just to roll the legs of my Bombay bloomers and look around as I paddled, because apart from the stooks of rifles and the chimney pots sticking out of the sand hills probably not much had changed since Marc Antony visited Cleopatra at her holiday home nearby. Furthermore, it was just possible the fragments I turned over with my porcelain-white toes were from shipwrecks back then?

The pressure had gone up a notch or two: exercises now were with artillery, transport, planes, armour (Bren carriers standing in for armour for now). If anything went wrong somebody got it in the neck and passed it on. We drilled for air attacks, tank attacks, gas attacks, for how to get through barbed-wire entanglements; there was talk even of us lifting mines. Railway Group was laying two miles of track per day: the amount of ordnance going by was nobody's business.

In the evenings we'd have a few beers and a singsong before tea; I recall popping out for a pee and hearing singing coming out of the ground all round me. Once every fortnight the Mobile Picture Unit would screen something on the footy ground. We hosted a game between the Division and a South African side. In the last series the Springboks had beaten us; this was our opportunity to set the record straight.

The day dawned cool and squally, showers drifted in off the Mediterranean. The slope behind the goalposts was packed solid, as were the sidelines. In our greatcoats and balaclavas we were probably better prepared for the weather than your average Athletic Park crowd.

Jack Sullivan, veteran of the aforementioned series, scored the only try. In fact, the South Africans did well to hold us to that given we had the home advantage, an international player not to mention a referee who was one of our chaplains. A shower lashed us as we returned to our dug-outs, but with the fire going and a few Stellas in us it was as good a post-match celebration as you could hope for anywhere.

Had the Navy not sunk a dozen Italian ships off Taranto that night, the game would have been our main topic of conversation for days, if not weeks. Then two days after that, on Armistice Day, we got told we'd be fighting in Libya within the week. A further two days, the sun rising, I was hopping off the back of a truck on the Siwa Road: in every direction there were trucks and tanks and guns all the way to the horizon, the camp would have been as wide as from here to Bridge Pa and as long as from here to Napier. Petrol Company was dropping off rations and POL, which meant reorganising a truck that was already packed to the rafters. However uppermost in my mind was the possibility of running into Frank, he didn't know me from a bar of soap, but I'd seen his wedding photo.

We headed due west in a convoy twenty-five miles long by seven vehicles wide – each vehicle 200 yards from its neighbours. Watching them pop up and drop over the crests we'd just popped up and dropped over brought a smile to our faces, till the cold got the better of us; its only match was the dust cloud we stirred up. Sand-boulders hard as concrete broke axles and springs, we were thrown this way and that and all over the show; all the while, because we knew we'd been seen, we expected a strafing.

When we switched to travelling at night, the gap closed to ten yards and slowed to a brisk walk, because the drivers couldn't use their headlamps. The only light came from the hooded storm lamps Provost Company had marked the route with: a ghostly green every five to ten minutes that was soon swallowed by the swirling dust. Near the end of the first night's 'march', red storm lamps marked a minefield; one of ours.

Another reconnaissance plane spotted us on the fifth day – the electrical storm that night was widely interpreted as the opening exchanges. On my father's birthday, the first of November and the march's sixth day, we crossed through a fence into Libya. Built by the Italians to prevent Libya from getting food and weapons from

Egypt, it was ten feet wide, as tall as a man and had three rows of metal stakes with loops top and bottom to hold what was now a rusting barbed-wire bird's-nest 200 miles long. Libya had contested its Italian occupation in two wars already; the last having concluded ten years earlier with the hanging of Sidi 'Umar al-Mukhtar before the 20,000 Libyans confined this camp, the first concentration camp. Of 100,000 prisoners about a third survived this and other camps.

The gap made by the sappers was wide enough for the convoy to pass though without slowing. There was no sign of the Germans or the Italians. We turned north and continued for a further hour before stopping. Heavy gunfire kept us awake – the Indians, after covering our crossing, had begun their assault on the Italian-held fort of Libyan Omar twenty miles to the north: what had sounded like German 88mm anti-tank guns turned out to be the equally effective Italian 75mm gun.

We breakfasted at first light then spent the day awaiting the outcome of tank battles to the north and west. In the middle of the afternoon we broke camp and shifted a dozen miles to the north. The day after that was one cancelled get-ready-to-move order followed by another before we settled in for another chilly night. We were getting a bit antsy by this time in spite the C.O.'s pep talk, or perhaps because of it – the British Bulldog was trained to approach on its belly in order to make it more difficult for the bull to get its horns under it, then to sink its teeth into the bull's nose and not let go; dogs lost their teeth and were bludgeoned to death but did not let go. We got the point all the same.

Meanwhile with apparent impunity, the RAF shuttled back and forth, lending weight to the supposition that we were holding our own, so we upped-stakes and continued north before swinging west onto the motor-track that crossed the top of Cyrenaica (where the supposed 'opening exchanges' had taken place). It was slow-going; the storm had turned the route to sludge.

On the afternoon of the twenty-second we were ordered to Sidi Rezegh – to support the support group that was supporting one of our armoured divisions (a support group in need of support?) We were going that way anyway and as there seemed to be no further urgency, our unanswered questions went unasked, indeed were all but forgotten when a squadron of Valentines rolled up.

The Valentine is a small tank that fires a two-pound shell and also has a machine gun port and a pistol port. Its rows of ventilation holes, each with its own little sheet-metal hood, and a wireless aerial pivoting on an arm similar to that which you'd adjust a fanlight with, give it a homemade aspect. Meanwhile tied to the fenders are the pickaxes and shovels and crowbars and a tool like a hockey stick for adjusting the tension of the tracks. It was only because it was supposed to be impervious to anti-tank fire that we withheld our misgivings. The drivers seemed cocky enough too, grinning ear to ear and gunning their engines like bikies at a set of traffic lights.

Enemy trucks accompanied by tanks were in our way apparently, so an advance party was dispatched to give them the bum's rush. By the time we got there, the tanks had shifted off to watch proceedings from a safe distance. We fired on the advancing infantry and in spite their being out of range, where my Bren was pointed figures fell: whether by my bullets, whether they were killed or not, I couldn't say; anyway that's the answer to your question. We rejoined the brigade.

Seven

The first hint of light was in the sky, there were no stars; only dozens of small fires like fallen stars. While trying to catch what warmth I could, I was watching the flames being batted back and forth by the chill dawn air. I had one ear on a leg-pull that was going on and the other on a noise I couldn't quite put my finger on when all hell broke loose . . . .

The fire had burnt out; our breakfast lay scattered and forgotten among the ruins. The Germans were pulling out one way and we the other, watching each other go over our tailboards; them on the route we had been on up till then, us up the side of the escarpment.

We came out on a vast flatland overlooking the Mediterranean and turning west ran into enfilading fire from the re-entrants (that is to say the notches made in the rim of the tableland by draining downpours). We shot across this tableland a good five or six miles till we ran into long-range fire from in front. We were close enough to where Barrowclough wanted to set up his headquarters anyway, so the drivers slammed on their anchors and we fanned out in battle order. The bullets whizzing over like drunken wasps stopped abruptly and the officers went off for a chinwag.

On their return the section I was with was ordered to clear one of two underground dwellings in the area. Its curving tunnel staircase, shiny from use, came out on an open courtyard with an empty pond in the middle. The walls had openings into living areas and sleeping areas, with notches for fitting curtain rods to separate them; the barrel-vaulted ceilings had been whitewashed. There were cubbyholes for storage, pegs for hanging shelves; a stable with a canny arrangement for dropping feed from the granary above it. It appeared to have been abandoned for some time. It was a relief to be out of the wind and my thoughts turned to the breakfast we'd missed out on earlier. I'd have happily let the events above ground tear overhead like the clouds were it not for a sense that what had happened at Bir el Chleta was just the beginning.

When the order came to occupy the hill and prepare to defend it, we looked around for the hill. Apparently it was a tableland we stood on, sufficiently prominent for a survey party to have calculated its height and put a cairn on it. The CO suggested calling it Hill 175 or Point 175; its highest point being 175 metres above sea level. After scrutinising the cairn through field glasses, Barrowclough was convinced there was nothing else there; one of the majors thought he saw earthworks. A march of a mile and a half brought us to within a mile and a half of it and a start line half a mile in length was laid over the terrain: sand, rocks, stones, pebbles, reefs of bedrock and saltbushes.

The officers pored over their maps; as well they might because failing to match up what was on them with what was under our feet had gotten us into trouble twice that day already.

In fairness, travelling at night hadn't helped; nor had some of the mapmaking: the contour lines south of Bir el Chleta for example had told a different story to the abrupt climb.

Chewing over the events of the morning, we could only conclude we'd set up camp cheek by jowl with the Headquarters of Deutsches Afrikakorps; that the fires burning nearby was them doing what we were doing, having breakfast; that the noise I'd heard had been one of their supply units approaching from the north; that these two groups had taken us for each other; that by the time the runner, sent out to identify the approaching column, had returned no adjustment of elevation was necessary; that from the point-blank broadside of our twenty-five pounders the column had careered through our tail like a stricken galleon; that several hundred prisoners, their radio sets and code lists for the day, had cost us six men and six vehicles; that more perhaps critically this had cost us time, hence why the Point hadn't been reconnoitred.

Our place on the far left of the start-line put us as far from the line of fire as it was possible to get. In addition to this we were in reserve, we'd have felt a lot easier all the same had our left flank not felt so menacing. 17 Platoon stood two hundred yards to our right, 18 Platoon was between us and 17 Platoon but further back. B Company occupied the northern half of the start line, its three platoons staggered like ours: 11 and 10 in front, 12 between and behind.

A Company, having sorted out the enemy to the right and rear of us, had caught up. After covering our withdrawal from Bir el Chleta, they'd been nicking out the machinegun nests in the re-entrants. They had barely had time to catch their breath before returning to the right flank to cover B Company.

My brow was cold and my legs were rubbery, I couldn't trust my voice. The cigarettes I'd been chain-smoking had turned to tar on my lips.

Eight

The pace we set out at would have been tramping on a road; we were busy enough without having to negotiate saltbushes, rocks and sand pools. We were also keeping an eye out on what lay ahead, on how our mates to the right of us were getting on and on the wadi that had just come into view on our left. The thing about this wadi was that with its side being convex, the only way to tell if there was anything in it we needed to know about was by going down for a jack nohi. We weren't too happy either with the tank tracks crisscrossing the ground under our feet or with what looked like the smouldering remains of a tank battle a mile or two to the south. So when the major ordered a part-right wheel we breathed a sigh of relief, which was all very well and good except that what happened next was straight out of the Keystone Kops: the men on the inside of the turn, as spooked by the wadi as anyone, forgot to slow down, which of course meant the men on the outside had to run to keep up. I was in the middle and my gear was going up as one foot was coming down and coming down as the other went up; I thought the Bren was going to dislocate my arm at the shoulder.

Half a mile out, B Company stopped and 11 Platoon went forward in rushes. Then the Valentines came over the escarpment lip like a flotilla of fishing boats on a swell in the Aussie Bight. Half took up positions in front of us, the other half went clattering and squeaking through B Company's extended files. It took them about five minutes to reach the cairn. At which point the Bren carriers tore in like bloodhounds, driving hundreds of grey uniforms from their holes, while 17 Platoon ran the last few hundred yards to round them up.

Snatches of cheering reached us from behind. We'd have cheered too if we'd had the breath, had some tents in the wadi not come into view; had Spandaus not started hammering away like heavy duty sewing machines to the accompaniment of Mausers and Schmeissers and the bullwhip crack of Granatwerfers – the crescendo reverberated round the wadi – had we not started getting hit from behind and in front and on either side. The lieutenant decided we'd better take cover and not before time either.

When I hit the deck, yellow sand and gravel went into my mouth and eyes and down the neck of my tunic. I gasped for air, my heart was going like billy-o; bullets and shrapnel were whistling and singing and dancing and clawing at our tunics, hitting the hardpan and skipping, rolling rocks end over end, spinning others, shredding saltbush and genitals and entrails and vital organs. We couldn't afford to stay where we were and we couldn't afford to move.

In the main it was due to the few blokes, game enough to stick their heads above the parapet of the curving ground that we learned the fire was coming from the edge of the wadi that curved like a bracket around us. It was do or die either way, so we regrouped and ran crouched-over into the fire, each section passing through the section before it, going on a bit more then dropping to cover the section coming through. In this way we got to within fifty yards of the nearest fire or the halfway line if you like. Men were going down all round me, partly through bunching up; I was waiting for it to be my turn. I got up and went, dropped and got up and went again; the same as the men before me and behind and to my left and to my right, those who still could. Every gun being fired at us now was going hammer and tongs and yet despite the odds we were knocking on the door of the twenty-two, which was enough for some thirty or forty grey uniforms to rise shakily from the dusty beds of their sangars with their hands up.

At a nod from the lieutenant we swarmed into the in-goal area and rounded them up. They were shock-eyed and shambling, unshaven and pinched, cowed and gawky, all ages and shifty; in short much like us. 18 Platoon arrived out of nowhere and out of breath to give a hand. Pat Oldham, in charge of 13 Platoon, which had been seeing to the machinegun nests on our left, was going on about how all the rifles he picked up were set to a range of between 1200 to 1400 yards, his point being they hadn't been adjusted as their target closed on them, in short they'd been as shit-scared as we were. The rest of 13 Platoon arrived to give us a breather.

The counter-attack wasn't far behind. In the scramble for cover, I dived into a scoop in the sand about a foot deep; you will appreciate my disappointment – it was the nearest cover to hand. Others thinking they had time to be choosey went for the sangars, the machinegun nests and the slit trenches; most had little more than the threadbare screen of a saltbush. Then the Valentines were seen coming our way till a series of explosions stopped them in their tracks, reduced them to a line of burnt-out wrecks; barrels bent, twisted and splayed. Black smoke boiled skywards from their gun ports and lidless turrets; two went round and round in circles like wind-up toys, three limped off.

We sent for entrenching tools; they were not forthcoming, which for my part was neither here nor there as I'd have been hard-pressed putting anything to use given the scrutiny we were under. For the same reason, using the Bren wasn't an option; I wouldn't have got it set up. Those with more cover made a pretty good fist of it till they ran short or out of ammo; other than that, contributions of any sort were at best sporadic. The barrage fell into a pattern of concentrated machinegun fire followed by concentrated mortar fire.

While I had made myself as flat and as still as I could, I knew or keenly felt that parts of me were still visible. All I could hope for was to blend in or be taken for a corpse. That said, I knew that having dug them the Germans knew where their pits were; that it was only a matter of time before a seven-and-a-half pound mortar hoisted me like a ragdoll; or a piece of shrapnel entering my shoulder, corkscrewed through my gut and exited somewhere lower down; before a bullet like the point of a jackhammer punctured my helmet. I sweated over whether I would scream like a pig or yelp like a pup or cry like a kid for my mother as I heard others round me doing. The sun came and went, the barrage continued; I remained in one piece.

Meanwhile, the shadow of the saltbush made its way round my head. I squinted at the twigs hanging on by a whisker, twirling and swinging, till one came away and hit my eyelid; my eye watered. I stuck out my tongue and drew the twig into my mouth and sucked on it. I was in the habit of adding a handful to our stews, but this was the first time I'd had it raw. We had a theory about the saltbush: that it survived the desert by drawing salt from the sand, shedding it on its leaves and branches and stems to attract the dew; hence the 'boulders' like leftover cement bags round the stems. And that was how I got rid of the acrid taste of nicotine on my lips.

Somewhere around the middle of the afternoon, the barrage dried up. My first thought was the Germans had run out of ammo and we had a stalemate on our hands. That was before I heard tank engines clearing their throats and the clank and squeal of tracks. I lifted my head an inch or two and saw a turret and a machinegun searching the ground, stabbing away intermittently. Behind it came a second then a third turret. When I heard the screams my hair stood on end. They came forward in bounds, their infantry taking turns to jump out and squirt off a magazine before jumping back to reload.

The Place Where
the Sun Sets

Last winter – our journey into Hell.
I dared not write about what I saw –
it was too burdensome & painful . . . .

[Those who were not there] will have the urge to relive it,
perhaps indeed to discern in the midst of that horror
the magic of great historical moments.

All we ask is never to see such things again,
to flee from them. To flee –
but in what direction?

Ηλιοδυσιο The place where the sun sets

One

Then everything – the clanking, squeaking and firing – came to a standstill and the noise from the battlefield was like a storm that had shifted off. After an age, perhaps of a few minutes duration, I lifted my head again. The nearest of them would have been the length of the section away, from the mailbox to the back fence: blood dripped from its tracks, smoke poured from an exhaust with the gauge of a downpipe. The lid was open; the commander, standing waist-deep in the turret, was intently studying something. Everything seemed to hang in the balance, to hinge on what he was looking at. The infantry, spread out on either side – trigger fingers a hair's breadth from hosing what was left of us to kingdom come – were intently studying this same thing.

The suspense having got the better of me, I very slowly turned my head and saw D Company's major, as cool as you like, picking his way forward among the bodies – as if this was merely a training exercise – every now and again pausing to have a word to somebody on the ground. As he proceeded, men got to their feet, lifting their arms in that familiar gesture we knew so well from our childhood games and the picture theatre, though as many of those at his feet didn't. It was the bravest thing I've ever seen, but you don't get medals for surrendering.

One bloke when he got up still held his Tommy gun: whether this was out of bravado or derangement, I don't know. The Jerry nearest him did his nut – in German but the meaning was unmistakable – he didn't get a second warning. There was a brief pause to see if anyone else needed further persuading.

There being no takers, we were bundled from the battlefield, catching on our way the tail end of a duel between a captured Valentine and a portée: the Valentine was dumbly grinding toward its tormenter when it erupted into flames.

Shells from our twenty-five pounders back in the Wadi esc-Sciomar

(Barrowclough's base) had begun tearing overhead: Intelligence having finally cottoned onto where the German reinforcements were coming from.

Once we were out of the way, we were searched. Everything went on the ground, only our Pay Books were returned. Attempting to retrieve his smokes was very nearly the last thing one bloke did. By now we had a fair idea of who was missing.

Following the German lines of communication took us past an anti-tank battery. The crews taking a moment to glance at us, we saw in their faces how we had felt, also possibly a suggestion of guilt or disbelief that anything could have emerged alive from what they had thrown at us. We weren't out of the woods yet of course.

At the dressing station, as it was at our dressing stations, irrespective of what side they were on, the wounded were attended to according to the severity of their wounds. Those who'd been treated lay on stretchers in the lee of the tents.

In another tent I gave my name, my rank and number and was cursorily dismissed. We continued down the wadi; shells continued flying overhead making tearing sounds not unlike sheets being torn for turning. Fountains of earth rose where they landed, leaving yellow dents in the hardpan and tassels of black smoke to drift off. We came out on the same low ground we'd been on that morning, albeit several miles to the west, and turned into the setting sun.

'For you, my friend, the war is over,' said the guards, handing us over to other guards and with a heavy step turning and returning to the battlefield. The quaint locution brought a smile to our faces (that our German wasn't a patch on their English didn't come into it). It was a gift of commiseration and equality and envy, the desire to be in our shoes.

The sun was dropping below the horizon when we lay down in long lines on the desert floor in our battledress stinking of explosives and burnt rubber and burnt flesh and unwashed bodies. When one bloke turned over, we all had to and we all got a turn on the ends at being three sides numb. *'For you, my friend, the war is over'* went round and round in my head. It could have been: *'A year and a half's training for one day's fighting.'* I was showing a profit.

When dawn came, I flapped my arms and stamped till enough feeling had returned to them for me to be concerned about doing myself an injury. Breakfast was a small cup of unsweetened black coffee of questionable provenance; it was warm and wet was all you could say for it. When the NCO put in a complaint about there being nothing to eat, the response was that it was our fault for having disrupted their supply lines.

In the late morning we were handed over to the Italians: the dust cloud approaching us; as big as the dust cloud approaching them. The officers strutted round like little Hitlers while the browbeaten ordinary ranks relieved us of our fountain pens and wristwatches (overlooking our fob pockets as it happened; my parents must've known something!)

Skirting El Adem aerodrome, we came under fire from one of our planes. Fortunately, the pilot recognised us, because he flew off waving his wings. Around midday we were joined by a column of South Africans; they'd been bagged in an even more torrid battle than ours. It was one interminable straight after another; one nondescript sand hill, one unnamed wadi after another and the further we got from the front the slimmer our chances became of being reunited with our units. The saltbush thinned and was replaced by sparse grassland, greened by the recent rain and laced with purple and yellow flowers. But for the coffee and a pint of water from a passing tanker, we'd have had nothing to drink; we'd had nothing yet to eat. We spent the night in a hastily-erected barbed-wire enclosure in the middle of nowhere. In spite of the cold and the nagging thirst, through sheer exhaustion I got a few hours shut-eye.

Headachy and light-headed, tongues swelling in our mouths, we passed the fort of Acroma, where Italy's first imperialist war against Libya had been adjourned: the Italians, despite having every other advantage, reeling from hit and run tactics they couldn't get the measure of; the Libyans out on their feet from drought and locusts and a blockade imposed by amongst others, us.

Around the middle of the afternoon we came out on the Derna-Tobruk road, where we were picked up by Italian supply trucks; Fiat six-tonners returning to Derna. It was fifty men to a truck, fifty to a trailer. How we stayed on, I don't know. In fact one bloke didn't; he went under the wheels of the trailer. The trucks didn't stop – there were shells landing in the fields on either side of us.

We climbed into the Gebel Akhdar (Green Mountain) – where

Sidi 'Umar al-Mukhtar and his men hid out between raids during the Italians' second war of occupation. They were getting the best of the Italians too, till Graziani was brought in: his approach was to concentrate the Bedouin (the raiders' support base) in fortified camps. At a rate of 12,000 a year, through starvation and lack of medical care, through disease and executions a hundred thousand people were reduced to 35,000.

The gullies were thick with oaks and pines; with cypress, olives, figs and almonds; quince and apricot, pomegranates and acacia; with myrtle and tamarisk. It was the first bit of green of any substance we'd come across since the Nile valley.

Going on twilight we became aware we were taking hairpin bends so tight they had to be taken in bites; the drivers backing up to where we dimly made out the wrecks of vehicles 1000 feet below. Plumes lifting from the cascading waterfalls of a river that cut through the sandcastle town made us faint with thirst.

The soup that night was hot water a cabbage had swum through, plus half-pound cans of meat shared between two; and between three, four hardtack biscuits so dry even ground up they repelled water. Water was the one thing there was no shortage of – we drank till we were bloated – then strip-washed and settled down in an Arab cemetery that was so crowded we had to sleep sitting upright. It rained in the night.

Two

To get breakfast – half a pound of bully and a biscuit – you had to get out the gates, preferably without also getting a jab in the head or the back with a rifle butt: *Via! Via!*

The trucks ground and whirred their way up the escarpment, till we looked down on the narrow orange hem of a vast azure canvas of sea and sky and fog. From there it was breakneck speed: we hurtled past Greek, Roman and Turkish ruins; an American fort from the Barbary Wars; what was left of Sidi 'Umar al-Mukhtar's hideout. What with our pilots and the Italian drivers, we didn't fancy our chances. Some lost consciousness and had to be hauled by their bootlaces back onboard. Somehow we got down in one piece.

It was well past our bedtime when we drove through deserted streets overhung with palm trees, before coming to an abrupt halt in the warehouse district.

'*Via! Via!*' shouted the guards.

Numb with cold and dizzy and exhausted, we milled round a warehouse which evidently had been a garage: it was heady with fumes and the concrete was oil-stained. It was too late for supper (we asked anyway) and much else besides a trip to the latrines (the inimitable pole over a pit), before settling down on the concrete. There, as in the desert we lay in long lines, knees tucked into the backs of the knees before us and turned as one and took turns on the ends.

Flies bred on our waste: germs spread everywhere; there was no soap and no hot water. Before long, disease was adding insult to the injury of malnutrition. Addled with dysentery, men fell off their perch and had to be fished out and doused under the one tap that served everyone and everything and dressed in borrowed clothing till theirs was dry.

Hunger lay round every turn: when you thought you had the better of it, there it was again. I avoided the schools of men sharing blow by blow accounts of twelve course meals in fancy hotels, preferring to daydream about the spreads on the *Mauretania*, the Sunday roasts at home; the feeds in the work camps, which I by default jacked up – the others finding the day's hard graft easier.

When the hut door banged behind the last man out, I'd swing my feet to the floor: add a stick to the fire and roll a smoke and smoke it while the water came to the boil. I'd scrub the table and sweep the hut, then breakfast on a slice of venison as thick as my finger: liberally seasoned, sandwiched between doorsteps of camp oven bread and washed down with a mug of billy tea.

After a lick and a spit and a dig in the grave, I'd peel and melt onions and brown the meat, before getting the lot simmering and starting the bread: rising it in the camp oven, putting the lid on, covering it with embers. I'd have another mug of tea then and dip into the hut's library – Westerns, whodunits, cliff-hangers, bodice-rippers, penny dreadfuls and potboilers and so on – before turning out the bread and getting the next one on. It was my job too to keep the meat safe stocked, which

I'd do on my day off and it was a rare occasion I came back empty-handed . . .

And just like that I was back where I started, only hungrier than before.

Breakfast was the usual mug of ersatz coffee and a smoke. In the late morning we lined up for a ladleful of vegetable and macaroni soup: in other words, hot water with a greenish tint to it, the odd globule of fat and if you were lucky a few bits of macaroni nosing around on the bottom.

In the late afternoon we got another ladleful, with for variety a few grains of rice instead of noodles: half a dozen grains and you thought you were doing alright. Every now and again we might get a small loaf of bread or a couple of biscuits. The loaf was about the size of your cupped hand; sometimes black, sometimes brown. It wasn't bad bread: for a while you felt you'd had something to eat, but with no protein to speak of there was always the nagging feeling of having been short-changed: starvation rations we called it.

Planes came and went through the day – there must have been an aerodrome nearby – they had corrugated-iron bodies and windscreens like flies' eyes. At night we listened to the drone of our bombers, to the explosions of the bombs they dropped just down the road. As the drone diminished, the singing began; the dark and freezing warehouse reverberating into the wee small hours.

We hadn't been there long when word got round a ship had come in. Those with better hearing than mine heard cargo being trucked away; others put the noise down to repairs being made at the port.

When we got the order to pack up, we looked at each other in amazement: all we had were the clothes we stood up in. Rations for the voyage were doled out: some got two small loaves, others got bully beef as well, still others got two tins of bully plus biscuits *and* the two small loaves – or so I heard. I ate one of my loaves then and there and was sorely tempted to follow up with the other immediately. I looked at my watch: hours had passed since we'd been ordered to pack. There was a rainbow in the sky.

The town was in ruins, palms lay like temple columns on their sides; the narrow streets were choked with rubble. Funnels protruded from the harbour, smoke churned from listing ships. The only undamaged vessel was a 6,000 ton merchantman moored to the one largely undamaged quay. And it wasn't the old dunga we'd expected either. In fact, going by the line from low stern to high bow, it was fairly newish; what's more there was something of the *Mauretania* about the bridge. The name on the bow was *Jason*. Not everyone was taken with it: one of the South Africans looked like he'd seen a ghost; the four lifeboats didn't impress anyone.

We were three abreast up to where bombing had nibbled the quay. Planks had been laid over the gaps: it was touch and go, but by sheer good luck I made it. We climbed the accommodation ladder, crossed the deck to the holds. It was tempus fidgets: no one wanted to be in port when the bombers turned up. The guards were even more on edge: their boots tied together were hung round their necks.

Most of the holds had an upper and a lower section, each had its own hatch-cover; both were battened down. We entered through a manhole in the top hatch and climbed down a narrow vertical ladder the ten feet to the lower hatch. I was about to continue into the lower section when it was decided it already had its full complement. The planks on the lower hatch were then covered with a tarpaulin and those who'd already claimed possies on it reclaimed them: clearly it was preferable to the deck. I found a vacant spot on the deck and made myself comfortable: it couldn't be worse than the concrete of the warehouse or the hardpan of the desert. In fact, there was a bit of give in it and it was warm from the engines.

I nodded off, thinking about the name on the stern; the nod to Jason and the Argonauts. If my memory served me correctly, there was an Iris in there too: Zeus had a child with her while married to Hera then put it about that the West Wind was the father. In keeping the peace, Iris earned the ire of Hera.

I woke near dawn to the stench of the latrine and sat up expecting the usual quips, but other than those with stomach cramps everybody was intently listening.

'What gives?' I said to the bloke next to me.

He put a finger to his lips with one hand and cupped an ear with the other. The engines were going flat tack; the pitch of the ship had steepened, the roll was more pronounced: if there were subs about, these were the conditions in which to expect them.

As the morning wore on, we felt the wind buffeting the ship as it topped the crests. Then the trapdoor opened: it was our turn for a breath of fresh air. We emerged into a sou'wester whistling round the cargo booms and cowl ventilators, spraying rain and surf across the deck. I filled my lungs with the bracing salt wind, let the rain wash my face then joined the debate in the lee of the superstructure as to what the land was to starboard.

Interest turned to the escort boat zigzagging about; its four inch guns and torpedo tubes, its Breda machineguns and depth charge throwers. It was lean and low; not in the same class as the *Achilles* but every bit as fast. Had we known it was there, we might have slept a bit better.

The rails were chocker with sailors with binoculars. The guards slopped past in their sodden socks, boots still swinging from their necks; they looked as if the world was against them. And perhaps with good cause: perhaps news of the attack on Pearl Harbour had come through?

Three

Back below deck, the discussion about what the land was or why the Italians seemed more on edge than usual was cut short by the ship lurching to starboard, by the engines cutting out; by our being thrown into a logjam.

While we were sorting ourselves out, we heard yelling and shouting and the thudding of stockinged feet across the deck. With the drop-off in speed, the lean to starboard eased: it still took some doing staying upright, especially when your neighbours – while not minding hanging onto you – weren't too keen on being hung onto themselves.

Meanwhile, the racket that had been clamouring for our attention below finally got it: somebody was going to town on the underside of the lower manhole cover. We knew they'd been doing it tough, being more vulnerable in the event of a torpedo strike; besides they hadn't had a turn on deck.

Through the thunder of the sea and the shrillness of the wind came pistol shots. They were followed by a bone-jarring impact and a crescendo of crashing and thudding and clanging. The men at the foot of the ladder shot up it: the first banged on the underside of the manhole cover with his fist; the second, squeezing himself up alongside, tried to hoist it with his shoulder. There came then a series of muffled explosions like a twenty-one gun salute. The lean to starboard eased, while the lean forward steepened. We hardly dared breathe.

The stroke of grace we expected was indeed a burst of light, but it came in the form of a silhouette in the manhole cover above of someone waving us up. You'd have thought the man ahead of you was going to be the last man out. The company in the lower hold wasn't far behind.

The deck we emerged onto was like a West Coast beach after a storm. Waves crashing over the bow surged through the splintered beams and twisted iron framing of the forward hatches and through the bodies, some of them still moving, and parts of bodies of the men who'd been on them. A South African medic caught my eye and waved me over. With some trepidation, I made my way toward him. The face of the man he was attending, also a South African, which to my mind already wore the pallor of death, was that of a lad in his teens. A flap of flesh was all that held his leg to his thigh. I was handed a pair of scissors.

'It's no use to him,' he said.

I needed both hands. I staggered to my feet with the leg, got to the rail and dropped it over, then everything caught up with me and I had to have a sit-down. When I had got my bearings back, I turned to check on the medic: he had someone else assisting him now so I left him to it.

There was a dull twanging sound at my shoulder and something flew past. I looked down and I saw a splash – the sea was surging along the ship's side like a river in flood – then someone surfaced and was swept round the stern. I saw others on this swollen river, some on life rafts. I saw someone leap from the ship and land on something: I don't think it did him much good.

There was land on this side of the ship too, about as far from home as The Peak: seeing a lifeboat heading toward it through the spindrift brought home the full force of my failure to learn how to swim. I thought about jumping anyway, though the chances of my grabbing something before I sank didn't seem too promising. It occurred to me then that the land I was looking at was the land we'd seen earlier: which could mean only one thing, that the ship had turned round. That being the case I thought I better check on the situation to starboard before I did anything rash.

The sea was calmer there for some reason; there was no land. I joined a couple of blokes perched on the rail like cockies at a stock sale barracking something below. Following their eyes, I saw a bloke floundering after a hatch beam in his boots and battledress. He got a mitt on it and pulled it under him and to our cheers, paddled off to his doom.

'Must've been shitting themselves,' said one of them, jabbing a thumb at the lifeboats bobbing abreast: one half-full of water, the other two upside-down.

'Eh?' I said.

'Couldn't wait for the ship to slow down; in too much of a hurry to get away.'

'If you dip in the well often enough,' I said.

'That's what the navy boys say. The quickest route between Italy and Libya – La Quarta Sponda, as the cheeky buggers call it – is the shortest; that's why that's where you'll find most of their shipping: they don't want to spend longer on the water than they have to. And they get their wish too, because that's where most of our lot are. That's why there was only one seaworthy ship in port when we left.'

'And why we're in the same boat,' said his offsider.

'So what's the land, do you know?'

'I'd say Greece.'

'Go on.'

'Greece is out of the range of the Fleet Air Arm.'

'But not the navy?'

'Not the navy, as it happens. All this talk is making me hungry. What about you. . . ?'

'Max,' I said.

'Ray, and this is Reece.'

'What did you have in mind?'

'We thought we'd have a look round to see if the Ities left us any going-away presents. If we're going down, it might as well be on a full stomach as an empty one.'

'Lead the way.'

The galley was packed to the rafters. Holding centre stage was a bloke who claimed he'd been a cook in the Grand in Wellington. I'd met a couple of the chefs there; they were larger than life and this bloke was no exception. He kept up a line of patter as he lifted eggshells above his head, two in each hand, draining the white before popping the shells in too to get the last morsel. Some blokes appeared behind us, looking as if they'd won the lottery, one of them with half a bag of flour on his shoulder.

Before long, we each had a pancake with a fried egg on it. After making short work of these, we were licking our lips and our wrists and looking round for more. Then someone turned up with some lemons. The galley had been gone through a number of times already; nevertheless a small dune of sugar was uncovered in one of the bins. It was the best lemon drink I've ever had, in fact I'll go further than that and say it was the best drink I've had full stop.

Of the 500 men in the first hold only a handful had survived. The rest, most of them dead of course, were sucked out of the hole. The explosion had blown off the upper and lower hatch-covers of holds one and two. It had also caused the bulkhead between them to fail. Hold two was a bloody backwater of body parts and screaming survivors desperately trying to catch hold of the ropes being lowered to them, at the same time trying to avoid the hatch beams sliding backwards and forwards like battering rams. The 'lucky' ones came up minus limbs and other bits and pieces and blotched all over.

The captain, possibly, in his haste to evacuate, had flipped the chadburn from FULL SPEED to DEAD SLOW rather than to STOP, which was why one of the propellers was still turning fast enough to butcher a man. And this was the fate of those who'd gone over the port side: the wash on the outside of the turn had dragged them into it. The 'twenty-one gun salute' would have been the escort dropping depth charges.

When my bladder drove me from the galley, we'd closed to within a mile of the coast. I could now see the north side of the hill I'd seen earlier. It was dusted with snow. In the foreground on the seafront was an old castle and it was this that we seemed to be headed toward: backwards because we had turned round so that the propeller, which had been reversed, could add its tuppence-worth. Doubtless the stern was also contributing, catching what it could of the sou' wester (someone clearly knew what they were doing).

It appeared as we closed on this promontory that the castle took up several hundred yards of seafront. At the southern end was a tower on a tiny island connected to the castle by a causeway. It was some storeys high and had crenellated parapets and a cupola. The battlements of the castle by contrast had mostly crumbled as had parts of the wall. Tiny figures lined the ramparts; the waves exploding on the sea walls sending showers of spray over them. At the northern end, other figures lined a small beach flanked by the remains of two forward defensive forts; presumably intended to guard the seaward end of what appeared to be an unfinished moat. Of more concern to us was the southern tip of a low island or reef about two hundred yards out from the beach.

There were still a few hundred yards to go, when the ship's stern turned north and the ship began to roll and pitch due to the waves bunching in the shallowing sea. My first thought was whoever was in charge had decided to look for a less hazardous landing spot further up the coast. But the ship kept approaching sideways. We were almost upon the shelf when a trough opened up and I saw the shelf's edge and heard the shouts of 'Take cover!'

Men with their backs to the wall, heads between their knees, their hands over their heads lined the passageway. I sat with a thump as the ship lifted on what was clearly a bigger wave than those preceding it: the timing couldn't have been better, because from stem to stern the ship was lifted over the shelf.

When the wave put us down, the hull went hammer and tongs at the sixty-five million-year-old saw-tooth rocks that had barely lost their edge since the previous ice age. We thumped, bumped, ground and screeched our way across the reef like a derailed train, expecting to go over at any moment. Eventually, the cacophony of braying and shrieking gave up the ghost; even the wind seemed to pause for breath.

Then the ship began rocking, first one way – grinding and chafing and rasping to a knife edge and teetering on it – then going all the way back, to the same sound effects. Over and back, back and over: pause, roll, lean; pause, roll, lean. Amplified by the 600-mile fetch from Tripolitania, the wrecking-ball waves thumped the starboard beam, broke over the superstructure, cascaded down the companionways and along the passageways; got to the engine room and shorted the electrics. The gale resumed its baleful whine. It was the middle of winter, the middle of the afternoon. I went out for a jack nohi.

Four

It was like Bombay, except the bigger ship was a castle; it loomed over us. With wind-assistance, it was almost within spitting distance; close enough to read the minds of the guards on the ramparts, who every now and again, being forced by a gust to take a step back, didn't look too happy about their duty. Others, Germans among them, stood on the patches of grass growing between the rows of rocks like beach obstacles before the unfinished moat. They must've thought we would skittle them; breach the walls and come to rest in the castle grounds. It was astonishing how close we were, fifty yards by my reckoning, a piffling distance compared to how far we'd come, yet the nearest of those yards would have been well over our heads and the farthest, with the waves breaking round the ends of the ship and going head to head over the rocks, would have souped our brains and diced our bones.

Above the moat, a white road loped past red-roofed, white-walled houses toward a snow-topped summit to the north of the one I'd seen earlier (which it turned out was not pyramidal but conical). Nor was it one hill but a cluster: mum, dad and the kids posing for a family portrait. The locals, who'd come out to witness our arrival, stood in groups on the road. Others, who'd come down to the shore, despite threats of beatings and worse, stood their ground and pointed at the bundles at their feet.

Snatches of 'There'll always be an England' whipped past us, then men I hadn't seen since boarding appeared and began tying ropes to the rails and lowering themselves, till one man got cold feet halfway down and while trying to haul himself back up lost his grip. The swell carried him in and might have deposited him on the ramparts, but failing at that, dropped him on the rocks; picked him up and dropped him again and again.

The light was fading when a South African seaman with a line round his waist was lowered overboard. After a long battle we thought he'd lost, he emerged from the tumult under the northernmost of the two forward defensive forts. He was met by the soldiers, yanked to his feet and strip-searched. After an exchange that was punctuated by pointing and finger-pointing, the heavier rope attached to the line round his waist was hauled in. By this time, all you could see were jiggling lanterns, however that didn't stop men grabbing this rope and sliding off into the dark. I left them to it.

I spent the night with one eye half open: on the brink of sleep, thinking the ship had gone over, I'd be wide awake. I must've managed forty winks however, because when I woke it was to stillness. The storm had gone off in search of greener pastures; the landline was unattended.

'Jesus, Mary and Joseph! Is that what I think it is?" I said to the other early riser.

As he put it, when the ship had leaned shoreward and the line went slack, the men on it had been dropped into the sea or onto rocks; some had managed to hold onto it and had used it as a guide and a means of hauling themselves shoreward. On the other hand, when the ship leant seaward and the rope went taut, those on it had been flung off. They also had landed in the sea or on rocks but from much higher up. The lucky few, who'd gone down when the rope was more or less taut, had pretty much had a clear run in. It wasn't till it began to get light however, that this was seen and the landline was abandoned. Those in charge of the operation had not heard anything over the wind or been alerted by lantern signals or other means.

Since then, a new plan had been hatched: two small cutters had been found below decks; these had been brought up and the accommodation ladder had been lowered. For the wounded, a stretcher was rigged to the landline.

Reece and Ray and I put our heads together: at a dozen blokes per cutter per trip it would take at least a day to get us off; that being the case with the guards on one side of the water and those in no great hurry on the other, the latter could go through the ship at their leisure.

We grazed on raw onions, chocolate, biscuits, apples, tinned fish and tinned meat, tinned beans and what-have-you. The afternoon was well advanced when I put my head up: the sun hovered over the sea; the water was as blue as a kingfisher's back while the hills were the yellow of its breast. No longer nagged by food, my mind turned to other thoughts – the possibility of a future with a certain other person perhaps; the occupants of the castle, who at a similar time of day must have entertained thoughts of a similar nature – when I was interrupted by a familiar voice.

'Plenty more fish in the sea,' said Ray. 'Quite some hole, isn't it?'

'You're not wrong there.'

The bow looked like it had been opened by a monstrous stab-and-drag opener. At its widest a man on his side could have passed through without touching the sides; height-wise, three acrobats on each other's shoulders could have walked through it.

'Thought we'd check on the bunk situation,' said Ray.

'I'll join you,' I said.

I put the stub away and followed him. Our eyes were still getting used to the dark when we heard a whoop.

'Sangiovese!' breathed Reece, in his best Italian accent, 'Panzano.'

'Pity you're on the wagon,' said Ray. 'Here, give it here.'

He wrapped the base in some discarded clothing and began thumping it against the doorframe.

'Bloody hell!' said Reece. 'You'll have every Tom, Dick and Harry in here if you carry on like that!'

'Move over and let the dog see the rabbit,' I said.

I worked a knife I'd found into the cork and twisted as I pulled.

'Bob's your uncle! Salute!'

'Pity about the cork.'

'All mouth and no trousers, if you ask me.'

'What about the plum and cherry notes?' said Reece. 'And here I was thinking I was in cultured company! *Sing, goddess, the anger of Peleus' son Achilleus and its devastation, which put pains thousandfold upon the Achaians, hurled in their multitudes to the house of Hades strong souls of heroes, but gave their bodies to be the delicate feasting of dogs, of all birds . . .'*

'And if the Wine you drink, the Lip you press, End in the Nothing all Things end in – Yes – Then fancy while Thou art, Thou art but what Thou shalt be – Nothing – Thou shalt not be less.' That was my contribution.

'If it wasn't for that Gerry we'd be drinking with the fishes,' said Ray, removing the bottle's little basket. 'What a fiasco!'

'What Gerry?'

'The bloke with the monkey wrench and the luger; he was going round telling everybody what to do?'

'A Gerry on an Itie ship?'

'He shot one of them! I wouldn't like to be in the captain's shoes when they catch up with him.'

'Eh?'

'Abandoning a ship that doesn't go down doesn't go down too well.'

'He shot one of our blokes too, I heard.'

'But what was he doing on board?'

'Boson, I heard.'

'Engineer: a boson wouldn't know how to stop a propeller and reverse it.'

'Apparently he got everyone to stand over the stern.'

'Not me.'

'Or me.'

'What was that about?'

'I think the idea was to take the pressure off the bow or more importantly off the next bulkhead in line.'

'So why choose the reef and not the estuary?'

'Maybe it was too shallow?'

'How would he know that?'

'The charts.'

'What does he look like?'

'Tallish, I think, fair,' said Reece.

'Average height, dark,' said Ray.

'Age?'

'Old enough to be your father.'

'Not mine.'

'Deserves a bloody medal, I reckon, even if he is German.'

The blankets had all been collected for the wounded, so we settled down with one palliasse underneath and another on top. From somewhere on board came strains of 'There'll always be an England' again. It was up there with the national anthem, according to the English. As far as I was concerned, the tune was alright. It was the lyrics I didn't go much for, the 'if-you're-not-with-us-you're-against-us' jingoism: too old-school-tie for my liking. Apart from which, I imagine it would have been a slap in the face for the bloke who'd saved our bacon, who'd apparently turned on his heel when they'd come out with it earlier, and gone back to looking after our wounded.

Five

The cutter skittered when I set foot in it and I almost got a dunking. With a full load, it was brimful. When I got up the courage to glance over the side, I saw greeny-yellow rocks through the dazzle and the reflections and between them men in brown uniforms and blue uniforms setting off tiny puffs of sand with their boots or unshod feet; their arms outstretched as if in resignation or entreaty; their heads thrown back, mouths wide open as if belting out some aria while tiny fish came and went.

We stepped over waves that wouldn't have said boo to a goose, trudged over drifts of egg-sized pebbles that knocked and rattled underfoot. Centuries of broken pottery, biffed from the castle, littered the beach. A mint green fragment caught my eye. I wanted to pick it up and turn it over, to reflect on the history it had been part of: who the people were who used it. But the mood of the guards hadn't lightened; maybe because they knew we'd been through their things?

The track over the neck of the peninsula narrowed toward the saddle: it was a bit of a squeeze between prickly pear cladodes as big as ashets and the eroded edge. On the other side of the moat, the northern wall of the castle, gaunt and spectral as the photos I'd seen of the Acropolis, cast its wintry shadows over us. I took a last look at the ship – the biggest fish out of water I was ever likely to see – and mentally thanked the German.

Beyond the rise, much to our surprise, a small town came into view. The people: women entirely in black (scarves, dresses, aprons, jackets, stockings, footwear, the works), some carrying babies, some with grey hair on their chins, some lobbing bread that by the look of them they could have done with themselves; children in skirts and shorts, jerseys out at the elbows, running barefoot alongside us, offering us water; white-bearded men on crooked walking sticks, grinning their heads off.

'*Aeì Libýē phérei ti kainón*,' an old woman said.

'*Kakòs anèr makróbios*,' the old man replied and they chuckled.

I turned to the bloke next to me: he'd been in Greece earlier in the year.

'Libya is full of surprises', he said.

'What about the old man?'

"Only the good die young': that's how we put it. Their way is: 'the bad live long.'"

We were in the southern Peloponnese, in the town of Methoni. In Homer's time it was Pedasos, known for its vineyards and for its castle; it being one of the seven Agamemnon offered Achilles in return for him giving up his suit and getting on with the war.

We had washed up on the shores of the *Iliad*. Methoni was on the trade route to Istanbul and everybody who was anybody wanted it: the Spartans, the Venetians, the Byzantines, the Franks, the Turks and the Egyptians, not to mention pirates. The Turks crowned their siege of 1500 with the slaughter of 7000 males over the age of ten; the sea round the tower ran red.

A short march brought us to the inlet of a shallow harbour that lapped the eastern wall of the castle. We turned left along its muddy-brown margin then left again into the cold damp shadow of a small stone warehouse. The shutters on the grilled windows had been closed, which was fortunate indeed because the metal doors had been taken off their hinges and the air off the bay was, to put it mildly, bracing. I think now that this warehouse was the source of the clothes which the men on the beach were hoping to give us, because as I later learned it was owned by a doctor with sidelines in property and secondhand clothes. I might add that within weeks of their deportation, suitcases of clothes belonging to the Jews of Macedonia had been turning up for sale in the southern Peloponnese.

The puddles on the floor were from the wrung-out uniforms of the previous nights' occupants; between them were the charred and waterlogged remains of fires. A sheet of roofing iron flapped overhead: apparently it had been prised up by the youths of the town, under the noses of the guards, so that bread and dry clothes could be dropped in. I shuffled from one foot to the other and when I got tired of that I shuffled from the other foot back to the first.

The locals saw us off with more gifts; it was like being given money by a beggar, which is not to say we'd have been too proud to accept, but we didn't get the chance: the guards ran at them with rifle butts and clenched fists and knocked the food from their hands and trod it into the road or put it in their pockets. It was par for the course: in the two-plus years of Italian occupation, the Greeks had been concentrated into camps and tortured, raped, brutalised and murdered by the thousands; they had been starved to death by the hundreds of thousands; hundreds of villages had been destroyed. And apart from the trial of a few individuals and the return of the Dodecanese (a mere fraction of a percentage point of the reparations claimed), there had been no come back. And that wasn't the half of it.

The women came to their doors and windows and some came into the street: some made guarded victory signs, others were just guarded. And I wondered if this in part was due to the song we sang – *She'll be coming round the mountain* – because their men had a version of it which made ours sound like children's song.

The town petered out and with it our audience and our oomph. Men fell out to relieve themselves; those who'd left their boots on the *Jason*, lest they drown in them, pulled up lame. Near the pass, the olives gave way to cushion-shaped shrubs of thyme and sage, of broom, horehound and asphodel; oil-producing plants that sometimes exploded in the hot summers. We passed under the snow-capped, cone-shaped summit of Ai-Nikolas then descended to the harbour where the battle that led to the Greeks' independence had been fought; along the way passing the remains of an aqueduct, which to all intents and purposes had once supplied the old castle it led to. At this point the column hooked left in through a formidable gate and we found ourselves enclosed by the curtain-wall that had once protected 600 houses. The houses had all gone: all that was left was the barracks block – in which the guards took up residence – and an acropolis; and a church that had once been a mosque – and between-times a church and a mosque. The freshly dug trenches round it held many of the bodies of our comrades washed ashore from the *Jason*.

A short path led to a second set of doors – studded like our hobnails – through them into a courtyard crisscrossed by stone partitions. Here we caught up with those who'd arrived before us, some of whom drew our attention to the letters and numerals engraved on the limestone walls.

I was looking at the grilled doors and barred windows of cells that had been made by blocking off the arches, when I heard yelling. Taking a step back to see what the fuss was about, I saw an aeroplane heading straight for us through drifts of low cloud, its engines screaming, its pilot and navigator-cum-bombardier hunched over the controls, steeling themselves for their reception. It dropped out of sight under the line of the west wall and not for the first time I questioned the RAF's choice of markings. A second or two later, the flak guns opened up, which in their turn were drowned out by the explosions of the 500 pounders.

We picked up the receding drone as it emerged from the cacophony. Whether or not they'd hit their target, whatever it was, much to the chagrin of the Italians they'd gotten away with it.

We resumed our wait for supper, which – par for the course, 'because we were late' – didn't eventuate, before settling like dogs turning this way and that. The flagstones were flat enough; it was the edges of the gaps between them that were the problem. Drops, condensing from the fog, 'exploded' all round us.

Six

We looked up and down the line. As far as we could see, there was nothing coming either way: evidently the guards knew something we didn't.

'*Tutti a bordo!*' they shouted, '*Tutti a bordo!*' getting evermore impatient.

Then it dawned on us they meant the pint-sized train on the far siding. They couldn't be serious, surely? It had to be a train for children. It was no spring-chicken either. Then incredulity turned to childlikeness as we raced each other for a window seat. Two giggling-gerties elbowing and shouldering each other lost their footing on the ballast. Another bloke tripped on a strip of concrete that served as a platform.

The carriages were dollhouse-sized; even I had to watch my head. The seats were miniature park benches: a single on one side of a narrow aisle, a double on the other. As it happened we all got a seat except for the guards, who stood outside on the pokey boarding porches, hanging onto miniature wrought-iron balustrades. It was none too tropical outside and they weren't too pleased with this arrangement, whereas two out of three of us got window seats.

A toot and a jerk and a clank and clouds of black smoke engulfed the carriages. As the speed picked up, cheering gave way to singing: there was the song about the bloke who gets pulled up for not having a ticket, the song about the bloke who leaves home because he can't find work, the song about the soldier who goes up north to have it out with his ex-sergeant and the song about the soldier who comes home in a box. Reece managed a creditable rendition of *McAbee's Railroad Piece* on a comb and a threadbare kerchief.

The snow-covered, forage-cap peaks above Kalamata dropped below the horizon. We rattled over bridges, through olive groves, through scrubland that reminded us of home; fell silent, nodded off, woke to the guards taking pot shots at sheep; woke again at the approaches to stations to take in the pinched faces of the long-suffering Greeks behind the hand-winch barriers, to exchange smiles and sympathetic shrugs with the locals on the platforms. On the basis of our efforts on their behalf, our stocks at that stage were right up there.

Stations were gathering places, windows on the outside world; opportunities to glean titbits of information that could prove useful. They were opportunities to show your contempt for your occupiers for robbing your country blind of the tools and materials of trade, of the implements and machinery of cultivation and harvest, of fishing boats, of infrastructure; for having to pay them for the privilege of being occupied, while your quisling government printed money to cover its depreciation till the economy was bankrupt; for the decree prohibiting contact with us – the concern being perhaps that if word got out something might be done about it.

Word got out anyway, something was done about it, but as is often the way it was of least use to those in most need. Money changed hands: aid fell off the backs of trucks and was sold on the black market to those who could afford it; which is not to say the black market was altogether a bad thing; without it more would have perished.

Meanwhile the very poor turned what few possessions they had into food and when this ran out, faced with the choice of watching their children die or dying themselves, left them to compete with the dogs for the scraps in the gutters and the rubbish bins.

This didn't apply so much to the places we passed through: in the country it was possible to keep body and soul together, as long as you didn't grow more than you needed. As for the farmers who managed to keep or get their plant back, they had to pay tax on what they produced and they had to sell it to the government. To get round this they hid their produce from the tax inspectors, bribed the soldiers at the check-points and profited at the townies' expense. At one of the stations we passed through, shots were fired over the heads of the locals to clear the platform: gestures of solidarity had been observed.

The sun had not long gone down when we stopped at yet another station in the middle of nowhere; this one with the inscription ΑΧΑΪΑ above its entrance. Our stupor from the nine-hour haul, coming as it did on top of weeks of malnutrition and dysentery and dirt-poor digs, was all too evident in our reluctance to swap the stuffy carriages for the frosty air. Needless to say this didn't go down well with our frozen guards.

We lined up beside the water towers then set off in the direction of a trio of peaks sticking up into the last of the light. A four or five-mile trudge into the freezing countryside brought us to a glow in the frosty air; the shadows of posts and barbed wire reaching out to embrace us. There being no suggestion of supper in the offing, we gathered an army blanket each and a wad of straw. We split the wads into five more or less equally thick squabs and laid them beam-wise. Four rows covered an area about six by six feet. Six Italian groundsheets, snap-fastened end-to-end over a ridgepole and laced at the sides, covered it neatly.

Seven

I opened my eyes at reveille and lifted my head: we were sardines in a can and no mistake. I lay back contemplating the dull green light coming through the groundsheets and decided that while I preferred the light through plain canvas, the Italian groundsheets were probably warmer for being water-proofed; nor did you get a soaking from brushing against them. In a week's time, the family (fifteen at the last count, spouses and children included; Mum in her element, Dad chuffing on his pipe) would be sitting down to my second Christmas dinner away. The bugler wasn't your usual glorified alarm clock; perhaps he was missing family too? There was a moment's silence then a clangour of steel on steel.

'From the sublime to the ridiculous,' said Richard and we waggled our heads from side to side.

The queue when we joined it, stretched halfway across the parade ground. The cookhouse (a repurposed hayshed by the look of it; the manger of our bedding) with its back to the prevailing wind, looked a dozen miles east to a wave of mountains. To the north, beyond the Gulf of Patras were mountains of a similar height and as far away; both had a sprinkling of snow. A battered wheel rim dangled from an oak tree, twisting and swaying in the wind. A cook or a kitchen-hand stepped out and gave it another hiding.

'All we need now is strings and woodwind,' said Richard. 'What are you like on the fiddle?'

'I wouldn't know one end from the other,' I said.

'I hope the same applies to the cooks,' he said, 'they look a bit shifty to me.'

After breakfast we went for a wander. The compound enclosed a clump of oaks; this was where those who'd missed out on a tent had bedded down. The latrine – a trench six yards by two with a pole over it – was in a dip by the road. Though the two houses a mile off were the only visible sign of settlement, we knew from the bells there were people around us. As for where we were, it sounded like the name of the station, only with something added: *Ana* or *Ara* or *Ano*. A lot of the Greek settlements had an upper and lower part and the lower part was generally prefixed by *Kato*, so I'm assuming *Ana* or *Ara* or *Ano* meant upper. Those who know their Homer will know that ΑΧΑΪΑ or Achaia is the ancient name for Greece.

I felt a familiar trickle in my beard, which was hardly surprising as I'd seen neither hide nor hair of a bar of soap in a month, or a pair of scissors or razor or that there was barely enough water to drink let alone wash and shave with. Doubtless the lice that glued their nits in our hair and dug their latrines in our skin and did their business there thought they were on starvation rations too. I knew the risk of sores; I knew I could scratch my skin raw and not winkle out the itch, but I also knew resisting the urge took a stronger will than mine.

'Bladdy goggas,' said Richard.

The extra tents had no sooner arrived, along with replacements for our sorely-missed greatcoats, when a vault of cloud enclosed us in an icebox, dashing our hopes of a long spell of late autumn sun, banishing our scruples about donning the greenish-grey Italian greatcoat; which aside from its chest pocket and patch pockets, its sewn-in belt and button-up tails was also lined. To expect to get a good night's sleep in it however, was asking too much.

Then the rain came and the epithet Pig Pen, coined by the South Africans. There was no denying the camp looked as if it had been rooted by pigs, nor were the tents unlike the A-frame sties of piggeries and of course the skilly bore more than a passing resemblance to swill. On the whole you'd have to say pigs were better off: they got better rations for one thing, for another the down-draughts dropped on us by the mountains wouldn't have knocked a sty over.

The pockmarks overflowed, rivulets ran across the treacly clag. We dug dykes round the tents to keep the straw dry: it disappeared down the maw of the swampy ground. The rain got into everything. The fug of mouldering damp was as dismal as the stench of the latrines. When the rain turned to sleet, calls of nature became life and death struggles: you staggered through the mud in the pitch black to find the latrine when it spilled into your boots then tracked the effluent back to your tent – it got into everything: your clothing, your bedding, your hair, your food. The dysentery that became endemic was blamed on the bread ration and the bread ration was withdrawn, it was not replaced. The cooks and the higher ranks increasingly looked out for number one. There were dingdongs over whose turn it was to scrape the coppers. It snowed.

It can only have been through sheer luck, but up till then I'd avoided gippy-tummy. Now I was foetal with colic, my insides gurgling like a downpipe in a downpour, my wind rivalling the thunder; I passed a bloody mucous that wouldn't have been out of place on the rear end of a lambing ewe. I'd stopped taking my boots off through sheer exhaustion and because when the time came I didn't have time to put them on. I'd get back to the tent feverish and parched, pull up my sodden blanket, once a shade of beige on a dog you'd call blue, now the colour of the mud and before closing my eyes I'd have to do it all over again. We called it Dysentery Acre.

It was Christmas before I was over the worst. On Christmas Day, up to our ankles in freezing mud, we endured one interminable roll call after another; the bells in the neighbouring churches tolling through the morning mist. Then the rain set in again, wetting the firewood, diddling us of the coffee we turned up our noses at.

'A monkeys' wedding,' said Richard.

After the midday skilly, the Commandante produced two cases of currants and we lined up again. However, what began as a dessertspoonful each, by the time I stretched out my hand, had diminished to a teaspoonful. I peeled off poking a dozen currants around in my palm, in half a mind to fling them into the mud. Bugger it, I thought and tossed them into my mouth. As luck would have it the largest missed. I looked down. Bugger it, I thought and planted it with my boot. Meanwhile, my teeth getting on with the job, the astonishing tangy sweetness of the Black Corinth grape was blossoming in my mouth.

That afternoon, on our perambulations, I bumped into the medic from the boat. Richard introduced us. I reminded him of our earlier meeting; whether he remembered it was debatable. We got onto Sidi Rezegh and he spoke about his truck getting stuck, how while digging it out he'd paused and looked up at the boiling column of smoke over Point 175, a mile high at least he reckoned, the base full of the flashing lights from all the ordnance going off. How anything could have survived it was beyond him he reckoned. It was beyond me too, I assured him.

'It was like the fires on the veldt,' said Richard, 'now I know how the wildebeests and the cheetahs feel.'

The Commandante's gift came up and I volunteered the opinion, he'd have been better off divvying it up amongst his own lot. As it happened, it had been the subject of the service he'd just taken; his voice dropping a couple of notches, so I had to lean in. The gravity of John Wesley's explications of the Sermon on the Mount came through loud and clear. I'd been brought up on the Presbyterian version. I knew it by heart; clearly I hadn't taken it to heart.

That night some blokes got under the fence. A few days later, they were picked up by the Carabinieri: the farmers who'd taken them under their wing knew the risks. They were dobbed in by their neighbours, not out of fascist sympathies, but for the reward. After the usual unspeakable atrocities, scattering the families to the four corners of their wits, the Carabinieri torched their houses and anything else they could burn.

It was hogmanay before the currant bun put in an appearance: on New Year's Eve the frozen mud clanged like an iron bridge as we marched over it, billy goats gruff in our long hair and beards, and out through the gates.

In and out of bays we swung and up and over bluffs, the guards on the tailboard hanging on for grim life, while over their shoulders we watched the stub-nosed ridges behind Missolonghi coming down to the gulf to drink.

Eight

On the outskirts of Patras, the drivers braked in the manner to which we'd become accustomed and we were drafted into warehouses with round windows in the gable: Cyclops' eyes. Some wit came up with 'The Bungalows' and the name, being suitably sardonic, stuck. Getting into them was another trial, not helped by the guards snapping at our heels.

Rows of tiered shelves rose from the gloom, with aisles so narrow to pass anyone you had to turn side-on. When we found out this was where the Greeks had kept their prisoners, the dottore's riposte returned to our lips: "What are you complaining about, don't you know the entire Italian Army is lousy?"

On hands and elbows and the balls of my feet I backed onto the bottom shelf. When I got tired of lying on my front I turned onto my back, when I got tired of lying on my back I turned onto my side, when I got tired of that there was always the other. It reminded me of stories I'd heard my father and his father sharing about the thinner seams of the Millheugh where only by lying on your side could you swing your pickaxe. That said it was a step up from being out in the elements, or so we thought till the cold seeping up from the concrete made our bones ache; while the cigarette ration, mixed with the smouldering fires of damp scrap wood, had us coughing our lives away; the draft between the Cyclops' eye and two wooden louvers in the back wall being about as strong as a royal wave.

The night guard, like a lobby concierge, sat at the front of the warehouse beneath a light bulb with a fluted metal shade. To his right was a forty-four-gallon drum with a ladder propped over it: you can guess what that was for. Jokers, singers, versifiers, tub-thumpers and tellers of tall tales used the front of the warehouse to stage the odd variety show. It was also where we lined up for rations and where the water-cart man did a roaring trade in a panforte of pressed fruit and molasses. A wristwatch bought you 150 of these 'pasties' (as we called them); ten cigarettes or a 200 gram loaf, fifteen. As I doubted whether any number of these 'pasties' could give me the feeling of having eaten something that I got from the bread ration, fleeting as that was, I didn't find out how moreish they were till Ned, trying to give up smoking, prevailed on me: two for a cigarette.

As if things weren't tight enough, winter put the squeeze on. We crouched over the smouldering fires, flushing the lice from the seams of our uniforms with a cigarette, crisping or crushing them between our fingernails, while thinking about food obsessively: about whether there'd be a piece of cheese the size of a pat of butter to go with the 200g loaf, or meat (a trace, a piece of gristle) with the rice instead of beans, or if neither then whether the rice would be salted.

The life and death issue however was not as we'd supposed – the starvation rations – it was the lack of fresh air and exercise; we weren't taking advantage of the available one hour per day in the yard. It wasn't till somebody's throat swelled up and he was carted off hospital, till spinal meningitis carted off several others, that we got off our chuffs.

Their places were taken by a couple of blokes who, while younger than us, carried themselves as if they were older. They'd been picked up making an attempt on the life of the one German we had any time for (other than the engineer on the *Jason* of course and one or two composers and philosophers and poets and whatnot). On the night of the storm widely taken for Crusader's opening salvoes, they were hauling themselves and their gear up knee-deep cataracts pouring off the coastal escarpment, on their way to a job that was as breathtaking for its audacity as for the shortcomings of its planning. That they lived to tell the tale they owed to the intervention of their target, because having been picked up wearing Bedouin jurds over their uniforms they could have been shot as spies. Rommel was more put out by our thinking his headquarters were as far behind the front line as we supposed.

Beda Littoria to us mere mortals was the kink in the main road – Arabs in tin huts on one side, colonists in villas on the other – where we'd hung on for dear life. To the mission, it was tower blocks and barracks and a tall building among cedars. Like his old man before him, one of the co-leaders (shot by one of his own men in all probability) was posthumously decorated for his role in a cock up. The other – who had one foot in the mission and the other on an escape route; a repeat performance of his effort on Crete, where he'd jumped the queue to get off the island – needless to say survived.

Not a day passed when the question wasn't put to the guard: *how much longer?* Not a day passed when the answer wasn't the *Domani*, till the day dawned when he announced we would be leaving the following day. So what did we do? Broke into song, of course:

Tell me the old, old story,
Of unseen things above,
Of Jesus and his glory
Of Jesus and his love;
Tell me the story simply
As to a little child
For I am weak and weary
And hopeless and defiled . . .
Tell me the story slowly
That I may take it in
That wonderful redemption
God's remedy for sin;
Tell me the story often,
For I forget so soon.
The early dew of morning
Has passed away at noon.
Tell me the story softly
With earnest tones and grave;

Remember I'm the sinner
    Whom Jesus came to save;
Tell me the story always
    If you would really be
In any time of trouble
    A comforter to me.
Tell me the same old story
    When you have come to fear
That this world's empty glory
    Is costing me too dear;
And when the Lord's bright glory
    Is dawning on my soul
Tell me the old, old story:
    "Christ Jesus makes me Whole".

Needless to say, he wasn't amused.

Seven Men
Under the Stars

Here in Italy we say if you count seven stars then straight away think of something, immediately that thought will appear in the mind of the person you love.

One

After a week of snow and thunder and lightning, we marched through the town to the wharves, blinking in the bright light. The Gulf of Patras can take some beating on a fine day and the soldiers in their garrison caps and 'Swiss yodellers' seemed to think so too; they were singing their hearts out and their heads off. It was bella Italia this and belle moglie that, belle ragazze this and belle madri that. It was as if we'd taken a wrong turning and ended up on the set of an opera production, as if when the lighthouse at the end of the wharf winked at us it would be our turn to raise the roof. Others meanwhile were busy stowing their luggage (and loot by the look of it) on an old passenger liner. We followed them up the gangway with a rousing rendition of 'Old Man River'.

The holds were crammed with bunks, so the usual queue had been dispensed with and our section commanders were serving us in our bunks; a turn-around if ever there was one and one we milked for all it was worth. It was the usual slim pickings of course, except with variations, so for instance the meat in the rice was polony, the bread was fresh (baked on board) and there was an issue of wine and fresh figs. That said after three days in port we'd had a gutsful: we were still pretty raw from our last voyage. Then in the early hours of the fourth day, the Tannoy clicked on and the tinny voice of the captain announced our destination. Which was all very well and good till he advised us to keep our bootlaces loose and our buttons undone and the fear we'd been keeping a lid on till that point got out and skittered round the hold like a beast that has seen the butcher's bolt-gun.

Up on deck for a leak, I gazed at the sagging dune-like hills of Albania, at the wake of a fishing boat going the other way, at an island to the west I presumed was Corfu: everything a pale blue it seemed we could disappear into and no one would be any the wiser; in short what was happening to the Greeks. I looked down: the sea jostling the hull was the azure of my mother's blouse; the flecks of spray were its polka dots.

To put us at ease, the captain set a course for Montenegro before making the crossing: sensing we were in good hands and lulled by the engines' rhythm and warmth, we were dead to the world when the boat nudged the wharf in Bari.

Nuggets of wisdom from the Dux in his dunce's cap decorated the bridges, the churches, the shops, the factories and the schools: *BISONGA SOPRATUTTO OSARE; Disciplina, Concordia, e lavo per la ricostruzione della patria; Il lavoro e la cosa piu solenne, piu nobile, piu religiosa della vita; CREDERE OBERIRE COMBATTERE; La Guerra è per l'uomo come la maternità è alla donna* and so on and so forth. *DUCE DUCE DUCE* goose-stepped alongside us on a wall. Young men in clean-pressed uniforms grinned slyly, while others grinned broadly. Children hopped and skipped while chanting nursery rhymes, stopped to hiff stones then ran to catch up. Men had to be picked up and put on a cart. The women wept openly. We knew, from the reflections of a wild-haired mob in a mishmash of uniforms on clothes-hanger frames, that we weren't much to look at; even so the tears struck us as a bit rich. That was before the penny dropped: the tears were for their husbands, fathers, sons, brothers, cousins, uncles, nephews and grandsons languishing in our cages in the desert, drifting in their coracles of bones ever further astern; and for the whole sorry state of the world. These were the beautiful women of the songs. This was the beautiful country.

The guard popped his head in the door (the only way he could get from one end of the train to the other was by changing wagons at stops). Looking along the forms and deciding we needed cheering up, he offered us his opinion that it wouldn't be long before we were looking back on this journey from the windows of our own trains. When I got the opportunity I asked about the stone huts in the olive grove we were passing. He looked at me warily.

'Ah,' he said, 'il trullo.'

'Trullo?'

'Cupola?'

'Dome?'

'Si!' he said, 'South African?'

'Kiwi.'

'Kiwi?'

'New Zealander.'

'Ah, Captain Cook, did you know there was Italian seamen on his ship?'

I shook my head politely.

'My English is not so good?'

'A trap for young players.'

'A trap for young players?'

I tried a different tack, got into muddle, then backing out concluded his English was streets ahead of my Italian.

'Streets ahead?'

'Più veloce?'

The hut, if I got his drift, was built from the stone excavated for the well; what was left over from lining it. It capped the well, it was a place to store the tools of cultivation and harvest and it provided shelter from the elements for the itinerant workers. At the last stop, he shelled out handfuls of coins and advised us to get ubriacarsi at our first opportunity.

The name on the station was Tuturano; it could almost have been a name from home. Less familiar was the shrine; the painting of the Madonna in its hull-like niche, fingertips of one hand in the palm of the other; the gesture not unlike that of the women of Bari. We shuffled beneath a hand-painted sign – the S of USCITA like a back-to-front Z – out into the yard at the front of the station to be met by a troop of teenage Germans: if looks could kill, that would have been the end of us.

At the end of a long straight we came to the town; the tramp of our boots brought the villagers to their gates and fences. On seeing us however, they retreated into their houses crossing themselves. We zigzagged through the narrow streets back out into the damp country night. After a few miles we passed through an ancient olive grove – centuries old judging by the girths – and came upon a paddock of tents. It was too late for food of course and for straw as well for some. It was Dysentery Acre all over again and not for the first time that day I wondered if I was coming down with something.

Two

It took some doing, but eventually I got my head up and wagged it from side to side. Drifts of rain swirled in the camp lights.

'What's that?' I said.

'Eh?' said the Aussie.

A bit later, I heard him again.

'All the mod cons,' he was saying, nodding at the flush mechanism.

My eyes had closed again and my chin was on my chest, when he spoke again.

'Better to have a roof over our heads and no walls than the other way round, but?'

I nodded.

The ablutions block lacked walls too. It was pretty flash all the same, with its rows of sinks and lines of spigots.

'I'll see you back,' said Dave.

'No need,' I said, but he must have all the same; how I would have got there otherwise, I can't imagine.

When I lay back, my head kept going; back, back into a bottomless pit. I woke with a splitting headache.

'One too many last night?' said Ned, while we were having a look round the camp.

Ned was one of a half-dozen blokes who had a go at what others only thought or talked about. After several days, tiring of the raw and cold food, they lit a fire. Well, they might as well have been sending smoke signals. They knew the game was up when they saw the soldiers on the beach. Just hearing about the beating they got made me flinch.

As a matter of fact, there's a sequel to this story. A handful of days after being crippled by the *Porpoise*, the commander of H.M.S. *Torbay* (one of the subs that delivered the commandoes to the coast below Beda Littoria), 'Crap' Miers (he got a V.C. for sinking some ships off Corfu around the time we were in those waters) sent a torpedo over the reef at Methoni to make the *Jason* unsalvageable. In other words, you could say the Italians did Ned and his mates a favour.

When the war was over – in what may be the last public reference to the German who'd saved our bacon – the George Medal was awarded to a Lance Corporal Bernard Friedlander of the Third Transvaal Scottish Union Defence Force on the recommendation of an unnamed German officer. Friedlander was the bloke who battled the sea off Methoni for an hour and a half in failing light to get the landline ashore.

Some said the engineer had been transferred from the escort vessel to oversee the rescue attempt. Under the circumstances, that seems unlikely to me. Another possibility is he transferred at Benghazi. The reason I say this is because Brigadier Hargest, who as a high ranking POW was on the escort, is on record as saying he was put up in one of the engineer's cabins. One other thing to consider while I'm about it: Friedlander was Jewish.

The guards had taken up residence in the old manor house (or small castle: one of a string built along the southern Adriatic coast as a first line of defence against pirates from the Eastern Mediterranean and bandits from the hinterland, these houses-cum-castles became the hubs of sprawling complexes of stables and sheepfolds, storehouses and living quarters, with kitchens big enough to double as cheese factories). The difference now was it was inward-looking; its main purpose was to keep people in rather than out.

We continued our tour. The piles of stumps beyond the eastern fence told a sorry story: a very old wood, having sustained generations of landowners and poachers, had made way for us.

Beyond the western fence, new huts were going up. *Campo Prigioniero di Guerra 85* was the southernmost of the Italians' POW camps. It had been built as a sorting camp; it was here we were sorted according to our nationality. It stopped the bickering, but at the loss of some good friends. The new part of the camp was called Campo Grande, which of course made the part we were in Campo Piccolo.

Campo Piccolo had three barracks huts: a hospital, a kitchen and a spare clothing store. The hospital was staffed by two Italian doctors, a team of orderlies drafted from our ranks and a dentist who, short of materials, could remove teeth but not fill them. The kitchen included a pantry and a canteen. For a lira a day of camp money (printed on coloured paper and bearing the Comandante's signature, a stamped seal, the denomination and the words *Valevole solo per lo spaccio del campo*; for use only at the camp shop) you could buy a piece of fruit or a vegetable that had seen better days. The spare clothing store was for men who'd been captured in their summer uniform; here they could trade it for an Italian or a Yugoslav or a Greek winter uniform.

We passed a work group emptying barrels of effluent into a shallow depression that was crawling with flies.

'So much for having flush toilets,' said Dave.

A bell sounded – in all probability, the bell that had summoned the workers from the fields for centuries – and we lined up for a ladleful of macaroni and cauliflower cooked in olive oil and tomato paste!

On about the third day, a convoy of six-tonners turned into the lane. And once again it was fifty men to a truck and fifty to a trailer: the big difference being the likelihood of a strafing was minimal. Within the hour we were at a Bathing and Delousing Station on the outskirts of Brindisi, enjoying our first hot shower since being rounded up. Some were so weak they had to be helped out of their clothes, helped in the showers and helped back into their clothes. As for the rest of us, we were like kids again and the guards indulged us.

The only quibbles were with the soap (the kind for scouring pots and cleaning floors) and with the steam-cleaner (our clothes came back crisscrossed with creases and all mixed up). For those who'd grown up scrubbing themselves with pumice, it was water off a duck's back. For others, the steam-cleaner was the last straw and did they do their nuts. The guards shrugged: there was no pleasing some.

The constant talk of a move made us restless – what was the point of getting yourself organised if you were about to move? Of course the point was it helped take your mind off the nagging hunger. It was for this reason that places in work parties were sought after; it wasn't only about the extra rations. One of these parties involved digging a garden; another, shovelling sand onto trucks at the local beach. We knew sand went into concrete and that concrete built runways, so enquiries were made to the Red Cross. They said they'd bring it up with the British authorities, in the meantime to carry on. I was reminded of their response to complaints about guard brutality in the transit camps of North Africa: insufficient detail.

At the end of the month, we were back in Brindisi. Whether by design or not, the route took us past the new airport and the sea plane base, which put a spring in the guards' step and took one out of ours.

We got a second shower on the way back. On our return, we were drafted into Campo Grande: it was under water, half the tents were awash; yet the new huts stayed empty. We scavenged for materials to keep our bedding dry: builders' off-cuts, stones.

A further two days passed before the huts were opened. They had double walls, windows all round, two-tier bunks with straw mattresses and a sheet, a long narrow communal area down the middle, a stove, a latrine for inside use at night and an electric light with a blue bulb. Hullo, I thought. And sure enough the jokes were soon coming thick and fast: blue being slang for cock-up, dingdong, difference of opinion, not to mention nickname for a redhead.

'Strike a light, Bulb,' said Ned, handing me a mess tin brimming with wine.

It was my birthday, my twenty-eighth; I'd forgotten. The blokes I knocked round with had not only pooled their wine issues, they'd gone into hock so there'd be enough for a skinful all round. There were a hundred Kiwis in the hut; it was as close to home as you could get without being at home. A toast was proposed, speeches were called for: put on the spot, I reminded my audience of what the guard on the train had said about looking back on this time through the windows of our own carriages; of the expression he'd used: *di ottenere ubriaco come una tegola,* to get as drunk as a tile. Blokes were still coming out with it weeks later.

It was a while before I nodded off. I was thinking about the photo I'd taken on my last trip home: of Dad in his newsboy cap and cardigan that was too short in the sleeves, waistcoat open on a collarless white shirt done up to the neck, pipe in a corner of his mouth; how Mum in her calf-length velvet dress and sun-browned skin wouldn't have been out of place in the mezzogiorno; of Agnes in the dress she'd made with the tie neckline, one hand on Mum's shoulder, the other in Dad's hand, her expression seeming to say 'for goodness sake get on with it' or 'since the earthquake, nothing would surprise me'. Then my thoughts turned to Iris and I shook my head and grinned.

Three

The rest of our mob caught up with us on the day we got our marching orders, among them some men who'd been on the loose on Crete, and again it occurred to me to wonder if I was about to run into Frank. Not that it bothered me unduly. Actually I was in no fit state to go anywhere: sweat bubbled from my wrists, I couldn't keep my tucker down; a migraine sent intermittent lightning bolts across my cranium. In fact it was just as well we were moving as there were no drugs in the camp, not even aspirin.

We lined up for lunch then as soon as lunch was over we lined up for dinner. I lost the lot. I'd seen men on all fours eating their own vomit and while I understood their reason, the thought of it was enough to make me puke. When we lined up a third time to hand in our blankets and mess-tins, it was all I could do to stay on my feet. It was time to say something, but what and who to? I'd been left behind before for reasons of a similar nature and I didn't want to make a habit of it. When we lined up a fourth time, this time for the march to the station, the matter was taken out of my hands.

I was aware of the discussion going on over my head. And I stirred at the station when I was stretchered on board, but that was it till I woke to the squeal of bogies, to pencil lights in the wagon walls playing jiggery-pokery with the dust; to the light at the vent that obliterated the heads of two blokes taking turns to crane their necks. The floor was covered with stretchers, the walls with men huddled together on forms.

'Thought you'd given up the ghost,' said a voice in my ear, Ned's; he was bundled up in a blanket under a form about a foot away.

'What's the light?' I said.

'Them's the Pearly Gates,' he said.

'Sunset?'

'It's morning mate; you've been away with the fairies. We've just come out of a long tunnel.'

I thought it was sunset, I thought we were travelling east. We had been travelling east, now we were travelling west.

'Have a look,' said Robbie.

'Is it worth it?'

The light stung my eyes. I was looking at a valley chocker with trees in blossom and every petal, every molecule of moisture shone.

'I see what you mean,' I said.

'There's someone I've got to see as soon as I get home,' said Robbie.

'Oh?' I said.

'I should have said something before I left. I thought I was doing the right thing, but since then I've been afraid someone will beat me to it. There's a little board and batten chapel in the village I grew up in. I want us to get married in it.'

'And where's that, Robbie?'

'The Drakensberg: I grew up in Durban, but that's where we used to go for holidays.'

'What do you do for a crust – if you don't mind me asking?'

'I'm in the newspaper business, it's a family business. Is there somebody waiting for you?'

I gave him the potted version and he nodded.

'Speaking of which, I had a look at those books you left behind last time you were here. And I came across something in one of them that reminded me of this valley; a poem about a bloke travelling up to London, who happens to look up from what he's reading and sees a wedding party on the station. The same thing happens at the next station and the next and the one after that and so on. It was the bouquets that reminded me of this valley in Apulia. The big difference was that whereas in the poem summer has come early, we seemed to be travelling back in time: the train pulled up in a town like a catacomb where people still lived in caves, where the water for cooking and washing ran in the same limestone channel in the floor that served as a sewer – not many by that stage, but some, I believe.'

I lay on my stretcher on the platform, listening to what the history teacher had to say and to the grumblings of his audience, till finally he'd had a gutsful.

'If that was all there was to it,' he said, 'I'd be out of a job. So tell me, when you've been hunting and it's time to go home, how do you know which way to go?'

There were no takers; I wasn't sure what he was getting at either.

'On your way into the bush, you're not only looking out for game, are you; you're looking round from time to time to see where you've come from, to see what it looks like so you know when it's time to go back that you're on the right track; because if you don't you could find yourself going round in circles, getting a bit panicky; you could have an accident, you could run out of grub. I'm not saying that getting lost is a bad thing necessarily: if it's only temporarily, it can be just the shake-up the doctor ordered. And if you don't make it, it's not the end of the world; someone else will take your place. The point I'm trying to make is: how do we know where we're going if we don't know where we've been?'

'And I thought you were trying to tell us this is the end of the line,' said one of his pupils.

'It is, as it happens. What does the name of the place tell you about where we are? Gravina means gorge; it means the river is probably called Fiume Gravina. People have been coming here for donkey's ages, since the Iron Age in fact. Why? For the rock and the water; water draws people too you know. It can get very dry round here . . .'

'You don't say?' muttered a comedian under his breath.

'Having tools made of iron meant people could make their homes here without too much effort or cost. To begin with they made their homes in caves, making them relatively comfortable by cutting shelves for beds and or seats and for places to store things. Then they made blocks to keep the weather out. Then they used the blocks to make separate dwellings. They made holes in the rock to bathe in, to wash clothes in; to collect rainwater to tide them over the dry months.'

'Excuse my ignorance,' I said. 'Who were these people?'

'They could have been Minoans from Crete or Arcadians from Achaia or Illyrians from Yugoslavia or Albania. They crossed the Adriatic some twelve centuries ago. Since that time others have come and gone – Samnites, Romans, Byzantines, Normans, Africans – each adding their grist to the mill. Gravina was established by the Greeks 1000 years ago. This whole region then was known as Magna Graecia. The Baroque church across the road is recent, perhaps only two or three hundred years old. The eagle is the coat of arms of the Giustiniani family.'

We looked at the church: the whole front of it, apart from the round window where the gut was, was the relief of an eagle with its wings spread, beak open, ravenous.

Meanwhile our transport had failed to turn up. Those who could had to get up off their sick beds and catch up; those who couldn't would have to wait for an ambulance.

A woman with a tray of bread on her head passed us in the street; the smell of the loaves made us faint with hunger. I was reminded of my first job; of the bicycle with the basket on the front. It was a step-through, a ladies bike; not that it bothered me: not many kids had bikes in those days and I was allowed to take it home. I wasn't supposed to use it then for anything other than getting to and from work, but I did – if word got back to the boss, he didn't say anything. At the end of my shift, he always gave me a loaf to take home and, being peckish by that time – I was always peckish – I couldn't help taking a pinch on my way. One pinch of course always led to another and my mother when I got home was always disappointed in me, not that it stopped me doing it.

Actually, she was more disappointed about my smoking; having started smoking at the age I was. The bread was good, but it didn't have a patch on this bread. This bread had a yellow glow to it; it was made from the local flour, hard flour, and barm and water and sea salt and was baked in a wood-fired oven. The quarter-inch crust kept it soft and moist. You didn't need anything on it; not that I'd have turned up my nose had I been offered what we were as kids: a spread of jam or dripping.

The camp was a six mile trek back the way we'd come. When the head of the column turned right off the road toward a collection of unfinished buildings, there were groans of disbelief: not only because the buildings had an unfinished look about them but because the railway line passed within 200 yards. The wind bundled us through the gates.

Four

The tableland was a blue-green ocean, as solemn and sombre as the farmland round here this time of the year. The crops were a different story: they were mostly wheat and oats; a good deal more cheerful than stock to my way of thinking. That said, they were months off harvesting: we could only hope the supply of flour held and it wasn't us feeding the crops.

The camp was on the top of a rise. In most cases you'd expect a hilltop to be dry, but the water that fell on this hilltop wasn't getting away, possibly due to a non-porous stone substructure or to poor drainage or the presence of springs; any of which would be a problem for farming but evidently not for a POW camp.

The first thing they did was call the roll. We shifted from one foot to the other through one interminable roll call after another, literally, we trod water. The range of hills bearing down on us from the nor-west, that got to within 50 miles then veered south, was the Apennines of our school geography lessons. They had nothing on the Southern Alps for height or on the Ruahines for that matter, and while the chill that cut through our serge knocked the stuffing out of us, we weren't averse to granting the livery of these mountains was top drawer.

The warmth generated by the march had long gone by the time our hosts were satisfied with the count. Indeed, had it not been patently obvious they were making it up as they went, we might have taken the long drawn out proceedings as a ploy to get under our skin. Their patience and civility was also ambiguous, because it didn't extend to the provision of supper. So when they issued three blankets instead of the usual two, we smelt a rat. And sure enough: the huts had yet to be glazed.

The huts had seven rooms or bays ('byre' wouldn't have been off the mark, given the amount of mud we tracked in). The bays at either end of the hut had six empty casements, while those between had four. They were twenty by fifty feet; six two-tier double bunks along one wall faced six two-tier double bunks along the other. A passage ran up the middle through a series of arches so that from either end you could see out the other. Accompanying us about a mile off, a farmhouse bobbled along on the same green ocean. All the bays had the same round vent we'd come across in Patras; the intention apparently was to keep them cool in summer; being winter the air came and went like a tide in a rock pool. I was out on my feet; I crawled onto the nearest available bunk and was dead to the world before my head hit the hay.

The following morning I joined the sick parade. If you didn't have something the medic had something for, he waved you away. For sores and cuts he had bandages and antiseptics. For dysentery he had an injection or a pill. I took the pill.

When I was back on my feet, I caught up with my mates. The current bun had put in an appearance and they were sitting with their backs against the white stone, faces like sundials. Most of the talk was about food, which was not surprising in view of the fact that our rations had just been halved.

We were staring down the barrel: that grim oxymoron 'starvation rations' had acquired a keener edge. We looked back on Greece as a land of plenty, on the suppers of the Karori socialites and the lashings of grub on the *Mauretania* as the stuff of legend. Meanwhile, the bloke who could talk for hours about a meal he once had in a posh restaurant, had added another course. I daydreamed I was opening a tin of sardines, the greasy bodies falling apart in my fingers as I lifted them from the oil bath with its tidemark of congealed fat and popped them into my mouth, tipped back my head to catch the last of the salty lees, drew the back of my hand across my chin and opened my eyes: puzzled and cheated and hungrier than ever.

We were waiting for the bugler's summons. At the first notes of *Come to the cookhouse door boys, come to the cookhouse door* we were on our feet, sorting ourselves in groups of a hundred, three per hut. Anxiously, we watched the progress of the pots, fearful a wheel would catch in a soft spot.

The servers ready, we saluted the orderly officer and shuffled forward; hoping, praying we had timed our run to perfection, that our serving would come from where the pot's contents were thickest, despite the best efforts of the stirrers. Then canteen cup in hand, like an egg and spoon race, we would make a beeline for our bunks; the steam wafting, flattening and spilling. There, the only sounds that could be heard were sipping and chewing; except if some lucky blighter got a few grains more of rice than the usual or a slightly bigger piece of gristly meat, when your only way of softening the blow was by congratulating him. Whether you wolfed it down or chewed every morsel a hundred times, the outcome was always the same: your head would come up and staring you in the face would be the forty days and forty nights of the twenty-four hours till the next summons.

Things came to a head when they tried to get a work party together to remove a hut roof: despite the usual offer of double rations, there were no takers. The roofs were made of terracotta blocks that had been reinforced with wire and plastered on the underside. We would be undermining our footing at every blow of the sledgehammer or pick; more to the point – given we were blacking out when we got up from our bunks and keeling over on parade – a slip-up could be the end of us; after five minutes on the end of a shovel, it took the rest of the hour to get our breath back.

When they got their work party at the point of a bayonet, a delegation was organised to see the Comandante. His hands were tied he said: the order had come from Rome; all camps on Italian soil were now on half rations. He produced the document as proof. Our warrant officers and sergeants conferred. What he could do, said the Comandante, was have extra vegetables brought in?

When these turned out to be dandelion leaves and turnip tops we thought, we'd been had. And so it was with no small degree of astonishment that we discovered how improved by their addition the watery stews were. All the same we had become so desperate that men trailed the vegetable cart hoping a leaf or a stalk would drop off. One thing led to another and an orderly officer was seen booting those who having stuffed their pockets, then hi-tailed it back to their bunks to get rid of the evidence.

We were mostly English and South Africans and New Zealanders and Cypriots – in that order. The Palestinians, Australians, Egyptians, Canadians and Montenegrins were a tiny minority. Rather than point the finger, let me just say that the main offenders were from two of these groups and that a few Kiwis and Englishmen and South Africans were amongst them.

But the fact was it was a poor show, because a handful of greens could be the difference between seeing your family again or being carried out the gates on your mates' shoulders. I lost count of the number of times we lined the road with our hats in our hands. The poor sod would be put on a truck and taken to the cemetery which was on the skyline at Altamura. The cause of death would be put down to dysentery or pneumonia or diphtheria or malaria or food poisoning, but malnutrition was the root cause, because its effect on the system was to make it harder to combat infection. One bloke got it into his head he would stop eating so that others could live. When his personal effects were collected, a small pantry was found under his bunk. But I'm getting ahead of myself.

Five weeks passed before we got our first issue of tobacco in this place, Gravina in Puglia: two dozen cigarettes, half a cigar and half a packet of tobacco. The die-hards quit smoking the straw and tea leaves and weeds that had been laying them out cold. We started talking again.

After seven weeks we got our first Red Cross parcel: a lucky dip of shredded paper containing eleven pounds in fourteen tins of oatmeal, meat roll, custard, cocoa, coffee, sugar, bacon, figs in syrup and sardines. We were like kids on Christmas day. The empty boxes became wall cupboards hung on nails hammered into the soft stone. The cans reappeared as plates, as utensils, as mugs and boilers; the string as balls, slippers and bags. In the six months we were in this camp, we got seven parcels (it was supposed to be one per week per man): four were one per man; the other three were a half or a quarter or a sixth per man.

In early July, we got our first mail in the eight months since leaving Baggush. In one of her letters, Agnes tells the story of how they found out I was still in the land of the living. When Prime Minister Peter Fraser conceded the events at Sidi Rezegh had made casualties of half the battalion, they had feared the worst. In mid-December, a letter from Army Base Records notified them I was missing in action. Then out of the blue, a letter arrived from America from a woman who heard a Vatican City Radio broadcast of a list of men known to be prisoners of war in Italy; among them yours truly. This news however was tempered by a second letter from Base Records confirming the report but warning it was not yet official. Finally in the middle of February, the official notice arrived and they were able to relax on that score (not knowing of course what we'd been through between times). In other news, Hammond had been in and out of the Sanatorium; Mum was getting more forgetful. It was the beginning of a long exchange of letters and photographs between Agnes and this woman in America.

Unfortunately, as Alzheimer's loomed, Agnes censored her past and the written part of this record went in the fire. My memory's not what it was either, so all we have to show of this woman's compassion are the photos with the names on the back of some of them: Joe, her husband; Gregg, her son and Jerry the dog. Other photos show her with her parents and sister before a house on the outskirts of Minneapolis on the shores of Medicine Lake; like messages in a bottle they ache with the passage of time.

Medicine Lake comes from Mdewakanton; Dakota for Spirit Lake. The name dates from the settlement of the area in the fifteenth century by the Eastern Dakota. One story connects the name with the disappearance of a warrior whose canoe overturned.

As the war approached its end, the University of Minnesota conducted a study of 'starvation rations', thinking there'd be millions of famine victims. It was called the Minnesota Starvation Experiment.

The wheat was mown in early June, then the rain arrived and we were surrounded by sodden stooks. There were two escape-attempts during this period; the first almost got us shot. Someone thought a guard had thrown a grenade during appello (perhaps it was a stone?); others thought a truck was being driven into us (it was some idiots mimicking truck noises). We were about that close to being mown down in the stampede.

In the second escape-attempt, someone *was* shot: he was about to drop from the one roof that overhung the fence when the guards, hearing the rattle of its drainpipe, arrived. The bullet grazed his jaw and he was carted off to hospital. His fellow escapees came back from solitary looking like the English actor Peter Postlethwaite (you know, the bloke whose face has been likened to a bag of spanners?). In late July, the Cypriots and the Palestinians packed their bags. In August I had another run-in with the medic.

'Malaria,' he said.

We had our own medics by this time. This bloke was English.

'Must've been caught with my trousers down,' I said.

'That's a new one on me,' he said.

'Oh?' I said.

'That's not the kind of bad air the disease gets its name from.'

'Perhaps it's from the opera then?'

He looked at me sideways.

'I was thinking of the gabinetto opera.'

He put me on a course of quinine. I was off my tucker for a week. It couldn't have come at a worse time, as it happened, as it was our turn to pack our bags. And since we couldn't take it with us (in case we did a runner) we were obliged to make short work of what we'd been spinning out. I put it aside for the infirmary.

The behemoth wobbled out of the mid-afternoon heat. The wagons had been hosed; hay had been spread on the wet boards. By a stroke of luck, I got the shelf under the vent.

We trundled out to the coast and turned north. Father Time put his feet up; Mother Nature smiled her winning smile. The tiny waves shuffled in, cocked a leg at the coastal defences and shuffled back out; houses wound round a hill with a spire at the top. *On a huge hill, cragged and steep, Truth stands/and he that will reach her about must and about must go/and what the hill's suddenness resists, win so.* How's that?

'Spokeshave?'

'Donne.'

At the stops, the locals competed with each other to refill our water bottles – sometimes with wine – and showered us with bread.

Late in the second day the train slowed and stopped.

'Water break,' said Ned.

The wind whistled round the wagon, the doors opened: it was the end of the line. We were in a town named after the Caesar who founded it two thousand years earlier: Cividale del Friuli. According to our history teacher, it used to be called Forum Iulii.

'How does that work?' I asked.

'Iulii: Friuli: Julius.'

'I'll take your word for it,' I said.

What struck me more was how the everydayness of a place could put its illustrious past in its place, so to speak; I was more taken by the fact that the hills where the street ended were in a different country.

We set out across a floodplain: mountains hung like sheets in the late sun, bell towers sounded and resounded all around us; they probably had villages at their feet, but we couldn't see them. Before long gibbet-like structures were looming out of the dusk. How's your glass?

Five

The shenanigans the following morning had to be seen to be believed. The six-foot-four Comandante, decorated like a Christmas tree and wearing a biretta on each hip, strutted up and down the apello lines in his shiny jackboots like Mussolini's heir apparent. If you looked at him, if you talked or coughed, or if your idea of standing to attention didn't come up to his you were frogmarched to the cooler.

Calcaterra was behind the murders and bashings of the Socialists that put them off their stride and made it possible for the king to appoint Mussolini as prime minister. The ear-bashings we got from him were right out of Mussolini's hymn sheet, as was the quote on his office wall: 'The British haven't got a hope in hell and any Italian who treats them humanely is even further beyond the pale, if that's possible.' I didn't see it myself, thankfully and thankfully he didn't see me looking at him: he was a cold-looking fish. We called him Piccolo Pete after the song that went:

Did you ever hear Pete go tweet tweet tweet on his piccolo?
Huh, no? Well you've missed a lot. Well you've missed a treat . . .

Not that I want to make excuses for him – he had enough apologists – but it's possible he was still smarting from a recent breakout. He was on leave – but the point was the security arrangements were his responsibility and his alone. Some Aussies, who'd been given the job of finishing off one of the huts, had discovered that the ground beneath it was softer than it was in the rest of the camp (the installation of the toilet blocks, all on the perimeter, had required the removal of rock, so it had been assumed the rest of the camp was on rock as well). Taking up the dare, these Aussies had lifted the flooring under one of the bunks, had gone as deep as the hut was high then out under the wire, intending to come up in the adjacent maize crop. They had packed the tailings under the hut till it was chocker, before spreading the rest over the parade ground (which conveniently they were responsible for levelling). Fortune favours the brave they say, or it did till the weather packed in. They went ahead anyway, thinking the rain would provide cover, it bucketed down and the only way out of the district was over the bridges, which was where the carabinieri were waiting.

The fifteen acres of treeless river plain that *Campo Concentramento Prigionieri di Guerran N. 57* enclosed had been a border outpost till the Italian invasion of Greece. The change of function, it was deemed, necessitated the addition of miles upon miles of barbed wire. On the perimeter, was a mesh-fence three times the height of a man (the posts supporting it looked like the trunks of small trees that had washed out of the mountains). Inside it were rows of coiled barbed wire followed by an apron fence (like a row of tent skeletons with coils of barbed wire inside them). The effect of all that grey was mind-numbing. Then there was a bed of white boulders ten feet wide; its purpose was to make anything of a different colour stick out like a sore thumb. Finally, there was a trip wire: put any part of you over it and you could expect the attention of every sentry in every sentry box, of every marksman in every guard tower. It's no wonder Calcaterra thought his camp was escape-proof.

The poles buttressing the huts were the other home-handyman element. They gave the place the look of a dry dock and thus were an opportunity for quips about floods and arks. We guessed the purpose, but it wasn't till the Bora turned up that we gave the installation of them credit, because the wind off the snow-covered plateaux of Carinthia and Slovenia was like a dam burst; it bowled us off our feet, tipped over anything on wheels and tore off with our nascent gardens. Through the windows, unable to hear ourselves think, we watched the flurries of snow and sleet slalom past the huts.

The south fence was on a slope that might have been a stop bank at one time or a river bank. I had a plot there I visited daily. I'd scratch around for a bit then roll a smoke and lift my eyes to the Dolomites. It was a hop, skip and a jump from these mountains to the freedom and apparently the boredom of a Swiss internment camp. It was a fraction of the distance the other way to the smoky hut in its various guises that had been my home in the decade leading up to the war: where up for a leak under the great galactic river, I would then follow the stream to a ford or drinking hole to settle among the dew-wet grasses to await the change like a sleight of hand to the visible ground before, between exhalation and inhalation, unleashing a thunderbolt.

Meanwhile, back at the hut, my offsider, hearing the reverberations volleying up and down the valley, would be stirring some life into the embers and sharpening the knives.

On this slope, I dug up an old rifle shell; as others had, who had made vases of them for the wild flowers that grew along the fence-line. I spat on it, rubbed it on my trousers and considered the markings. It was a Mark VII: the type we used, but from the first war. I was contemplating what others might find at some future date that marked our passage (a piece of bitumen impregnated with crushed metal, a piece of heavy white china?) when I heard a noise behind me and swivelled round. The guard was all but upon me. I held up the shell and in my halting Italian remarked that we had once been on the same side.

Luckily, the Comandante he was accompanying had moved on (we were supposed to salute him) or I might have got what we called a Gruppignano greeting: a jab in the puku with a rifle butt. I wasn't spared a spell in the cooler all the same: five days in handcuffs on half rations, with no tobacco or reading material. When I got out I made out it was water off a duck's back: we all did.

The hospitals in the district were full of us lot: they had pulmonary tuberculosis, beriberi, pleurisy, pneumonia, appendicitis, fractures, tumours and mental disorders; they were too sick for the camp hospital. And as if that wasn't bad enough, there was a reward of a thousand lire and a fortnight's leave for any guard who shot one of us.

It was duly collected following a cricket match. The Red Cross had sent us a box of sports equipment, which the guards had largely destroyed on the pretext of searching for contraband. Never mind, somebody made a ball out of twine, a stone and a pair of boots that was beyond repair. A bat was made out of a headboard.

Matches were hotly contested both on and off the field, any guards brave enough to wander by generally copped a bit of stick. One of the guards (a surly character at the best of times; he had a birthmark on his neck and jaw) decided to take a shortcut through the field of play and got told in no uncertain terms where to get off. He altered course abruptly, took the bottle from the Aussie corporal's hand, and told him to follow him. The corporal refused. His mates pleaded with him. The guard lifted the barrel of his rifle and fired it point blank. It must have been loaded with dum-dums, because he staggered back with a hole in his chest as big as my fist. When the padre turned up, he almost copped a bullet too, till things settled down and the corporal was taken off to the camp hospital – still mouthing off – where he died shortly afterwards.

When the bullets were flying round the medical tents at Point 175, this padre was carrying water to the wounded and reading to them and listening to what they had to say. He didn't have to come into captivity with us. On Sundays, some wished he hadn't, because he went from hut to hut giving hour-long sermons. His followers were as humourless as he was when anyone read or smoked or talked while he was talking. He could have had them boobed; the Comandante would have thanked him for it.

When he visited the local hospitals, he made a point of popping into the waiting rooms and browsing the local papers. It was thanks to him that a story, that had been picked up on a radio built from parts provided by compromised guards and concealed in a bunk post, was confirmed: the Germans had indeed been given the bum's rush in Stalingrad and North Africa.

As I think I've alluded to already, the Comandante had his supporters. They pointed to the pride he showed in our inventiveness, for instance when delegates from the Protecting Power or Comandanti from the neighbouring camps toured: the latest burners, powered by fans and bellows, could bring a pint of water to the boil in a minute. They pointed to the regularity of mail and parcel deliveries, to the availability of alcohol and to the relative absence of the inveterate rackets of previous camps.

And there was a grain of truth in this, but only a grain because the deaths of a number of men could be directly attributable to the jungle juice distilled from the dried fruit that came to us in the Red Cross parcels. The priest like the padre, didn't have a bad word to say about anybody either, which the Comandante took as a personal affront and had him shot.

Within a year, the partisans had caught up with him; he might have been executed anyway for war crimes. According to his apologists, this was another point in his favour: he hadn't changed his spots to save his neck.

While the Comandante took after Mussolini, with one or two exceptions the guards took after him. One of the exceptions was a bloke we called Twinkle-toes: in reference to his shuffling or stumbling gait.

His family name was Moronia, but because he was learning English we kept our thoughts to ourselves. At lights-out in order to prolong the inevitable, we'd endeavour to engage him in a discussion; it was an opportunity for him to practise his English so this wasn't difficult. Most people like to be right and to have the last word and Twinkle-toes was no exception, which played into our hands too.

'It's not often you're right,' said Ned, 'but you're wrong this time.'

Twinkle-toes had paused and was beaming, his hand on the light switch, when the first seeds of doubt crossed his brow and he looked up at a hut full of grinning faces.

'*Che c'è da ridere? Non c'è niente da ridere!*' he bellowed like a wounded bull.

Gales of our laughter followed him out the door. He wouldn't talk to us for a week.

In March, the Italians finally got around to sorting out a problem they'd been aware of for some time – that they couldn't afford to keep us in the manner to which we'd become accustomed – and we were given forms on which to list the kinds of work we were familiar with.

Naturally, I wasn't about to put down ditch-digging, nor did I suppose there would be much call for rabbiters or tree-planters or bakers' delivery boys, so I put down 'gardener'. When my name came up, I thought I'd won the lottery. The company, the Agricola Millecampi, was desperate for 60 labourers; the station at Piove di Sacco was already expecting us, it was action stations, but I'm getting ahead of myself again.

Even fully dressed, the two thin blankets weren't enough; the wood lasted a couple of hours, then those nearest the stove were as cold as those furthest away. We were woken by exaggerated body noises, by the guards clattering through the hut in their hobnails at all hours, by the drunken outbursts of card players and by the voices of the young women of the neighbouring villages who, after a night on the town, would pass close to fence to get a rise out of us. What were they to do, with their men away? As it happened, the huts being at right angles to the fence and close together, not to mention the veil of the wire, getting more than a fleeting glimpse was well-nigh impossible: not that it stopped us or some of us anyway. What were we to do, being away from our women, but make a beeline for the windows?

Six

The Venetian Lagoon's perennial flooding hadn't stopped people from shoring up their homes and livelihoods by, as it's disingenuously called, reclamation. Fogolana (the name harks back to the notion of jack-o'-lanterns luring unwary travellers to untimely ends), once an island of linden trees and fish ponds, had a new pumping station, stop bank and bridge.

The company put us up in its new barn with its glass-panelled doors and louvers. The tip of the Campanile, twenty miles to the north, peeped over the stop bank. Twenty miles to the west were the cones of the Colli Euganei, where Francesco Petrarca composed his sonnets to Laura de Noves and through which passed a sniffy George Gordon on his way to his banal and tragic death on the shores of the Patraikos Kolpos.

Work at *Campo PG120/VIII* began at seven and after lunch and a siesta, finished with a further four hours; six days a week. Many of the vegetables were new to me: these included the chicory-endive crosses, preferred by the locals after their bitterness had been enhanced by the frosts. One of these crosses, radicchio, looked like a lettuce splashed with blood. I'm not shy of bitter, but it was like going from the sublime to the ridiculous.

There was a pumpkin with leaves like camp shovels that grew on stalks like green snorkels which went off like popguns if accidentally broken. Its name was Marina di Chioggia (Sea Pumpkin of Chioggia or something like that); its turban-shaped fruit was a dark green, its skin smooth or covered with sugar warts, its blossom-end patterned like a spiral staircase.

From time to time, a Great White Egret would lift from the canal or an animal with a rat's tail and the head of a beaver would swim out from the bank.

'Movite! Movite!' the guards would shout, if we paused too long. On the other hand, they'd turn a blind eye (one or two of them) if a discarded vegetable was picked up and pocketed.

As the season waned, we had all the seconds we could eat. Not since we'd been rounded up, had we been this well fed and with the work some of the old fitness returned. Meanwhile, time was running out for Mussolini: the king had had a gutsful of him and arrangements had been made for his party to dismiss him. When he tried calling their bluff by turning up for work as usual, he was arrested.

When the news reached us, we could barely contain our delight: the guards were more circumspect, their relief nevertheless was palpable. Night after night, we talked, long into the night in the days and weeks following, but short on further detail, we could only weigh-up the various options and risks in the event of a capitulation.

One was to head for Switzerland to put our feet up in an internment camp; another was to attempt to meet up with our armies advancing from the south; a third, to hole up and wait for them. What we didn't know was that Allied Intelligence had sent out a message to the Senior British Officers of the various camps to order us to stay put: their concern was that we'd get in the way of the advance or team up with partisans, triggering reprisals on the locals.

Five days after the signing, the armistice was announced: their fear being that none too happy with the turn of events, the Germans would pour over the Brenner Pass. It was a case then of getting on with it, before we didn't have a say in the matter.

Allied Intelligence knew where only a quarter of the work camps in our region were and so our Comandante had a free hand to follow the terms of the agreement and issue us with a Red Cross parcel each and a map of a route to Switzerland. Those heading south would be escorted as far as Ravenna by our chaplain, Father Domenico Artero. The guards had already changed into their civvies and jumped on their bikes and gone home. We scoured the place to see if they'd left anything – not a skerrick – said our goodbyes and slipped into the night.

I had teamed up with a couple of Kiwis. Blue was an Auckland Grammar old boy, whom I had to step back from to avoid getting a crick in my neck. Robert was the camp's oldest prisoner; obsessed with his young wife and kids, he spent hours poring over their pictures and was only too happy to share them with anyone who showed the slightest interest. We made a beeline for the Ponte della Rotta (the new bridge, the old name) then cut across the fields to avoid the farm workers' houses (to think they wouldn't notice).

The grass beyond the embankment was greener and springier, the mud was softer; the 'rafts' of dead reeds made a sort of boardwalk, but were squeaky, so it was slow going. After a few hours, we were done in. And that was day one on the loose: not at all as I'd imagined it.

Despite being windy about the tides, I must've nodded off, because it was getting light when I stuck my head up. Swathes of reddish brown reeds writhed and bowed and jigged and poked and scraped. Somebody was on the stop bank: I ducked.

We spent a muggy day dozing and battling insects. When dark fell, we set out again, looking for somewhere to lie low for a couple of weeks (while we waited for our mob). After a few hours, the clouds parted and a stand of trees stood before us like a cliff. It looked promising, till we caught the gleam of a canal some 15 feet between us and it. Had we been desperate, it may not have mattered, even allowing for the fact that I wasn't the only one who couldn't swim. Then Blue dropped to his hands and knees and crawled off into the undergrowth; Robert and I weren't far behind. A minute later somebody went past.

'Bob!' said Blue and indeed Bob's profile, short and round, was unmistakable. With him were Jacob, an Englishman, and Thomas, a Canadian. Thomas had hollow cheeks and deep set eyes and rarely opened his mouth unless he had something to put in it, which wasn't that often either. There being little to be gained by either party going over the ground the other had covered, the six of us returned to the bridge.

There was a small forest to the east of the farm called La Boschetta or Boschettona (or Small Forest). The original forest had been whittled away as the salt marsh became cultivable. Why we hadn't gone there at the outset was because others had beaten us to the draw by saying that was where they were going. They would just have to put up with us now. We followed the embankment till we came to a broad beach; the forest began to the south of it. In the starlight, it didn't look all that small; perhaps there was room in it for us all?

We slithered over the stop bank and followed a ditch till it came to a road; here it turned into a drainage canal that ran along the west side of the road. We followed the road till we came to a bridge that crossed another ditch where it met the canal. At this point, we decided to leave the road and see where the ditch to the east went. There was a path on the north side of it that seemed to get a bit of foot traffic, which we followed till we got to where there were a couple of planks over the ditch. The trees here were mostly oak and alder and willow and poplar and ash and robinia. Most were struggling: too much salt from the lagoon, I suspect.

Only the robinia thrived. We tried pushing our way into a thicket. The stems were springy and covered with thorns, which was another point in its favour: if it was hard for us to penetrate, others less interested might not bother (who that might be was a consideration that didn't bear dwelling on too much or too little). When we found a clearing in the middle, big enough to accommodate all six of us, it was problem solved, for the meantime anyway. We cleared away the branches with our boots and settled down on the sandy floor. And that was our second night on the loose.

I opened an eye, saw where we were and shut it again, but unable to drift off again because of the cold and whatnot, I sat up and rolled a smoke. While I was doing that, I noticed the dried blood on the backs of my hands. Actually, the scratches looked worse than they were. I drew the gummed edge along the tip of my tongue and examined the bush for thorns. I found them at the base of the leaf stalks, cunningly paired; what ruminant had brought on this development, I wondered. Meanwhile, Robert's breathing didn't sound too good.

I got up and poked my head out and looked up and down the track: there were no obvious signs of passersby and in any case being a track, footprints would not be unusual; prints of hobnails might be of course. I struck a match and watched the smoke lift. The leaves were on the turn; turning an insipid yellow colour. The veins were like the barbs of a feather. The dense undergrowth of suckers carried an abundance of seedpods. Among the branches we had cleared were stumps with sawn ends that suggested the tree had its uses: firewood perhaps, fence posts? I picked up an old seedpod. It was rust-brown and dried up like an old leather purse. I closed my hand on it and poking among the silk-lined fragments counted five tiny black seeds the shape of beans.

By the afternoon, I wasn't feeling too flash myself. Over the following couple of days, we all developed headaches and aching muscles and fevers. We had food for three days; four if we were careful, but our canteens were empty. Nobody used the track that day; that we were aware of anyway and by evening we were desperate. When night fell, we formed a circle at the hub of the clump and held each other's hands to keep our spirits up, steeling our bodies against the chill of the wind off the lagoon that flooded through the forest and needled through our serge. Getting a poke in the ribs from Blue, I got to my feet and got to the lookout in time to glimpse a receding back.

'*Un momento!*' I said, '*un momento!*'

The figure swung round.

'*Auito! Pieta! Noi avere la febbre.*'

The figure retraced his steps and we sized each other up through the parted branches. He and I were about the same height; he was older though judging by the beginnings of a receding hairline. I motioned to him to join us, to enter the thicket, and parted the suckers for him to squeeze between. I shook his hand. He looked over my shoulder.

'*Acqua! Chinino! Coperte!*' the others chorused like chicks in a nest.

His face relaxed. We invited him to sit with us.

'*Più siamo, meglio è,*' I said.

We widened the circle and took each other's hands again. Going by his grip, our visitor was no stranger to hard labour. After a while he leaned back and looked up at the starlight illuminating the thicket's interior, then withdrew his hand from mine and brushed away a tear. We grinned. He grinned and soon we were all grinning and shedding a tear. Eventually he got up for a stretch then he took his leave.

'*A presto,*' he said.

We resumed our vigil, thinking we had seen the last of him. An hour passed. Then we heard a low whistle.

He knew someone who could put us up for the night.

We emerged from the forest into the backyard of a cottage with a tile roof and wooden shutters. The chimney also had a tile roof; sparks flew from the vents below it. There was a lean-to: a woodshed by the look of it, which I'd gladly have swapped the robinia for.

Our friend spoke again of the need for quiet: there were children in the house who must on no account be woken. There was another condition: we must be gone before dawn, again because the children could not be expected to keep our visit a secret. If we kept our word, the blankets we would be provided with for the night would be ours to take back to the hideout.

The kitchen had a woodstove along one wall and a long narrow table along the wall opposite. A middle-aged woman in black appeared from the adjoining room, closed the door quietly behind her and beckoned us to sit. She served us bowls of polenta and shrimp and squid, swimming in squid ink. A large bowl of salad and a jug of wine were for us to help ourselves to: the salad was mostly fennel and radicchio, the wine a prosecco. The jug was refilled a number of times.

From what I could gather the woman and her husband were from Chioggia, having moved here when the port was bombed. He was a fish trader. We never saw the children, so whether they were grandchildren or children of friends or neighbours I couldn't say.

Seven

Our friend turned up the following evening, with a friend of his who had recently returned from Albania. Given the option between more of the same under a revamped Nazi-Fascist alliance or a German labour camp for the duration, this friend had put to sea and been lucky to survive. We called him Lucky.

On hearing our story, Lucky made it his duty to do the rounds of friends and family in the district asking them for food and medicines for us. Some of these medicines (perhaps the greater part of them) came from a Doctor Flavio Busonera (another name we were not privy to at the time; another man who risked his life to help those in peril and was publicly hung for it. As a matter of fact, I've seen the photos: in one of them he is standing on a chair with a noose round his neck, having his last rites read to him; in the other, only the rope is holding him up, his knees are bent. This is in a public square in Padova. 'Grim' doesn't come anywhere near unravelling it: the viewer is both complicit and victim).

Our friend's name was Alfredo – we called him Alfred. In a similar vein, Jacob became Giacomo, Robert became Roberto Vecchio, Bob became Roberto Giovane, Tom Tomaso and me Rosso on account of my hair; Blue stayed Blue. It was all just banter.

Alfred too was a wanted man; in his case for his involvement with the Committee of National Liberation. When the Italian version of the German SS (the *SS Fasciste Italiane*), guns blazing turned up on his doorstep, he acted like he was the gas meter reader and let himself out. His wife (and courier), Lionella Moda didn't miss a trick either: on the way to the Palazzo Giusti for interrogation, she managed to dig out an incriminating receipt from the case file and swallow it. She was in the Santa Maria Maggiore Prison in Venice for two months.

Both the Palazzo Giusti and the Santa Maria Maggiore were notorious due to their unsavoury conditions and because the accused were often tortured. Nella wasn't physically tortured, but she agonised over the fate of her young family (Alessandro, the youngest, had pleaded to be taken with her). In a repeat performance of what had happened to their father and his brother in the First War (when their father was at the front and their mother was ill), Alessandro and his brother Gianni Cesare were sent away. Now Alfred's brother was being sent away a second time – he was one of 700,000 Italian servicemen who spent the last years of the war in a German labour camp. No wonder Alfred was out walking that night: he had plenty to think about.

While Lucky was getting his stove going, Alfred warned us about the local fascists who, with the arrival of the Germans, had their tails up again. As he put it, we had to be as quiet as church mice and as vigilant as kestrels – easier said than done once the locals got wind of our presence, because they began dropping in at all hours of the night and day with news of the war's progress and morsels of food. From them we learned that the Allied advance had come to a standstill; that the Germans had flushed out some Englishmen near Chioggia, killing one and wounding others (the shots had carried to us on the fog); that witnesses had heard their helpers being beaten to within an inch of their lives.

One of our visitors, a Londoner who'd been with us in the camp at Fogolana, came and went on an ancient bicycle he'd wired blocks of wood to the pedals of. This bloke could talk the hind leg off a donkey in Italian as well as English; his references to Manzoni had even Alfred scratching his head. We envied his freedom. On one of his visits, he informed us he'd been given the use of a boat, which he could get us on if we were interested? He could take us to Termoli (where our lot had got to by that stage). This was something we had talked about, dreamed about: we had seen ourselves pushing off, poling between the reeds, paddling across the dark lagoon, slipping between the litorale's barrier islands then sailing down the coast. And after all, as Alfred was fond of reminding us, the sea that lapped the Gulf of Venice lapped the beaches of New Zealand; so just as both had their origin in creeks and rivers, we would have to begin with punts and fishing boats.

There were however, one or two drawbacks: we couldn't swim and we couldn't sail. Who better then to ask advice and assistance of than Johnny on the spot? Besides, he was in as much danger as we were.

He was flattered, so we went and had a look at this boat.

'You'd be lucky to get across the lagoon in this,' said Alfred, laughing, 'let alone down the coast. In fact, you'd be doing well just to get to the lagoon!'

We'd been on the loose for a month, when it came to our attention notices had been posted offering 1000 Deutschmarks just for information leading to our capture and/or that of anybody helping us – which explained the sudden drop-off in visitors; apart from Alfred and Lucky.

Carolina Emilia Donà, the woman who had put us up for a night and given us blankets, continued to send food. As soon as it got dark, we headed for a patch of scrub between the hideout and her cottage: there we would wait for her nephew (I think it was, or a grandson) to make the delivery. There were occasions when no one turned up and there was nothing for it but to return to the hideout and go to sleep on empty stomachs.

The weather blew hot and cold. There was an unseasonably warm spell: the marsh steamed, the wildflowers bloomed: fennel, golden samphire, pink and yellow asters, the blue-green glasswort and something that poked its yellow flowers from trumpets that looked like exploded cartridge cases. Coots ran across the water like waiters – white plates balanced on their foreheads. Blackbirds flew from trunk to trunk round us, pouring their hearts out before pausing and cocking their heads to see if we'd noticed them; to see if we had anything to say for ourselves.

'Turdus,' said Jacob.

Jacob was the twitcher among us. From him we learned the builder of the flask-shaped nest was the male penduline tit, which would settle a female on a clutch of eggs then make another nest for another female. We learned that the monogamous female and male pigeon both produced milk in their digestive systems; that in lean times the shrike stored prey on spikes; that the chicks of the marsh harrier ate their diminutive siblings; that bitterns disguised themselves as reeds to elude predators; that plovers feigned injury to divert threats to their young; that the starling was the great archivist of the bird world: in its song you could hear for example early mechanical harvesting machines (generations hence might hear the Thompson submachine gun). Never having been taken much with the starling's goosestep or its table manners, I looked at it anew; coming to the conclusion its plumage wouldn't make a bad feather cloak.

Then one morning we woke soaked to the skin. The hideout was a sodden sandpit; all the leaves had come down: the better view of the track was a mixed blessing because anyone passing had a better view of us too.

Alfred sent a sheet of plywood with instructions to lay it across the ditch. It beat holding our sodden blankets over our heads but not by much, especially when the wind funnelled along the ditch or fat dye-yellow drops fell on our heads. So it was good riddance when a violent gust picked it up and smashed it against a tree.

Thereafter when it rained, we sheltered under the bridge by the road. We were staring at the stagnant water one day, when I looked up and saw Alfred emerging from the hideout with a bag over his shoulder: I gave him a whistle. After a bite to eat and a smoke, we went back to staring at the water, at the bubbles rising from the mud and popping, at the rings rippling outwards.

Alfred plonked himself down next to Tom (we knew what was coming, because Bob and I had already been 'interviewed'). Tom, who had little to say at the best of times, responded to each question in the shortest way possible: he had no father, no mother, no wife, no children, no home and no girlfriend. Exasperated, Alfred asked him if he'd ever been in love.

Tom kept his cool and Alfred changed tack. Then he told Tom about himself, how he'd worked as a labourer in France and as a miner in Belgium; how he'd laid cobblestones, read gas meters, run a picture framing business and art gallery and written books; that, moreover, he was thinking about writing a book about us, which he would call *Sei Uomini sotto le Stelle*.

We pricked up our ears: reminded of a conversation on the evening that our hopes of sailing down the coast had been dashed, when on looking up at the night sky, Alfred had started counting.

'Here in Italy,' he had said, 'we have a saying that if you count seven stars and think of something, that thought will immediately appear in the mind of the person you love.'

'Sounds like an old wives tale,' I'd said.

'Try it.'

'How would that prove anything?'

'You could ask when you get home.'

'Not my cup of tea,' I said.

But at his insistence, for the sake of peace, I went along with it. It just so happened that night that between the treetops there were seven stars; no more, no less. But counting them was the easy part, because as soon as I thought about Iris the tears came.

'*Piagnucolona*,' chided Alfred. 'You're letting the side down; you who have always made it your job to keep our spirits up!'

So I gave him the potted version: substituting the name Kitty for Iris, having not long finished *Anna Karenina* and, somewhat to my embarrassment, including our pet names.

He put his hand on my shoulder and pushed himself up. I pulled out my watch. It had stopped. I tried rewinding it.

'Ah,' said Alfred, '*a Doxa*! Let me have a look? What's a Lothario like you doing with such a virtuous model? That's twice this evening you've disappointed me. It just so happens I know somebody who fixes watches – leave it with me, he owes me a favour.'

I was reluctant to part with my watch, whether or not it was in working order; but this is by the by. The long and the short of it was we put it to him he should call his book *Sette Uomini Sotto le Stelle*: not only because it fitted with the gem of local folklore he'd privileged us with, but also because we considered him to be one of us.

Eight

It was getting on for midday; I'd had my nose to the lookout since daybreak and I was ready for a spell. I rolled a smoke and put it to my lips.

When I looked up, the view had changed. It was as if a spider's nest had been torn open: men in black uniforms were poking round in the bushes at the side of the track. The rifles slung over their backs looked like muskets (inclined to be as fatal to the shooter as to the target). In their hands they carried pistols; tucked into their belts were daggers; ammunition belts crisscrossed their fronts. It looked to me, for all money, like a tip-off. I backed away slowly, holding up four fingers behind my back then I crouched and turned. The others were already on their feet. I turned back to the lookout.

The nearest Blackshirt had a large round head, wavy black hair and a pencil moustache; behind him was a man with a long nose and a thin face, while further back was a man with a ruddy face; the last was a clean-cut, well-built looking man who looked to be in charge; he was scanning the ditch.

With the wind behind us, we could still hear the occasional curse: what they were directed at wasn't clear, unless they hoped to flush us out? If on the other hand they were cursing the weather, then perhaps all they knew was we were in the general area? If this was the case then perhaps we could call their bluff and sit tight? With only a few clumps of robinia between them and us, they changed course, crossed the ditch and disappeared among the trees. Maybe they'd had enough of the rain, maybe it was lunchtime, maybe they'd done what they'd set out to?

When they reappeared a few days later something had to give and that something was us. I didn't stop till I was near the edge of the forest; then when I looked round I found I was on my pat. The shooting and the shouting had long since died away and the light was dimming when I heard a twig crack.

I stared into the gloom till I thought I was seeing things as well as hearing them: it was time to move, I crawled through the remaining few yards of vegetation till I could see the stop bank luminous in the twilight. Cautiously, I poked my head out and looked to where it curved out of sight both ways. I was about to make a move when a hand grabbed my ankle.

'Jesus, Mary and bloody Joseph!' I breathed.

We caught up with Robert, whom Blue had been following till he saw me. The plan if we got separated had been for the three of us (now that we were back to our original groups) to meet up at the copse where Signora Donà sent food. We went there anyway, but nobody came, so we continued on, looking for another hideout; giving Signora Donà's house a wide berth in case it was being watched. Beyond her house, was all hay paddocks and grazing. The boat we had inspected was out of the question of course and the boatshed was draughty. It was a toss-up then between continuing southwards or keeping to the southern side of the forest. We chose the latter and soon came upon a likely-looking clump of robinia, not as spacious as our old one but more sheltered from the prevailing wind.

In the early afternoon of the following day we watched a farmhand cross the fields. After he had done his business, we got his attention and explained our situation as best we could. He said he would have a word with his boss.

It was going on dark, when he reappeared with the farmer. The farmer had lumps of bread and cheese in his pockets, which he doled out to us. While we ate, he commiserated with us over our situation; lamenting the pace of the Allied advance, the fiasco of the armistice, the failed attempts to have us taken off by submarine. In regard to the latter, our chaplain's name came up several times; it appeared that he had been co-ordinating the various unsuccessful attempts from this end on our behalf; unfortunately, his profession notwithstanding, he had no control over the weather. We also learned that some of our mates were back at the Agricola Millecampi – the perfect cover – mind you, their Italian was a good deal better than ours.

It was a case of the blind leading the blind: it was only by holding onto the coattails of the bloke in front and by the feel of gravel under one foot and the grass under the other that we were able to follow the farmer's directions and avoid tumbling down the steep bank into the canal. He met us at the door and led us through the stirring, snorting, breathing stable to a trapdoor and down a flight of steps. By candlelight we saw we were in a cellar full of old harnesses and farm implements in need of repair – awaiting the return of the former farmhands from the German labour camps. The cellar stank of rotting leather and rust and damp and mould and wine. Wine barrels lined the walls; we couldn't take our eyes off them.

'Help yourselves,' said the farmer, 'have as much as you like.'

We didn't need a second invitation. He sat with us for about an hour or so but didn't drink with us. Then he took himself off to bed and with his blessing we continued drinking. It was cold and damp in the cellar but not as cold and damp as the forest. The wine was a bit on the rough side, the alcohol content wasn't up to much either, but it was food and with the bread and cheese the only food we'd had in days.

The terms of the arrangement were the same as at Signora Donà's house: we had to be out by dawn and as long as we kept our end of the bargain, the cellar was ours for as long as we wanted. And this was the pattern for the next week or two – twelve days I think it was – till the night we heard a commotion upstairs.

We cast round – hiding would have been about as effective as shutting our eyes – snuffing out the candle would have been equally pointless – probably disadvantageous – as the smell of the wax and the burnt wick would have been a dead giveaway. Nor would getting to our feet have improved our situation: we stayed where we were, sitting round the table with our hands on our mugs in clear view.

The trapdoor was lifted, torch beams shone on the steps, jackboots appeared on the steps and the barrels of Schmeissers. Having hardly dared breathe, we were very nearly breathless.

'*Hände in die Luft, langsam!*' said the first soldier or something to that effect.

They were not young and nor was the Hauptmann who in schoolmasterly English asked to see our Pay Books. When he got round to mine, he slipped the photos from the pocket at the back.

'Your parents?' he said, nodding approvingly.

I nodded.

'And this is your girl?'

He could only have been looking at the photo of Iris and Winnie mocking the Nazi salute.

'A long story,' I said.

'A long story?'

'She is married.'

'Some men have all the luck.'

There followed the obligatory questions about where we had stayed since the armistice, who had fed us, housed us; the numbers and locations of other escapees and so on to which we were obliged to give the standard response. He wasn't happy but he didn't press the point.

'Finish your drinks,' he said and left us.

The soldiers marched us to a truck at the end of the road. Through the mist we heard the rap like a sprung-steel doorknocker of a woodpecker.

'l hope that's what I think it was,' I said to Blue.

'*Ruhe!*' said one of the soldiers.

The driver made no concessions for the corners or very little, as if concerned about one of our planes showing up, the sun flickered through the plane trees . . . Next thing I was sprawled on the deck, blinking like a new-born to the wry grins of my cobbers and the guards alike: the bruise stayed with me throughout the winter.

We spent a week in the former barracks of the 58th Fanteria, the Caserma Oreste Salomone. Oreste Salomone had made a name for himself as a pilot in the war between Italy and Turkey over Libya. The barracks stood cheek by jowl with the Santa Giustina Abbey, the domes of which looked into our exercise yard. It was through the shared wall that with the help of the monks and the Resistance some fifty or sixty men had escaped.

We went to another collection point a few days later. It was in Mantova, some fifty miles to the west and it was from there that we were sent by train to Germany.

We were no sooner underway, than we took to the floorboards with an assortment of knives and pocketknives, with a view to lowering ourselves through the underframe, under cover of darkness, while the train was slowed by the Alpine incline. At a latrine stop, our efforts were discovered.

When the two armed guards who then boarded with us herded us to one end of the wagon, drew a line on the floor and warned us that anyone stepping over that line would be shot, we thought we'd gotten off lightly. However, we spent the remainder of that day on our feet and that night and the two days and the two nights that followed with no water, no rations and no toilet stops.

Our blood pooled in our legs, our feet swelled in our boots, the boots effectively became foot presses; our joints ached. We were a sorry lot, I can tell you, when the doors rolled open.

The Black Vein

We who lived in concentration camps can remember the men who walked through huts comforting others, giving away their last piece of bread. They may have been few in number, but they offer sufficient proof that everything can be taken from a man but one thing: the last of the human freedoms – to choose one's attitude in any given set of circumstances, to choose one's own way.

And there were always choices to make. Every day, every hour, offered the opportunity to make a decision, a decision which determined whether you would or would not submit to those powers which threatened to rob you of your very self, your inner freedom; which determined whether or not you would become the plaything of circumstance, renouncing freedom and dignity to become moulded into the form of the typical inmate.

One

Thirty miles to the northwest of Munich, on the outskirts of a small town called Moosburg, was a camp that had been built for prisoners who had been captured during the invasion of Poland: the event that set the ball rolling that had brought us to this pass. Being built on a river-flat, it didn't take a lot of rain to turn it into a puddle, and that winter there was no shortage of rain.

As *moos* means mudflat or open country and *burg* means fortress, I'm guessing there was a Roman garrison here once; unless, that is, the name harks back to a much earlier time when a roundel was built here by people who came up the Isar to trade and stayed to graze cattle.

If you think of the river-flat as the foot of a saucer, then the town was on its rim. We could see its two belfries like hare's ears sticking above the forest. From time to time, we'd be drawn from the huts by the fiery skies and they'd be backlit by the bombs falling on Munich. When the booms reached us, we would cheer, which evidently didn't go down too well in some quarters: that is to say if the payload of concrete blocks that was dropped on us is anything to go by. But I'm getting ahead of myself.

The camp was a hop, skip, and a jump from the station (not that we were doing anything of the sort for some time following our arrival; it was as much as we could do to put one foot in front of the other). We crossed the Isar, where it had been diverted into a spillway for the town's grain mills, and passed a sign: *Kriegsgefangenen – Mannschafts Stammlager VIIA*, (*POW Camp for Other Ranks*). Through the guard tower's reflections we saw figures looking down at us, then the gates opened and we hobbled along Hauptstrasse, which was the main street of the camp. It was half a mile long. The camp occupied an area the size of Soames Island; there were as many people in it as there were people living in Wellington at the time.

The huts mirrored the herringbone layout of the camp. Row upon row of three-tiered bunks ran off a central aisle; each tier slept twelve men – these were the twelve men you shared food parcels with when there weren't enough for one each; more often the case than not. The same twelve men took their turn serving the soup to the rest of the hut. I say soup, but it was little more than hot water a swede had been dunked in, with perhaps the odd wisp of rehydrated cabbage, a few grains of barley or semolina, and if you were lucky a piece of horsemeat the size of your eye.

The bread was rye: it was black, it was sour and it wasn't bad bread. Cutting twelve equal slices under the scrutiny of a dozen pairs of starving eyes, however, took some doing. We took turns choosing, everybody that is but the bread-cutter, he (or I, I should say, as more often than not the dubious honour of cutting the bread was delegated to me) got the piece no one else wanted.

The mattresses were stuffed with either wood shavings or straw. It didn't matter which you got, because both were soon lumpy and crawling with vermin; we were soon covered in weals from scratching the itches where the bedbugs had punctured the skin, sucked our blood and left their business. There was always someone worse off than you of course. In this case it was the last to arrive: they slept on the floor or on a table or on the sodden straw in a tent.

At reveille we put our boots on and went back to bed – till the dogs were sent in – before making a beeline for the parade ground because before Oberst Burger was satisfied we could be shifting from one foot to the other in the freezing winds for two hours or more. Then as soon as we were dismissed it was back to the huts as fast as our little legs could carry us: to get some warmth back in our bones, to roll a smoke if we had the makings, to join the queue for the hand pump or the latrines before they got any longer.

Consignments of toilet paper were few and far between and when they came, might last a week then it was back to the labels off the Red Cross tins, our precious writing and reading materials, the cardboard of the Red Cross carton; anything in fact that could be softened by working the fibres back and forth. We ought to have a leaf out of the Indians' book: they took a can of water with them.

Nothing was spread over our waste to soften the blow. Only when the overflow seeped across the parade ground, were the pits emptied; only then was the honey wagon sent for. The contents were spread on the farms of the district. When I heard about some blokes escaping through the walls of their latrine, it occurred to me to wonder if that was their inspiration. If nothing else it was an interesting reversal of the usual course of events.

An easier way was to put your name down for a work detail. It was a day out; you got an extra ration plus the opportunity to trade (as long as you were careful, of course, because the guards took a dim view of fraternisation). At five cigarettes for a loaf, I was tempted. Some blokes fiddled the count and spent a fortnight with the wife of somebody at the front; where they got the energy from I'm blowed if I know.

It was an early start and a long day. For starters, the station was half an hour away. It was a long day to be on your feet all day too, as it was standing room only as often as not; there were long waits for supply trains to pass. We looked over the heads of the guards – who sat on forms in the open doorways, nursing their submachine guns – at the passing countryside, the villages; at a dozen Americans struggling to shift a rail into place that down the line we saw four Russians manage: it was all about showing their contempt for their guards; showing us a thing or two too. On which subject, let me add: of the thousand deaths in Stalag VIIA, half were Russian. If you saw a body on the wire, you could bet your boots it was Russian. They went to the nearby camps to be shot by the hundreds.

The streets of Munich were chocker with rubble. All that was left of the buildings were the sockets people stood in or came and went from. Our job was to clear the rubble, but we never made much more than a show of working and nobody seemed to mind: neither the guards nor the locals.

Jacob and Bob turned up in March or April. They had stayed a few days with Alfred at Ca' Rossa, before trying to get to Switzerland: they had been picked up at the station at Piove di Sacco. Tom had eluded capture, but it was the last we heard of him.

In August we were split up again and sent to different work camps. By this stage, the Japanese had been driven out of India, the Germans had withdrawn from Paris and the British had gotten as far as Florence (it would indeed have been a long wait).

On the platform opposite a guard with a German shepherd was going up and down a line of men who were wearing what looked like a cross between prison garb and pyjamas. They were skin and bone, these men; they looked like death warmed up. The line rippled as the dog lunged. Meanwhile another group of these men – their feet wrapped in blood-stained rags – was approaching the station at a jog; a guard dog snapping at its heels.

Two

In my Oxford Atlas, the black lines standing for railway lines converge on Berlin like the veins of a heart or the radii of an orb web. Not that I had it on me at the time, needless to say or indeed that I needed it to appreciate that on the day of my enlistment I had set in motion the train of events that had brought me to the black heart of Germany. By the same token, you didn't hear any complaints from me when we pulled up 60 miles short.

The floors of the distribution centre were stained red and white and black, except where the presses had been; dotted round their outlines were the holes in the floor where they'd been bolted. The operation – the printing of flags – had taken up several floors of several large buildings. Clearly they had the wind up, and for good reason as the day was fast approaching when Russians and Americans would be shaking hands on a half-submerged bridge over the Elbe.

With a dozen others, I went from here to a farm an hour's drive west. The rear of the canopied Opel panned this way and that across a backdrop of Renaissance art treasures: a chocolate box town hall, a jigsaw puzzle castle. I should have been impressed and might have been, had I been able to shake the feeling there was something untoward about this town. As it turned out, Torgau was where the Nazis confined their deserters, their resistance fighters and those who refused to join the Wehrmacht or its firing squads. They were tortured, starved, ground down by brutal exercise regimes and this it seemed to me had cast its shadow over the lanes and cobblestone squares.

Onion domes disappeared down the maw of interleaving hills that were crowned with poplar and beech and the occasional small castle. Before long, I was up to my usual tricks: the rumble of cobblestones roused me.

"*Raus! Raus!*" barked the guards and we scrambled down into a courtyard surrounded by farm buildings with exposed framing timbers.

The guards had their quarters in the machinery and implement building, where the harvest was also stored; the animals were stabled on the ground floors of the two barns; we shared the first floor of one of the barns with the farmer and his family, while the Russians had to make do with the cramped and dusty attics vulnerable to air strikes.

The fields were bounded by lines of trees, in which buzzards waited for field mice or small birds to come in range. On the brows of the rises, windmills on spindles caught the changing winds.

Years of overproduction had taken their toll: everything looked worn out – the land, the buildings, the workers, the animals – and despite the recent harvest being a poor one, the seed had gone into meeting the quotas.

Rations had been cut. We ate from the same pot as the famer and his family, so we knew the cut applied to them as much as to us. Because the farm was behind on production schedules, they were on edge. The Hauptmann was especially on edge. The farmer put on a show of being tough on us, but only when the Hauptmann was around, otherwise he left us to get on with the job. No leniency was extended to the Russians. They did the bulk of the work (they'd been spared slaughter on the steppe for this reason) and they did it on spoiled produce: on the rotten potatoes and the rotten swedes. If a job wasn't completed on time, if a machine broke down, they were beaten. If they were too sick to work, they got no food. If they were caught stealing, they were shot.

It was getting on for dark, when one of the Russians was carried in from the fields. We knew there'd been an accident that morning, because he'd been dragged to the edge of the field and left there till the meal break, when his wife was allowed to take him water; after that he was on his own till the day's work was done. He should have been taken to hospital, but that would have meant being two men and a vehicle short, not to mention the fuel.

Some days passed and when he hadn't reappeared, his wife turned to us. Like the other Russian women, she was dressed from head to toe in black, even her clogs were black; they were black from the mud. She was fair-skinned, her hair was straw-coloured; she could have been twenty-five, she could've been fifteen. She picked her moment. But we had no knowledge of medicine or none to speak of and no medicines, besides I doubt we'd have been allowed to see him anyway.

She put the acid on me – perhaps knowing a soft touch when she saw one? The only language we had in common was German: she was fluent; I had barely enough to get by on. Could I look out for an egg, her husband desperately needed something he could keep down?

I looked at her sideways. She knew as well as I did that food that was found had to be handed in – sooner rather than later. The rules were posted round the farm – accompanied by the nature of the punishment that could be expected for not adhering to them. In our case a beating, solitary confinement, the withdrawal of rations; any of which could be the beginning of the end of us. I held her eye and said nothing.

Of course, then the others wanted to know what had passed between us: she was lining me up before the old man was in the grave; food for favours, that sort of carry-on. I had to take a ribbing to keep mum. On the premise 'promise nothing, deliver everything,' I started keeping an eye out; getting to the barn ahead of the others, so I could have a quick look round.

Days passed, during which a quick glance was all that was required when our paths crossed for her to know what there was to know, and while there was never any suggestion of recrimination or disappointment, with each passing day we both knew the situation was getting increasingly critical.

The following morning, when I opened the stable door, the early sun over my shoulder lit up the very thing I was looking for: it was both like a Nativity scene and a set-up. I looked round and when nothing out of the ordinary occurred, I picked up the egg. It was still warm. A swarm of thoughts flushed my mind and brow: handing it in would be the simplest solution, but how could I then meet the eyes of the Russian? I could eat it raw and be done with it, but what to do about the shell: stuff it down the crevice I was planning to temporarily hide the egg in? In that case I might as well do what I had planned. I popped the egg it into the gap where the drying dung had shrunk away from a pole and covered it with a handful of straw. As I turned toward the stable door, a shadow cut the sunbeam.

'Hullo,' said Shelley, 'what gives?'

'I got caught short,' I said.

'You weren't thinking of helping the Russian lass, by any chance?'

'Not on your life,' I said, feeling a flush in my cheeks and a shortness of breath.

'It wasn't my life I was concerned about.'

I spent half the day sweating on the egg being found and the other half sweating on it not being. When we knocked off, I returned to the barn on the pretext of having left my jacket behind. I tucked the egg up the left sleeve, gathered the unbuttoned cuff in my fingers and joined the implement queue. I had let it down into my palm and was shuffling forward with my pitchfork, when the Russian lass appeared alongside me in her queue. Next thing I knew, the egg was gone. I had a sudden panic I'd dropped it and glanced down, expecting to see yolk and egg white and broken shell in the mud behind me or worse on my boot.

Her husband shouldn't have been working. He wasn't up to it before the accident; it might've been why there was an accident in the first place. Before the accident, he couldn't afford either to work or not to, now he didn't even have that Hobson's choice. At best, the egg would have given him a brief respite and I think the same applied to his wife: in her case from not being able to do anything. Or at least, that's the impression I got the next time our paths crossed.

Three

We were warming our bones in the early sun, when we got a signal from Alf (on duty in case someone: the farmer, the Hauptmann or a guard popped by to check on us).

And then we heard it, a low rumble like thunder, except that there were no clouds. Shelley closed his eyes, Alf cocked his head, Sandy studied the ground then we looked at each other. It was hard to know where the sound was coming from; because of the wagon-wheel arrangement of the buildings, sounds seemed to go back and forth between them. In the few weeks we'd been there, we'd had a number of visits from the Luftwaffe and this rumble probably heralded another.

When Alf got our attention again, the hum had sharpened and

gathered tempo. We joined him at the corner of the barn and looked along his outstretched arm. Where the leaves on the nearest shelterbelt were thinnest, we caught flashes of something racing along behind it; the pitch of the engines had changed to a deeper tone.

'What's it doing there?' said Sandy.

'What is it, more like?' said Alf. 'I'd be a lot happier if I could see the markings.'

'I don't like the look of this,' said Shelley.

'Sounds like a Merlin to me,' said Sandy.

'Two Merlins, you mean.'

'Two planes?'

'A twin-engine.'

'I've never seen a Messerschmitt go that fast, said Sandy, 'have you?'

'It's tramping alright,' said Alf.

I'm no expert in these matters, but from where we picked it up to where we lost sight of it, it must've covered half a mile in a matter of seconds.

'There it is!' said Shelley.

I was looking for a receding tail. What I saw was three bulbs: a nose like the head of a praying mantis and an engine on each wing. At the back was a tailfin like a shark fin; the tail wings were straighter, not quite parallel with the main wings. More to the point, they were coming straight for us.

'I can't see any guns,' said Sandy.

'Must be reconnaissance,' said Alf.

'Whose though?' said Shelley.

If it was one of ours would suggest the war was further along than we thought; that Allied Intelligence was plotting the locations of work camps with their liberation in mind. In which case, one of the two heads we could see would be the pilot; the other, the co-pilot or navigator, his head down looking at his charts or perhaps through a camera lens.

When the flaps opened, the plane was lifting over us. It took the appearance of bombs dropping from their cradles, their tailfins grabbing the air like parachutes, for the penny to drop.

'Jesus, Mary and Joseph!' said Alf.

'This is going to be a close one!' I said.

We dropped our pitchforks and turned and high-tailed it back into the barn; not because we thought the bombs would miss us, but because when shrapnel and shattered cobblestones were flying round, any shelter was better than none. Sandy and Alf dived into the stall we'd been mucking out. Shelley and I kept running, thinking the further into the barn we got the better. The plane snarled overhead; the pitch changing again. The first blast picked us up and flung us further into the barn, the second blast spun us sideways; the third, of which I was only dimly aware, seemed to reverse the effect of the first.

My first thought when I came to, because I couldn't breathe, was what do you do when you're drowning? I thought I couldn't see either, till the blackness appeared to waft or billow. I still couldn't get up. I could move my head from side to side and I could lift it; I could move my hands and feet, but I couldn't budge; I couldn't roll over. And the blackness was giving off a terrific heat. I lifted my head again: through the darkness I saw what looked like a roof beam, except it wasn't where it was supposed to be. It was right in front of me, in fact it was lying on me; no wonder I couldn't breathe. I tried wriggling again, but not for long and not with much expenditure of effort either, because there was a pain in my chest that made me wince. I might as well have been drowning for all the difference it made.

Then a face appeared, Shelley's, looking very solemn; Shelley's ghost perhaps come to say goodbye? At last, the penny dropped: Shelley thought I was a goner. I would have to persuade him otherwise; I opened my mouth but nothing came out. Then he was bending over me; his hand, fingers splayed, was reaching down to close my eyelids.

'Christ all bloody . . .!' was as far as he got.

Again I tried to speak. What I wanted to say was if you don't get this thing off me, you'll see a bloody ghost alright! He got the picture. As luck would have it, the beam was broken where it lay on my chest and he was able to lift the shorter end of it sufficiently for me to explode in a wheezing, coughing fit of dust and smoke, before very nearly fainting with the pain.

'Move!' he shouted at me.

I shuffled and wriggled down and away from him and he dropped the beam.

I could have done with a breather then, but the flames had become visible through the smoke and were spreading; besides the smoke was burning my lungs and eyes. After some effort, with Shelley's assistance

161

I managed to roll onto my hands and knees and from there get to my feet. We stumbled from the barn just as the work parties from the fields were arriving. Not that they paid any attention to us. Pulling their jackets up over their heads, the Russians plunged into the smoke. Then the farmer's wife arrived with blankets. I was laid onto a stretcher and removed to the middle of the courtyard.

When Shelley followed the Russians, I presumed it was to check on Alf and Sandy. How they supposed there could be anyone to help was beyond me, because the attic had gone. Then Shelley was standing over me again.

'Not a sign,' he said, 'that whole end's gone.'

The next time I opened my eyes, there was a stretcher beside mine; in it was the Russian, his wife was kneeling over him, bathing his brow.

It was one step forward and two back for the Russians, or in his case half a step forward and two and a half back. We were taken to a hospital in Leipzig – had the Russian been alone in needing attention, I doubt they would have bothered.

Four

'Sounds like a De Havilland Mosquito,' said the bloke in the next bed. 'They can tramp: balsa wood and bombs, no armaments. The Germans had nothing to catch it with when one of them bombed Berlin while Goering was giving a speech to the Wehrmacht in honour of Hitler's first decade in power.'

Leipzig had had more than its fair share of bombing already, but with the marshalling yards up and running again, the bombers were overdue. We were half a mile away; between us and the yards was a zoo. When the bombers rumbled over and the windows rattled in their frames, a God-awful scream rose from it. We lay in our cots listening to the racket; the walls pulsed red through our closed eyelids.

I had chest contusions; I had a touch of pneumonia: I'd have considered myself lucky to have got a week. It was only because he knew where I'd be going next, that the doctor kept me there a bit longer.

The doctor's name was Frederick Webster. He got around the hospital with a pipe jammed between his teeth and he made no bones about his contempt for the Germans, even to their faces. He was English, very proper; a captain and former medical officer with the Green Howards. He ran the place. We called him The Doc.

The hospital was in a four storey apartment building. From the street frontage, you looked up at alternate pointed and curved pediments. The buildings to either side were the same. There were blocks and blocks of these buildings, each with a central courtyard. I was in a ward on the fourth floor overlooking this courtyard. The Doc's office and quarters were across the corridor, he looked down onto the street. The orderlies were along the corridor. The Germans' offices and guard room were on the ground floor, their quarters in an adjacent building; they came and went through a door on our floor. On the floor below us were the Russians, the treatment room was on the first floor.

We saw the Russians in the treatment room on Mondays and Wednesdays and Fridays; their days were every day. They were unshaven, their eyes were sunken, their clothes threadbare; there was nothing to them, till one of them picked up the balalaika and they sang, tears streaming down their faces. The whole hospital stopped to listen, even the guards smiled.

The treatment began with food and rest: large heaps of potatoes, horsemeat, bread, cheese, jam, sugar and a blob of pig fat. On top of this, I was getting my allocated Red Cross food parcel weekly. I'd got down to seven and a half stone so I wasn't complaining. Rest was all the sleep you could get and hot baths: all the hot water you could want for as long as you wanted – I didn't get that at home. Once on the mend, the sessions began. They weren't optional: it was show up or get shown the door.

The sessions were low-key to begin with: they were about how I was sleeping, whether I was having nightmares, was I constipated; that sort of thing. At that stage I could get away with a yes or a no. Later when the Doc started homing in on the real business – the nature and circumstances of the causes of my Post Traumatic Stress Syndrome or Shellshock as it was known then, my responses got even shorter. That was the last thing I wanted to talk about or even to think about, because that just brought it all back again along with the tics: the shaking, the trembling.

'Take your time,' he would say.

It didn't help; the silences got longer.

'Have a spell,' he'd say and roll a smoke for me.

'Ready?' he'd say.

'As ready as I'll ever be,' I would say.

And he would put his paperwork aside and off we'd go again and it would be the same thing all over again: the racing heart, the sweat, the jiggling knees, the dry mouth . . . . I knew what he was up to because he'd been over it with me. I looked out the window while he went over it again. I had no problems with the theory; it was the practice I wanted nothing to do with. I'd have a crack at it I thought off my own bat one day when I was ready; when that day would be, I didn't know, but it wasn't now. I couldn't tell him this because of course I didn't want to be kicked out. And I think he knew all this because from that day on he didn't push it; we were just going through the motions.

'You've got a visitor,' said the orderly. 'You better make yourself decent.'

'What,' I said, 'who?'

He tapped the side of his nose. I was sure it must be a mistake, but I did up my top button, retied the cord on my pyjama trousers, straightened the bed clothes as best I could and tidied up the top of my bedside cabinet.

Who could it possibly be, I wondered? Who did I know in Germany other than my fellow POWs? What were the chances of them being allowed to visit me? Unless it was our Man of Confidence wanting an eye witness account of the bombing (fat chance he had of that), besides neither possibility quite accounted for the grin on the orderly's face. I was sure someone had got their wires crossed when there was a knock on the door.

'Come in if you're good looking,' said my neighbour.

The door opened and a beautiful young woman appeared: my visitor; was this a joke? Someone most certainly had got their wires crossed. And then the face began to fall into place: the smile; the clothes too – the ones she wore on her day off when she did the washing and mending. I was speechless, I reddened. She smiled again and looked around. Unable quite yet to trust my voice, I gestured to the chair beneath the window. She stepped toward it, took a quick look down into the courtyard and moved away again.

'The guards,' she said, 'they don't know I am here. I am visiting my husband.'

'Of course,' I said, astonished to hear he was still in the land of the living, 'how is he doing?'

'Not so good,' she said. 'That is why I am here, as you may have guessed. I was hoping you might have something, but only if you can spare it, of course?'

'Shit!' I said. 'Excuse my language, of course.'

I reach over the side of the bed and pulled out my Red Cross carton and got out the bar of chocolate I'd been saving for later.

'Here,' I said, 'give him this.'

'Are you sure?' she said, her eyes widening. 'All of it?'

'I'm sorry you had to ask. I should have thought.'

She slipped the packet down her collar.

'Be careful it doesn't melt,' I said.

'*Wie bitte?*'

Preparations for Christmas were well underway when I got my marching orders: the Doc had stuck his neck out for me for as long as he could. I would miss the place. I would miss the Russians, despite their seeming to pity us precisely because we had all the advantages; despite their not being too impressed by our singing or the orderly's violin repertoire for that matter. I would miss their singing, their indomitable spirit. Above all, I would miss my visitor: it was no odds to me that the reason for her visits was the weekly bar of chocolate that came with my Red Cross parcels. It was good chocolate too: dark, bitter, sweet. Perhaps the guards would miss her too: they always seemed to turn a blind eye to her visits.

I was going to miss the long baths; the orderly, who after a night on the town always made a point of dropping in to regale us with the details of his latest run-in with the SS; who it seemed, he was forever bumping into in parts of town he hadn't a permit to be in and managing to talk his way out of it. What I wasn't going to miss, needless to say, was the air raids or the sessions with the Doc.

From time to time when I'm reading something, a Russian novel generally, I'll see something of my visitor in one of the characters, which will set me off thinking about her, wondering if she survived the war and got back to her village.

As a matter of fact, I caught the tail end of a documentary not so long ago about a woman who was bringing up her grandchildren in an apartment in Odessa. I wouldn't have given tuppence for her old man's chances, but you never know; some of those Russians seemed to survive on spirit alone.

Further to which – perhaps you'll remember this – I used to get in late on a Friday night after a session in town, always with something for your mother of course: flowers, grapes, chocolate. Always, your mother said, it was the chocolate that was her favourite. It wasn't a peace offering only.

Five

Stalag IVF had 25,000 prisoners on its books, spread over ninety-five detachments. Saxony was one of Germany's biggest coal deposits, the farmers used to dig it up for heating and cooking; now they were turning it into synthetic petrol. As POW number 274194, I was about to follow in the footsteps of my father and his father. With any luck, I'd get to compare notes with the old man, as he had with his.

The headquarters and the main camp of Stalag IVF were housed in a former industrial laundry on the banks of a stream in the village of Hartmannsdorf. On the way to the mine, we stopped in to pick up others who'd been reassigned; they were as apprehensive as I was. I couldn't for the life of me see how I was going to cope with the controlled detonations, let alone anything else.

The year just gone had brought a shift in emphasis to the Allied bombing. It had gone from being a softening-up/preparatory-to-invasion approach to the shutting down of the German fuel industry. Had the shift come earlier, the war might have been over and many of the lives that had been lost as a result might still be going about their business, to say nothing of the lives of their unborn children. Hundreds of tons of incendiaries and high explosives had already been dropped on Dresden that year and yet the bombers returned again and again.

The war was in its twilight. We were following the Russians' progress by the sound of their artillery, getting more and more antsy about finding ourselves in their path. Among the stories doing the rounds was one about some prisoners being shifted ahead of the Russian advance getting slaughtered by the SS; another, that we would be traded for high-ranking Nazis and kept on under the Russians. Circumstances were beginning to look every bit as grim as those which had accompanied the Italian armistice.

The guards had even more cause for concern: they knew what would happen to them if the Russians arrived at the camp gates before the Americans. The thing was, they were taking it out on us, which would explain the increase in the numbers of complaints the Man of Confidence was receiving. What neither party knew was that the deputy *Kommandant*, having got the drop on the *Kommandant*, was sitting on those reports. Nor was our case helped much by those – among us, I might add – who took the view that the victims had got what they deserved.

It was a short march from the barracks to the pithead, where we changed into our wet work clothes. My boots had given up the ghost. I'd tried nailing the uppers to bits of broken pallet I'd picked up in the mine, shaping the wood with my pocketknife, but my boot-making skills weren't in the same league as those I was attempting to copy, so it was a case of squeezing my feet, raw with fungal infections and bound in rags, into the camp-issue clogs.

My heart would be in my mouth when the gate was shut, but I never blacked out as others did as we plummeted (the gleam from our carbide lamps accompanying us on the dripping wall), nor did I lose teeth clenching them; fearful we wouldn't pull up in time. It was 15 men to a cage, including staff, despite their objections to having to accompany us when their clothes were dry. At the bottom, we transferred to the empty coal tubs, roomy enough for one but a squeeze for two. There were two boys on the payroll. It didn't look good and it was what it looked like: for a loaf of bread or a canteen of soup they would share a tub with a prisoner.

A tiny diesel locomotive pulled us through a maze of tight-cornered, low-ceilinged, rat-infested and narrow dripping passages, past recesses like display cabinets full of obsolete machinery and instruments. From time to time a rock fall or a squeeze (that twisted and buckled the tracks like an earthquake) brought us up short. After some miles of this, there might still be a mile on foot: tough-going in clogs on uneven ground full of cables and pipes and tubes; taller men caught their backs and the backs of their heads on the sagging bars.

The walls were ribbed and lined with larch and steel and packed with rocks, making them look like dry-stone walls. There would have been acres of larch in this one mine alone (larch is close-grained, strong and flexible and splinters under pressure, thereby providing warning). The props were hewn to a point and mounted on rubble and splayed when any weight came on them. In spite of the precautions or because of them, we were made more aware of the hundreds of yards of rock hanging over our heads. Nor could we forget we were below sea level.

Most of the work would be done in pairs on long-walls: one man on the jackhammer, the other on the end of a shovel; except where the jackhammer was worked above waist level, then one of you bore its weight while the other operated. We'd be stripped to our loincloths or in nothing but our boots or clogs. Every now and again a face as high as the width of our shoulders had to be wriggled up to and chipped away at with a pickaxe: the kind of work some men would maim themselves rather than tackle, even at the risk of being shot.

Steinkohle was rock hard coal. The shovels, *Frau Hintern*, were light and round and capable of holding more coal than we could lift. The cutters and the chain-driven conveyors filled the air with coal dust. The noise was deafening, except during the lunch breaks when everything was turned off so we could listen for the creaking that meant further propping was needed, or when charges were laid and we retreated to a safe distance (or in the case if some, to endure insults to old injuries).

The mine trembled, gouts of coal dust cascaded from the ceiling: the order to down-tools couldn't come soon enough, even though getting out of the mine might be going from the jaws of one monster into those another, because as often as not the sky would be lit by flak and searchlights and the occasional cart-wheeling Lancaster, which meant hours in the air-raid shelter, all night if there was more than one raid and no supper because the cooks would be in there with you. This went on day after day, week after week and month after month on four weeks of rations spun out over five.

Breakfast was 300 grams of bread, 25 grams of marmalade, the same of sugar and half a litre of ersatz coffee. Lunch was 400 grams of potatoes, 300 grams of spinach or uncooked vegetables or 50 grams of noodles or meat or gruel with a dab of margarine. Supper was 400 grams of potatoes or pea soup. Sundays were a bit different: Sunday lunch was 100 grams of meat; Sunday supper, a piece of sausage and instead of the ersatz coffee a brew tasting of boiled weeds. The mining company pittance had dried up and so even the few rubbery vegetables for sale in the canteen were out of our reach. The Red Cross parcels, a casualty of the new bombing strategy, were otherwise being pillaged on the sidings by the SS or black-marketeers.

I'd survived Point 175, I'd survived being torpedoed in the Mediterranean, I'd survived being bombed by a British aeroplane, but the bombing of Leipzig had overridden my limits. I'd seen it in others and now I saw others see it in me: see me wake to my own shouting, see my hands shake so much I couldn't perform bread-cutting duties. I'd stopped smoking, not because I was too proud to ask someone to roll and light a cigarette for me, but because the weak got picked on. The Polish tobacco had to be boiled and redried anyway, so I wasn't missing much. I couldn't read, I was peeing more, I had back pains and stomach pains, I fell over from blackouts and fainted from headaches, my appetite came and went (most of what I ate went straight through me anyway), explosions brought tears to my eyes. In short, I was at the end of my tether.

Six

In April we heard the Americans in the west; after a few days, they were battering their way into Erfurt. Then it was Jena then Weimar then Buchenwald came to light: ovens choked with partially-burned human remains: no sign of the gas chambers but rows of naked bodies facing the sky, stacked like cordwood; floor-to-ceiling shelves of people deranged by malnutrition and disease; men in striped uniforms hunting the guards; photographs of gruesome tortures. The Yanks brought their troops in to witness the atrocity as a safeguard against denial.

A fortnight later, in the woods on Gera's eastern approach, a hundred Germans put up some last-ditch opposition with small arms, machineguns and bazookas. With the end in sight there was no time to waste: infantry regiments were leapfrogging tank battalions.

That Saturday, I awoke thinking I'd gotten my days mixed up, because a hut full of men on a working day was unheard of. I pulled the blanket over my head. Next thing, Ned was shaking my foot.

'The guards have gone!' he said.

'Eh, what's that?'

'The guards have buggered off! Come on, shake a leg, we're going for a walk.'

I sat up; the room was empty. I put my feet on the floor, turned them this way and that, considering their condition; then swaddled them, eased them into my clogs and went downstairs: nobody.

I poked my head out the door: not a soul in sight. I looked round a corner of the building and saw the gates shifting back and forth in the wind, squeaking. I wasn't too keen on leaving the camp on my own, so I went back through the dining room, the recreation room, the washroom, the toilet block, the basement, the kitchen: it was eerily empty. I was on my hands and knees, picking up grains of rice when I heard footsteps.

'What the fuck are you up to?'

The sun shone on the trunks of the trees and the roadside grasses. I kept turning round, expecting a rifle butt in the back or a boot in the jacksy. Low hills scarred by coal-workings stretched away to the west, a steeple appeared over a hedgerow. We passed boarded-up houses, others with slopes of masonry pouring out of them; patches where the plaster had come off. It was a good drying day but nobody was availing themselves of the opportunity. We passed an elderly couple.

'*Tag,*' I said.

'*Tag,*' said the old man, touching his hat. The old lady's eyes wrinkled.

When we caught up with the others, they were milling round a public house.

'What's the guts?' said Ned.

'Not open till 2.00.'

'Bother, I'll miss my shift.'

'Hurry up and open or we'll open up for you!'

A window went up and the proprietor stuck his head out and waved us away. Next thing there was a roar of engines and the racket of tracks over cobblestones and we turned to see an American tank and a Deuce-and-a-Half come shooting out of an alleyway and across the square. It skidded to a stop, the lid flew open and the up popped the commander like a jack-in-the-box.

'Who in God's name are you?' he demanded.

The senior N.C.O. was cut short and we were ordered back to the camp and told to stay put till arrangements could be made for our evacuation. This drew howls of protest; the N.C.O. explained that as many of us had been in P.O.W. camps for several years, returning to the camp was out of the question. We then got a tirade about how the war wasn't over, how if we were caught in the crossfire it would be our lookout, how if we didn't comply he'd call in the MPs and they would shoot us if there was any more trouble. There were more howls of protest, the N.C.O. tried again; the commander handed him a bit of paper.

'Read it out,' he said.

'"Administrative Repatriation Procedures and evacuation and Disposition of Recovered Allied Military Personnel: Eclipse Memorandum number eight: POWs who don't remain in their camps after liberation will be classified as displaced persons and will lose their priority for evacuation . . ."'

'We haven't been liberated,' said Ned, 'the guards just disappeared. What were we supposed to do, wait for you to find us?'

'We'll think about it,' said someone else, 'when we've had something to recover from.'

The Commander reached for his RT then evidently thinking better of it, paused.

'I'll make a deal with you,' he said. 'If you return to your camp immediately and stay there, I'll see to it you have food and medicines by the end of the day.'

'What about something to drink – for medicinal purposes only, of course?'

'We'll see what we can do.'

With heavy footsteps, we returned to the camp.

Dusk was turning to night when two trucks drove into the yard, one with food and medicines, the other with pallets of beer and cartons of Lucky Strike.

We ate and drank and smoked – not necessarily in that order – and talked and sang and ate and drank and smoked some more till it was daybreak. The party was still going on when a convoy of empty trucks arrived and we had 10 minutes to do whatever we had to do and get onboard. It was just a case of shifting venues: the party continued till the beer was drunk, the smokes smoked and the food eaten.

Seven

We followed a stream for a few miles then it was uphill and down dale through one village after another, each with its tiled, octagonal, domed *Kirche*. We overtook all manner of vehicles: wood-fired trucks, late model Mercedes-Benzes, hand carts, bicycles laden with cages of chickens, piglets perched on household goods. It was like waking from a bad dream: on the one hand, you didn't dare hope; on the other, you couldn't help pinching yourself.

We were processed in Gera, given cartons of K-Rations and pointed in the direction of houses that had been emptied because shots had been fired from them; lives had been lost clearing the town. The occupants had been permitted to take food and clothing, nothing else. We slept in their beds and ate our K-Rations at their kitchen tables: a different carton for each meal, though all had meat and cigarettes, coffee and chewing gum, candy and pemmican biscuits and soup powder, not to mention toilet paper, a small wooden spoon and a key for the cans; all in a carton a foot long by three inches wide and an inch and a half deep. Some blokes swore by them; after eating nothing else for several days, others fainted from a lack of vitamins.

After breakfast we changed trucks: the new ones had been hosed down, but the smell of corpses was unmistakable. More uphill and down dale followed. Thankfully, the machineguns mounted on the cabs were not required. As evening approached, rain condensing out of the mist spattered the windscreens and canopies.

We got into the U.S. camp in Namur in the early hours: here we were checked to see if we were carrying anything infectious then sprayed with disinfectant anyway. Most complaints were malnutrition-related:

swollen tongues, lips and other extremities; gastrointestinal problems from over-consumption of food or from having rich food too soon.

The physical examination took longer: blood tests, X-rays for tuberculosis and pulmonary disease, urine tests, tests for depression, anxiety, lack of self-confidence, authority phobia, attitude toward the prospect of further military service, domestic concerns and the like. In the middle of this, a poster caught my eye: it was a call for volunteers to get Europe back on its feet. As soon as I was done, I went looking for the office.

'What can I do for you, Private?' said the bloke behind the desk.

'I've come about the poster, sir,' I said.

'What poster?' he said, looking me up and down.

I told him.

'Get yourself on the first available ship, private,' he said, 'you've done your bit.'

'Thank you, sir,' I said, unsure whether to feel offended or relieved.

Because I couldn't hold a pencil, let alone make a legible mark, I was excused from having to fill out the Liberation Questionnaire. Ostensibly, this was about what camps you'd been in (main ones, work ones); hospitals (illnesses, treatments); ill-treatments; war crimes witnessed; names of known collaborators; whether you'd been interrogated, had sabotaged anything or escaped from anywhere. What it came down to was they were looking for bad eggs (spies, fascists, Nazi sympathisers); they were gathering information for war crimes trials. Most blokes wrote Yes or No where they could and I expect I would have done the same.

On receipt of a new Pay Book, I discovered I was worth the princely sum of 205 pounds and 14 shillings. My old Pay Book went into the bin: if only I could have put the time it represented behind me as easily. Meanwhile, I had 205 pounds and 14 shillings burning a hole in my pocket.

The following day, somewhat the worse for wear, we boarded a Dakota.

'Watch your head,' said the pilot at the door too late.

The benches along the sides had all been taken. I had to sit on the floor where the freight would otherwise have gone; I had to hang onto the nets that would normally have hung onto it. The propellers were already rotating, the engines were coughing clouds of smoke;

the air crew were chewing gum and making wisecracks. Door closed, the engines began powering up; the body began vibrating. The chocks were removed and the plane swung round. As much from nerves as from the cold, I shook so much my stomach muscles hurt. The plane shook too: I was sure it was coming apart. How we made it into the air in one piece, I'm blowed if I know.

The one thing in its favour was there was only one hill. It was as bad as the one fairground ride I'd been on – either the seat would lose me or I would lose something. Needless to say, I passed on the opportunity to view the White Cliffs of Dover. As we came in to land, I held my breath. The plane hit and bounced and hit and bounced again. Never again, I swore.

There were wrecked and blackened aircraft all round the airfield: bulldozed into piles, some still smouldering. The wind flattened the grass, combing it this way and that; harried it mercilessly. We had been told Manston was a long runway, presumably to assure us there was no danger of missing it. It was long alright: from the hangars I couldn't see the other end. In fact, with the Channel sweeping its bow, Thanet wasn't unlike the deck of an aircraft carrier: *H.M.S. Thanet*, I thought, catching up with the others.

The welcoming party was almost all female: mothers, daughters, wives, widows, spinsters and grandmothers. The sun made bright badges of their foreheads, while the wind got up to no good with their dresses. The speeches done with, we were ushered into a hangar full of trestle tables covered in newsprint, utensils, beverages and condiments. At the sight of the food, the wooziness that had been threatening seized its opportunity; I just made it to the Gents.

Margate's thirty odd hotels and lodges and boarding houses were all booked up. The Kent coast – Margate, Westgate, Broadstairs, Folkestone, Hythe – had been requisitioned for eight and a half thousand Kiwis. The proprietors weren't too happy: they'd been putting up (and putting up with) military units for five years solid; they were in the middle of long overdue renovations, looking forward to hosting their first English holiday season since war began. As far as they were concerned, it was high time other resort towns had the pleasure of our company. It being a hop and a skip from London's nightlife, the Dominion's representatives had other ideas: they put their foot down and the War Office came to the party.

I got accustomed to the whoops and carry-on heralding the new arrivals. Of course, like everybody else, I looked round to see if they were blokes I knew; and when they weren't, couldn't help thinking about those I knew would not be among them. When I learnt about the death of Tom Gray (he'd been sleeping on a boat near the Ponte Della Rotta, was on his feet with his hands in the air when the Cappo's son, a boy of some 12 or 13 years, shot him in the head with a single machine gun round) I was sick to the heart: a few more months and he'd have been home and hosed. A court case was pending.

In other news: my Company had just cleared the Senio and was on its way to Padova (it would indeed have been a long wait). Meanwhile, two-thirds of those in Stalag IVF had been on starvation marches: had the Americans continued into Chemnitz, rather than turning south to Nuremberg and Munich, these could possibly have been avoided. We had come within a whisker of being among them; the American tank commander had done us a favour, more than a favour in fact, he'd probably saved our bacon.

The rest, the sea air, the copious quantities of food and drink all did their bit in getting us back into the saddle. I've never been much of a one for beaches (too readily inclined to sunburn) so I was as surprised as anyone to find myself paddling in the icy saltwater twice-daily. It had the desired effect though: the scales and the inflammation were already receding. Mind you, I was one of the lucky ones: some were, as it was put, 'oedematous to the nipple'. I had my teeth seen to. I put on my new uniform. I boarded the train to Glasgow.

Eight

We were late getting in, so I booked into a hotel. And who should I run into at the bar but the orderly from Leipzig. He'd just come from Culloden.

'Oh,' I said.

'I did a project on it at school and I thought this would be as good an opportunity as any. I always wanted to go there.'

'Oh?'

'You haven't been there?'

'No.'

'Well, you haven't missed much. Apart from the clan graves and the cottage where the government-wounded were tended to, there's not a lot to see. What got to me more than anything was the piping of a blind boy.'

'What was he doing there?'

'It was the anniversary. It was the best anniversary of anything I've been to. This boy's piping covered me in shivers. It's the closest I've come to seeing a ghost.'

Culloden, as you may know, was the last act in a civil war that had been going on since William of Orange took over from James VII of Scotland. James VII's leadership was as uncompromising as his intolerance of the Protestants and as far as the Highland chiefs were concerned he was one of them.

Well, it was a bad day for them and a bad day for Scotland. Everything was against them, the weather included: they were outnumbered, they were tired and hungry; they were poorly equipped and badly led. They were routed within the hour then hunted and butchered. The wounded were burned to death in the barn where they lay waiting to be tended. What little land was left to them, was looted and laid to waste. The clan system was dismantled. They were exiled and outlawed, transported and replaced by sheep.

Had we not been amongst Scotsmen, I might have said the English had done me a favour: I might still have been in Scotland. It wasn't the only instance of Scots stabbing themselves in the back: had they invested in Scotland, for example, rather than in where they could get the best return . . . We got onto Leipzig, the hospital, the inevitable raid.

'I was at a sick parade at a munitions factory in one of the suburbs,' he said, 'when a shadow passed over us. We looked up, the sky was full of B-17s, hundreds of them then the leading plane got hit by flak: we saw its engines arcing away from the fireball.

'When everything was over, I headed back to the hospital. The trams were out of action, so it took a bit longer; also because of the amount of rubble I had to negotiate and because the city had been altered beyond recognition. Along the way, I ran into a man who'd been working in the locomotive workshops. He told me he'd dived into a ditch seconds before the blast passed over, that it had knocked over several locomotives. He'd picked himself up and gone scavenging. Along the way, he'd met a woman who was looking for her husband's head and saw the corpse of a Russian POW that had been split down the middle like a stick of kindling; its intestines still contracting in the dirt. But the strangest thing of all, he said, was hearing people quarrelling.

'Eventually I got to Gneisenau Strasse. It was intact, except for where a stray bomb had landed in the road outside the hospital. The only death was a horse; the only damage was to the windows and to the road: there was a great hole in it and that was where the horse lay. When I got upstairs, I heard a commotion in the street and went to one of the broken windows to have a look. The whole of the neighbourhood had descended on the carcass with axes and saws and scythes and cleavers. Within minutes the street was deserted again and all that was left of the horse was the stain of its blood in the crater.

'Before I forget, did you know Parliament was talking about you the week you joined us? I couldn't say anything before, for obvious reasons. Yes, they had quite a discussion about it. It wasn't the first time we've killed or injured our own, of course. There are thousands of camps across Europe: the reason their locations are largely unknown to us is because we have the same non-disclosure policy as they; which is why we have to take our chances alongside the civilian populations.'

I got the train to Lanarkshire the following morning. Larkhall was a small town when I left and it didn't seem to have grown much since; probably largely due to mine closures. I wasn't expected till later in the day, so I checked out various points of interest I remembered from my childhood: the church we had to go to daily and twice on Sundays; our last house looked just the same; the river (the Avon River) where I used paddle, I paddled in again, picking up a couple of rocks and turning them over as I had then.

I almost walked past the house I was born in. The footpath outside, where we used to have to tip a bucket of water in winter – along with the other kids on the street – so we could slide to school, wasn't as steep as I remembered. The house itself was far more substantial than anything we had lived in since. What I remembered was the cavities in the walls where our beds were; my embarrassment at how primitive it was.

I was admiring the colour and detail and texture of the stonework, when I noticed a woman at the window. She opened it and asked if she could help me with anything. We ended up having quite a chat. Then the school bell went and I was surrounded by school children.

'That's a funny hat,' said one of them.

'It's a lemon squeezer,' said another.

'Where are you from, mister?'

'Mind your own business,' said the woman.

'No harm,' I said. 'New Zealand.'

'Where's that?'

'It's on the other side of the world. I tell you what if you ever dig a hole in your backyard deep enough that's where you'd come out.'

'That's why it's called the Antipodes,' said the woman.

'Is that how you got here?'

'No silly, he came by ship or plane'

'Ships and a plane,' I said.

'You're a long way from home, mister.'

'Actually,' I said. 'I was born in this house. What's more, when I was your age, I went to your school.'

'Why did you leave?'

'It's a long story: perhaps another time. In the meantime, perhaps you can help me? I'm looking for Victoria Street.'

'It's the next one on the left. Do you know someone who lives there?'

'Yes, as it happens.'

'Who?'

'My aunt.'

'What number does she live at?'

'Eleven.'

'She's a witch!'

'I beg your pardon! That's no way to talk about your elders and betters, Millie! Perhaps as you seem to know where it is, could you show Mr . . .?'

'Gunn.'

Millie and I parted company before a two-storey, semi-detached, stone house. The stone was a light brown colour. Clearly my uncle and aunt had done alright, but I already knew that before the letters petered out. My uncle had managed the local Scottish Co-operative (or 'Co-oper-rative,' as it was pronounced here) Wholesale Society store. It had been part of our lives too: my father and his siblings had grown up in a Co-oper-rative house.

A lad in his early teens answered the door. He immediately wanted to try on my hat. Though my uncle had died before the war began, Aunt Rachel still dressed from head to toe in black.

I followed her up the stairs to the 'children's bedroom', as it was still referred to, though her children would have been in their early fifties or thereabouts by then. My cousin Elizabeth still lived in the house. She and her husband worked for the Co-operative: she at the cash desk, he as transport manager. Elizabeth had clearly had a stroke. In fact there was something of a pall over the house: the boy had hit his mother and his grandmother had beaten him 'to within an inch of his life'.

'It's the one and only time I've hit him,' she said, 'he was black and blue by the time I'd finished.'

After supper, I offered to help with the dishes, but got shooed off. As the rest of the family had already retired, I asked Aunt Rachel if she would excuse me and popped out for a drink.

In the Clydesdale, I got talking to a bloke I'd gone to school with as it turned out. When the pub closed, he took me back to his home to meet his family. His children were asleep; he woke them anyway. They sat up, rubbing their eyes, said hullo and went back to sleep. He got out his album, flicked through a few pages and there we were: the two shorties sitting cross-legged in the front row.

It was after midnight before I got back. Aunt Rachel had waited up.

'You better take the key,' she said to me, when I made motions to go out the following evening. I got back somewhat the worse for wear that night and woke in the early hours, cold and cramped, only to discover I hadn't made it up the stairs – what's more, that somebody, had covered me with a blanket.

'So you're fond of a drop, laddie?' said Aunt Rachel at breakfast.

Clearly, she didn't approve, but that was her only comment on the subject.

Back at Margate, we had the option of attending a course or getting work experience in a factory or business: one that might come in handy for when we got home. Only one thing appealed to me: having had my appetite whetted by the professors of Gruppignano, not to mention our history teacher, I was keen on doing a course on the ancient Greeks. My only misgiving was the essay writing that went with it.

I was still umming and ah-ing, when a new notice went up: a list of those who'd been allocated a berth on a ship that was due to leave Southampton in a fortnight. So instead of the course, I spent what time I had left to me acquainting myself with some of London's less salubrious – indeed somewhat notorious – watering holes.

Along the way, I found myself in Kew Gardens. I'd been at a party in the neighbourhood and, losing my way while retracing my steps to the station, had spent the night on a park bench. It was the middle of summer; I was mooching along, having a good old gander at the various specimens, when the ropey bark and coin-like foliage of one of them caught my eye. I stepped over the herbaceous border and studiously ignoring the sign on the grass, went up to it to read the label – Black locust, *Robinia pseudoacacia*, U.S.A.

Roll for Me Bones

My father said that the meaning was: "ovunque il mio cuore ti segua" (wherever my heart follows you). He said it was a wish for good luck pronounced by the women of the tribe living under the mountain massif of TAHOMA. The wish was addressed to their men and accompanied by a gesture, whereby they laid their hands over their hearts then turned them over toward their men saying "TA HO MA". . . . In the language of the tribe (of which there were several in the territory of this glacier), the meaning was simply the name of the mountain: "mother of the waters".

Just before Queen's Birthday weekend in 1947, between 15 and 20 young men gathered in the State Advances offices in Hastings St, Napier, hoping their names would be among the six drawn out of a box for a ballot orchard at Grasmere.

One

It was the dock we left from a quarter of a century earlier; whether it was the same berth or not is another matter and neither here nor there.

Haskell had gone out ahead, working his passage as a stoker. He was 18: it was a great adventure and a big responsibility. There was some concern about the reception we might get and it was his job to report back. When there was still no word from him, the bookings were made anyway.

Between his departure and ours, Aileen, the youngest, had died from diphtheria or complications arising from. She was 18 months old. Perhaps that was the nail in the coffin. They had lost their first born too; he managed only five weeks. They would be in good hands: my father's father and my mother's mother and umpteen uncles and aunts and cousins and hangers-on would keep an eye on the graves and each other. They would be in good company: the centuries of family dead in the cemeteries dotted about.

And so we became the latest offshoot in a stream that has been breaking with the past from the year dot; because apart from the odd visit to see what the future might have held for them by those who could afford it, or in my case had their fare paid for them by His Majesty's government, there would be no going back. There were cousins who went to Canada and Queensland we never heard from again.

By the time Haskell's letter had made the return journey, we'd had its contents from the horse's mouth. Cousin Hilda was a hard taskmaster, to put it mildly. Suffice to say, we weren't about to overstay our welcome. She soon had others doing her bidding.

We cut our cloth, changed our tune: some overnight like a change of clothes. We kept the Lallans for the hearth or a corner of the after-match functions of weddings and funerals, where to the amusement of in-laws and outlaws alike we went at it hammer and tongs. Others

– Agnes and I would be prime examples – being a bit slower on the uptake, paid for it in the playground and in the gauntlet we ran between home and school and back again. When Agnes went to work for Mademoiselle Bignon, the detours became longer and more circuitous. By the time I got in, the tea Mum had made me had long since gone cold and she would be fidgety.

As the years passed, the letters to and from home dropped off. Mum missed her friends and the wider family. She missed the Central Lowlands; the dialect and the pipes and the heather. As for Dad, the practice of insurance in the colonial companies did not sit well with his Presbyterian conscience, so he gave it up and became an odd job man.

It may not have been the berth we left from in 1920, but it was the berth the *Titanic* had left from eight years earlier. Furthermore, the onshore Master-at-Arms was none other than Frederick Fleete. The fate of the *Titanic* was one of the stories we'd grown up on and this detail caused a bit of a stir. Fleete was the bloke who had raised the alarm: too late as it happened, but that was no more his fault than other's; the part of each being a domino in a row of dominoes. The one before Fleete's being the failure of Second Officer David Blair to hand over the keys to the binocular boxes. It did for Fleete all the same. He became a ship repairer with Harland and Woolff – Harland and Woolff being the company that had built the *Titanic*.

By 1945 Fleete was with Union Castle: the owner of the ship we were about to board. The *Stirling Castle* was also built by Harland and Woolff; in the same Belfast yard the *Titanic* had been built in, which perhaps explained the same bucket-shaped crow's nest?

There were a thousand of us. The swimming pool had been drained and shelves of canvas bunks on tubular frames had been installed in them. 'Standee bunks' we called them because you'd have been better off sleeping on your feet: because the space between them was so shallow, you couldn't turn over unless those above and below turned at the same time. So much for thinking we'd seen the last of this caper.

The sun winked on the grey-green water as the *Stirling Castle* motored out on the double tide. It would be the third time I had turned my back on summer; not that I was complaining. I did my share of spine-bashing, drank my quota of beer; tried my hand at deck bowls, cabled home: TIME TO PUT THAT BEER IN THE FRIDGE.

LOOKING FORWARD WITH ALL OUR HEARTS was the reply.

I tagged onto a tour of the ship and was duly impressed by the ten-cylinder engines, one for each propeller, not to mention the size of the boiler: it was as big as a small house. On the whole I thought it wasn't a bad-looking ship – the forward-sloping stern and bow and the backward-sloping masts and funnel gave it an appearance of speed that matched its performance. It had taken a fair hammering of course in the course of carting thousands upon thousands of troops to and from the war. According to the pictures that peered up at us through the bottoms of the ashtrays, the funnel had once been red-and-black; the superstructure had been white and the hull lavender. In those days it had had its own baker, butcher, carpenter, lamp-trimmer and printer. You could get the daily news, typed up from Morse code, brought to you on your breakfast tray.

We were still getting the odd report of a submarine attack (not everybody had heard about VE Day) and knowing the *Stirling Castle* once held the record for the run between Southampton and Cape Town (13 days and 11 hours) or that it still carried its wartime complement of depth charges was small comfort.

After four weeks and three days, the curtain rose on a familiar outline. I turned to the bloke on the rail next to me. Gordon was one of Ned's mates; I hadn't seen him since Tuturano. By and by, Egmont caught the sun's early rays – it appeared to be meditating on a cushion of cloud – and I don't think it was the salt air alone that Gordon was squinting from.

Before long we were turning in at the heads and I was switching my focus from the hills above Eastbourne to the hospital nestled behind the commercial centre, winking in the mid-morning sun. The engines cut the ship surged forward and snatches of song floated up. Children on the hips of their mothers, grandmothers, aunties and siblings looked shyly along their upward-pointing arms. Some blokes stood on the ends of the lifeboats with their hands in their pockets, others dangled their legs from the side-benches; I was hanging onto the rail for grim life. There was a bump and another cheer rose to greet us.

I wasn't expecting to see anyone I knew so wasn't disappointed and was disappointed in about equal measure. Mum and Dad of course had been too old to travel when I left and Agnes would have her hands full keeping an eye on them. Haskell and Chas were still in the Pacific and the others all had young families to look out for; that left one other person and her not being there could mean only one thing and that of course was something to be thankful for.

'Thursday,' said Gordon, 'a working day and besides the sailing's supposed to be under wraps – not that you'd know it.'

'As it was when we left,' I said, 'if my memory serves me correctly?'

'It does, Max, it does.'

The lot from Wellington were off first. We heard the cheers greeting the announcement of their names as we shuffled into the wharf shed. The Women's Red Cross Transport Auxiliary would be dropping them off at their doors.

Special cars had been added to the Auckland train; it was due out at three. Buses – two to Taranaki, one to the Hawke's Bay and one to the Wairarapa; the latter carrying onto Gisborne – were due out late afternoon or early evening. The Pig Islanders would be boarding the *Arahura* and the *Wahine* about the same time. That gave us the afternoon to fill and what better way of filling it was there than by reacquainting ourselves with our old watering holes?

Somewhat the worse for wear, I boarded the bus and was dead to the world when it pulled into the station at Palmerston North. Paper bags were being picked up by whirlwinds; sheets of newsprint were being shunted along the platform. The urinals reeked: talk about home sweet home. The queue for refreshments stretched out onto the platform. I had barely got my foot in the door, when we got the call to re-board. However, our dilemma had not gone unnoticed: trays of pies and cups of tea were ferried out to us, compliments of the proprietors.

'Welcome home,' said the waitress.

'You'll do me,' I said.

She wrinkled her nose.

We got into Hastings in the wee small hours. In the dusty light, I thought Agnes and Hammond looked a little shy or nervous or tired. When Hammond went to pick up my kitbag, he got an earful from Agnes; I expect because she was concerned about him doing himself an injury.

'How're Mum and Dad?' I said.

'Oh Max,' said Agnes. 'There's something I haven't told you: I didn't have the heart to.'

Two

They put me on the path and left me to it – there were graves in the old part that needed attending to. I walked up and down, windy about what I would find and more to the point, how it would find me.

It was a slap in the face and no mistake. It felt like the public notice of a private failing and I looked round to see if I was on my pat. When I looked back the stone was blurred. I blinked and in my mind's eye saw an outrigger swamped by sand, a couple hand in hand disappearing into the mist up a beach. It was a few visits over a few years before it was just dates and names on grey granite.

'You wouldn't *believe* the number of times I sat down with pen and paper,' said Agnes. 'I wouldn't have been able to live with myself, if anything had happened to you. Not that I'm saying it would have, but you know what I mean?'

I nodded.

'She could be as bright as a button one moment and as silly as a two-bob watch the next. He was away with the fairies too. I didn't have a moment to myself; I was washing and hanging out clothes and taking them in and folding and ironing them and putting them away; I was cooking for them and cleaning up after them and doing the shopping for them. I had to get a neighbour in to keep an eye on them while I was gone. She was forever leaving things on the stove and he was forever going out the gate. I had to stop working and then of course that meant less to come and go on.

'I could have done with a hand. You would have thought with seven of us that one of the others could have leant a hand, but three of you were overseas and the others all had families and jobs. Hammond, of course, when he eventually came home, was still getting back on his feet, so he wasn't much use either. But no, as the only one without children, the job was left to me: I couldn't have children of course because Hammond had had TB. Anyway, seventy-two's not a bad age, don't you think, or sixty-seven?'

'I'll let you know when I get there . . .'

Hammond's eyes were smarting.

'It was so like him, sticking it out so she wouldn't be on her own.'

It wasn't all bad news, of course. A manila envelope arrived stuffed with newspaper clippings. Over several days, a trickle of items had appeared in the Wellington papers. The *Evening Post* carried a list of the men whose next-of-kin resided in the Wellington region. They followed this up with a photo of some gaunt-looking Wellingtonians waiting to go ashore and below it, us lining the rails and lifeboats. There was no mention of the ship's name, which was standard practice at the time.

Under the caption 'Back in the Dominion', the *Dominion* had carried a list of those residing in its circulation areas; yours truly among them. But there was no accompanying note and no return address; I could only assume Dougal had sent them.

I'd been saving it for last; now I turned my attention to the flash-looking envelope postmarked Trentham (Dougal, who had flat feet, had spent the war there, rising up through the ranks as an administrator). And sure enough, it was what I thought it would be. A day later and I wouldn't have made it.

Iris wasn't at the wedding either. It was none of my business who they invited or didn't invite to their wedding, so I kept my thoughts to myself. I had my hands full anyway: getting the hall set up and going over in my mind what I would say. As it happened, Iris's absence made my job easier: it meant I wouldn't have to pussyfoot around how the happy couple had met.

There were so many guests wanting to congratulate the happy couple, that we didn't have a proper catch up till things were winding up, by which time we were all pretty much kaput. Anyway, that was when Winnie asked me if I'd been in touch with Iris.

'I thought I might see her here,' I said.

'She was going to be here. She was going to be my bridesmaid till her father took a turn.'

'Oh,' I said, 'I'm sorry to hear that.'

I hadn't met her father, of course, though I'd heard enough about him to know they were close. Mostly, I was relieved to find out that the reason she hadn't come wasn't because I was likely to be there. Meanwhile, Dougal was having a dig at Winnie for having asked Iris to be her bridesmaid at all.

'How many times do I have to tell you? She's not married!' snapped Winnie.

'She was,' said Dougal.

Winnie rolled her eyes.

'Am I missing out on something here?' I said.

Dougal and Winnie looked at me aghast, then Winnie looked at Dougal and he thumped his forehead with the heel of his palm.

'Sorry, old man,' said Dougal, 'I was supposed to tell you.'

'What?'

'Frank copped it on Crete.'

'Alhamdulillah!'

At the station, the following day as I was boarding the train, Winnie asked if I had her number.

'I'm assuming she's still at the hospital?'

'She went home to help her mother two years ago.'

'That's Westport, I take it?'

'No, Hamilton; they moved when her father retired.'

'And she knows about this?'

'About getting in touch? I had to promise I'd give it to you, as long as you were still interested?'

I looked at the note and tucked it into my breast pocket.

'You'll remember to take it out when you take the suit back, won't you.'

'What makes you think I have to take it back?'

'The label . . . . Sorry; just kidding.'

'Actually, you're right, I do.'

I must have taken it out half-a-dozen times at least before we got into Plimmerton, though I had it off by heart by then. I was already imagining what she would say to me and rehearsing my replies. As far as Frank was concerned, I thought I would leave it up to her to bring him up.

We were stopped outside Waikanae for track works for some time. I was looking out the window, still in a bit of a daydream, when I found myself marvelling at the girth of a pohutukawa tree and the spread of its branches. I was still getting used to the newness of being back: the blueness of the sky, the greenness of the grass, the exoticism of everything; my certainty that this was where I belonged.

The winter light reminded me of my elaborate routes to and from school and of the feeling I had then of being at the farthest and most lonely ends of the earth, of being out on a limb. I still had that feeling from time to time, but it was no longer accompanied by a sense of homelessness. When I went for a leak and the dithyramb of a magpie floated in through the fanlight, I knew I had done it a disservice; that its vocal productions were on a par with the one-man-band of the tui.

It was getting on when I got in: too late to go disturbing folk's beauty sleep, so I turned in.

The following evening I got her mother. Iris had gone to the pictures with a friend, she said, as she always did on a Monday night; before adding, as an afterthought, a girlfriend. I told her I'd try again the following evening. I had not long put the phone down, when it rang.

'For heaven's sake,' said Agnes, 'are you going to answer it; because if you don't hurry up, I will!'

'What makes you think it's for me?'

'Who else would it be for at this time of the night?'

So I jumped up; Hammond wasn't far behind, turning the hall light on and quietly closing the door behind me.

'Gunn here,' I said and a voice I hadn't heard in five years, but which could have been five weeks, warbled and trilled in my ear. I choked up. That set her off. We both had a good old cry then apologised to each other. It took a bit to regain a modicum of composure then we were on the phone well into the early hours.

We were at it again the following night and the night after that and so on till the weekend was upon us and I was looking through dusty windows at roads I hadn't been on since the Depression.

When the Americans arrived in '42, Frank had been dead a year. There were 11 camps in the Wellington district alone: eight between Titahi Bay and Paekakariki, two in the Wairarapa and one on the hill below the hospital. The city was awash with Marines and after a decade of belt-tightening, was experiencing a small boom: taxi-drivers, publicans, milkbar proprietors, market gardeners, the wharfies were all doing alright.

'Not to mention the womenfolk,' I said, 'from what I heard.'

'Would you have rathered it was the Japanese?'

'Touché.'

On nightshift together, Iris and Winnie had continued their pattern of meeting Dougal in town for tea. On by herself, Iris caught up with correspondence, knitted and walked. On the one exception to this routine, she'd been caught out: at the top of Willis Street, she'd gotten the 'Hi-honey-wish-I-knew-you' routine from some Marines going the other way. She had smiled politely and thought no more of it.

Where the road climbed steeply through the park, there were two street lights on Ohiro Road and she was between them when she saw some figures pass through the lamplight ahead. As the two parties drew closer and as one of them was making no attempt to make room for her on the footpath, she stepped out onto the road. At which point, they stepped out onto the road in front of her. She went to go the other way; they went that way too.

It wasn't till later that it occurred to her, they were the men she had passed earlier. If this was so then they must've hurried through the park and up the hill to cut her off. I won't go into the details. Suffice to say when she got back to the hospital and into the room she shared with Winnie, without running into anyone (which neither had managed previously and not for want of trying), she thought she might be able to keep it to herself and might have succeeded had Matron not called her into the office to explain her lateness, at which point everything caught up with her.

'They think they were killed in the landing at Tarawa. That was their last night out. At least I've still got my life, but have I still got you?'

Of course, I thought that went without asking. Needless to say, I had to spell it out.

Things at the hospital, meanwhile, had been going from bad to worse. Vagrants were coming onto the grounds and getting into the kitchen and having a go at the staff. Intervening, Iris had had a knife thrown at her. She'd plucked it from the wall and run screaming like a banshee after the man.

By this time, her father had retired and her parents had moved to Hamilton to be nearer her brother. But his health was deteriorating, so she got leave to help them settle and then had stayed on.

The following weekend, it was Iris's turn to come down. And that was the pattern, till Agnes put us on the spot.

'For goodness sake,' she said, 'why don't the pair of you get married and be done with it?'

It wasn't as if we hadn't thought of it: the trouble was I was on a pittance; sometimes not even that, because getting money out of Hammond's old man could be like getting blood out of a stone.

'Get your own orchard then?' said Agnes.

It wasn't as if we hadn't thought of that either. As an ex-Serviceman, I was eligible for a State Advances loan, but as things stood, it was up to me to find an orchardist who was willing to sell.

There were 50 members of the Young Fruitgrowers' Club in Hastings alone and we were all in the same spot. That being the case, in our view, if there weren't any orchards for sale then it was up to the government to acquire and make available to us bare land, so we could get the trees in and crop between them till the trees became productive. Its response was we would then need to be 'A' grade certified for market gardening as well as orchard farming. And so it went on.

In the meantime, we got married in St. Peter's Anglican Cathedral in Hamilton. It was no skin off my nose what the denomination was; it was the cathedral part I wasn't so keen on. Anyway, so it was that Eddy and I found ourselves 'hurdling' the long steps of a pathway up to a church that wouldn't have been out of place in *The Adventures of Robin Hood*. When I said as much to the Dean, he said it had been modelled on a 15th century Norfolk church, so I wasn't too far out. That said I'd have preferred the hill to have still been covered in the rangiora it got its name from. It was the fourth church to occupy the site and, according to the Dean had been built like the proverbial you-know-what, but then its predecessor had been built from the sapwood of untreated kahikatea.

'And you can imagine how long that lasted? Thirty-eight years. And I'll tell you something else, make of it what you will, the head of the common house borer bears an uncanny resemblance to a monk's hood.'

'I take your point, Dean,' I said.

Iris arrived on her brother's arm. In her other arm, she cradled a bouquet of roses and lilies and ferns: maidenhair and baby's breath! Her hair had been done in reverse rolls and was pinned beneath her black hat; black garnets dripped from her earlobes.

The dress was a fine wool crepe with a tie in the same material hiding among the pleats; the bodice was embroidered with tiny crosses. She turned up her nose.

'What's the matter?' I said.

'Don't you think I look a bit daft in this get-up?'

'Nonsense,' I said, 'Olivia de Havilland would give her eye-teeth for an outfit like this!'

'You scrub up alright yourself,' she said.

'In no small part due to you.'

We signed on the dotted line: my dirty blue downstrokes and pale blue upstrokes, dots like comets in a medieval sky; Iris's Futurist 'I', followed hard on its heels by consonants and vowels tripping down steps, before pulling off an 'o' to eclipse my comets.

We had our own place by then. It was just round the corner from the last house I grew up in. Had my parents still been alive, we could have popped in from time to time and given them a hand with this and that; we could have taken some of the load off Agnes's shoulders. They'd have been as taken with their latest daughter-in-law as they had been with all their others.

The walnut was still there, but not the timber Dad had seasoned against it, or the dog kennel. This led onto the hunting expedition we'd been on when we surprised a Captain Cooker with her litter; how the first thing I knew about it was when 150 pounds of wild pork came hurtling out of the scrub straight for me; how in taking a step back, I had tripped on a fern root; how Kari had shot past me and sunk her teeth into its snout, giving me time to get my knife out and slit its throat; how by that time, Kari was breathing her last breath.

'She's buried in the garden?'

I nodded.

I had drawn my last Army pay in September, but I still had my three-month free rail ticket, so between the thinning and the picking we had our honeymoon. We got the train to Wellington, the ferry to Picton and the mail boat to our own little bay with its own little jetty and beach and bach. The sun was still shining on the tops of the hills, so we dropped our gear off and set off up the hill; climbing above the treeline to a place where we could gaze across the sound at the strait's blue islands.

Iris was quiet. I asked her if everything was alright and she leaned into me.

There was just enough light, when we got back down, to gather some mussels and an armful each of driftwood. I took the top off the bottle I'd left cooling in the creek. The bush was quiet, watchful. The wood fizzed and popped, the salty smoke got in our eyes; the tiny waves shushed.

Sometimes it was the stars that woke us, sometimes it was the sun. Two wet days kept us inside, so we swept the place out and got the pot belly going and pan-fried some fresh cod in butter. We talked and played cards and made love, then talked and played cards and made love some more. I'd have quite happily spent the rest of my days there, but when the mail boat appeared we were on the jetty waiting.

Three

Among the letters and bills was a small package postmarked Chioggia.

'The book,' I said.

'What book?' said Iris.

'The one I was telling you about.'

'You're always telling me about books.'

'The one the Italian bloke wrote.'

'The one you're in?'

'Possibly; you might be in it too.'

Alfred got around a bit: a lot of it to do with the resistance. He could talk the hind leg off a donkey, he stuck his neck out; he was well-liked. Chioggia was where his girlfriend lived.

The package was like a party trick. When I thought I'd got to the bottom of it, I found I was holding a slipcase. It was a beautiful piece of work in itself: the smoky yellow paper over the cardboard was covered in tiny eight-pointed gold stars with tiny gold dots between them. I was looking at the night sky of the southern Veneto.

'You do the honours,' I said.

'You; it's your book.'

'We'll do it together then.'

And so while Iris held the slip case, I pinched the half-moon slots with my thumb and forefinger and we staggered backwards from each other.

Half the cover, longitudinally, was the creamy white of the spine. In the top left-hand corner was Alfred's battle name – Tahoma – in gold lettering with a gold line under it. Beneath that was the title, in capitals, also in gold. Under that again was an emblem that looked like bells of two flowers on a diamond-shaped ground. The stars and dots on the slipcase were repeated on the other half of the cover. The back cover was the same, minus the embellishments. It was what was called in the trade a compact or pocket-sized edition.

I opened the cover: myriads of stars and dots from one horizon to the other, both over the top and exhilarating. I knew that Alfred had a thing about the night sky, that the house in Chioggia was like a planetarium, that this reminded him of the tough times he had endured as a child and young man, that it was the wellspring that shaped his politics and artistic leanings. If the contents lived up to the packaging I was in for a treat.

I flipped to the colophon. If my scanty knowledge of Italian served me correctly then the typeface had been designed by Zanocco (the publisher of *Pinnochio*) and the printing had been completed on the twenty-first of July, 1945.

'Tahoma Libertā?' said Iris.

'His nom de guerre; this is his given name here.'

'I can see that, what does it mean?'

'What does what mean? The nom de guerre? Hang on a minute. There's something in the *Prefazione* . . .'

'You're good; you sound just like an Italian.'

'Ha ha, kidney pie will get you everywhere. As I was saying: *L'appello di Tahoma* . . . Wait, I think I'm getting my wires crossed. I should know what *appello* means; I heard it often enough. I was getting mixed up with 'appellation'. But I don't think that's what's intended either. I can see I'm going to have to get myself a dictionary.'

'What about the title then, what's that about?'

'That I can help you with: *sette* – seven, *uomini* – men, *sotto* – under, *le* – the, *stelle* – stars. When he first put it to us it was going to be 'Six Men under the Stars'. We thought it should be 'seven'; as far as we were concerned he was one of us, we were all in the same boat, all on the run. In fact, as a member of the resistance, he was probably more sought-after than we were. But more importantly it fitted in with the local custom he had told us about: if you count seven stars then think

195

of something that thought will immediately appear in the mind of your beloved.'

'Is that what you think?'

'In the situation we were in, it was more a question of hope.'

'Tell me what you thought of.'

'You, I thought of you!'

'Well that's alright then. What was your nom de guerre?'

'Didn't have one, no call for it in my case. Not my cup of tea anyway. Besides, I've been called enough names in my time to last me a lifetime.'

'What about 'Kiss'? Was it not derring-do enough for you?'

'It's not what I'd call a nom de guerre. I'd be more inclined to say it was a nom d'amour.'

'You could have smothered the enemy in kisses, had you thought of that?'

'Here, here you are.'

'Kitty?'

'A character in a book I'd not long finished.'

'I gathered that. I suppose I should be grateful you didn't call me Anna. I hope you didn't give away any of our trade secrets?'

'I didn't let the cat out of the bag, if that's what you're concerned about.'

It was getting on. I went out and checked the garden. It needed weeding and watering; mostly it needed watering. When I got back in, I found Iris asleep on the bed. I covered her with a blanket and tiptoed back out to the kitchen, where I picked up the book again. I tried sounding out the words and discovered my ears knew more than my eyes. When I turned in, Iris turned over, her cheeks glistening.

'What's this?'

'Nothing.'

'Did I say something out of place?'

'No.'

'About that Venetian custom, I never knew whether it worked or not.'

'Maybe you were thinking about me because I was thinking about you?'

'But had you counted seven stars first?'

'They were raining down. I couldn't keep up with them.'

'Are you thinking what I'm thinking?'

'Have you been eating sardines?'

By midday when the library closed, I had the gist of the first several pages, enough to know I'd seen the last of my watch: it, a fountain pen and two sheets of writing in English had been given to the Commander of the Vittorino Boscolo Brigade who had passed them onto the Governor of Chioggia, a Captain W. Cubberley, presumably for safekeeping. I thought this was an extraordinary thing to find in a book and I didn't quite know what to make of it.

'Don't worry about the watch,' said Iris, 'we'll get you another. Would you like your name engraved on it?'

'Never mind,' I said.

It had been a gift from my parents. It hit me hard.

'How are you getting on with Tahoma?'

'Better: I was having another crack at the Preface when something Alfred said about his nom de guerre came back to me. I suspect the reason I hadn't taken much notice of it was because I thought it was a bit on the airy-fairy side. It turns out there's a mountain in the state of Washington which used to be called Tahoma but is now called Mt. Ranier. Tahoma means 'mother of the waters', which granted is a bit on the poetic side. Given, however, that the rain and snow and ice melt that comes off it feeds the flora and fauna and people in its catchment, it's quite literally true.

'That's one side of it. Another, which I believe Alfred was equally drawn to, is that 'Tahoma' is a cry or ululation the women of this region addressed to their menfolk when they set off to hunt or go into battle. There was an action accompanying it: the women would place their hands over their chests then turn them over: the implication, as I understand it, being that wherever the men were, the women were with them in spirit.'

'The Italian folktale.'

'I hadn't thought of that, but you're quite possibly right. I was thinking of the feeling we get when our heart 'goes out' to something, a person or a pet, for instance: heart strings.'

'Kari?'

'That's right.'

'Me?'

'Yes. Where Alfred got it from though, I couldn't tell you. Perhaps it comes from the German fascination with things Indian; something he'd read in translation? Perhaps it's in all cultures? It's at the heart of the word aroha, I know, because I've felt it. Maori ceremonial traditions surrounding food and prayer and singing generate it. It's like a wave of wellbeing that sweeps over and through you.'

It was slow-going all the same and I was beginning to think I'd bitten off more than I could chew. When I said as much to Iris and to Agnes they were of the same mind: that I should get someone else to do it, someone who was as familiar with English as they were with Italian.

'There must be someone round here, surely?'

There were: I'd worked with Italians, drunk with them.

I could see it was one thing to know what you were reading and another to copy it in a language you were new to. I imagined there were people who did this for a living. Who they were and how to get in touch with them were the least of my worries; it was the fee they would ask that put me off. Meanwhile, I owed Alfred a response.

A week or two later, when I ran into Guido in the Albert and explained the situation, he said he knew someone who might be able to help. More weeks went by. When I saw him next, he was apologetic. He hadn't gotten round to contacting his friend.

'Never mind,' I said, 'I'll keep plugging away.'

'I could have a crack at it myself?' he said.

'That would be a great help,' I said. 'It wouldn't have to be perfect.'

'If nothing else, it will help me with my English.'

'How's the fight?' I'd say when we ran into each other. 'Are you winning?'

A year passed. I had all but given up on seeing Guido or the book again, when I ran into him in the bottle store.

'I've got something for you,' he said, fishing the book and a sheaf of papers from his flagon bag.

'Alhamdulillah!'

'I know what it's about in my language,' he said, 'whether I have managed to put it in yours is, how do you say, another story.'

'Never mind,' I said, 'all you can do is your best.'

'Do you want your book back?'

'You keep it,' I said. 'Consider it part-payment for your efforts. I'll try to make the rest up in other ways. What are you having?'

'I'll have a whisky.'

'I might just join you.'

Guido's translation had me scratching my head at times. The gist of Bob's philosophy could be summed up by the expression *in vino verite*, which I had some sympathy with. Blue's idea of paradise was socialist; I had some sympathy with that too. Robert's be-all and end-all was his family; I had no argument with that either. Tom's response to every question was in the negative. He wanted no part in the book, he wanted no part in life; he was as Alfred put it 'the loneliest of the lonely'. And while I didn't go along with it, I could sympathize with where he was coming from. As for my part, aside from the occasional part that made my cheeks colour, I thought I got off pretty lightly. I wondered too if the representation of our poor Italian was a dig at our tendency to belittle things Italian.

Jacob's story was curious, to say the least. A version of it had done the rounds at Gruppignano, so it wasn't new to me. In a nutshell, a famous painter, a lieutenant in the first war, had cuckolded his father. His father had invited the painter to stay with him when they went on leave. The painter had spent his entire leave making pictures of Jacob's mother.

When he next got leave – supposedly to visit his ailing mother – the painter visited again.

Jacob's father, meanwhile, looking for a match among the painter's bits and pieces, had discovered the letters his wife had written to the painter and determining not to stand in their way, had left the trench and been killed.

Following the marriage of his mother and the painter, Jacob had been sent to boarding school. He remembered his grandmother denouncing the painter and her daughter-in-law for killing her son.

As I say, I'd heard a version of this story before and I'd thought then there was something odd about it: why for example, had the painter not been named, especially when sufficient detail had been provided to ensure speculation. And, given Alfred's knowledge of art, I felt sure he would have speculated. If he'd come up with an answer, however, he'd kept it to himself – and in all probability with good reason.

Haskell was up and down from the capital a number of times that year. His wife had died after a long illness and a memorial had been placed in the local cemetery: it was in the old part for some reason; the tombstones of the long dead throwing the shortness of her life into relief. Their two youngest, having barely known her due to her having been in and out of hospital throughout their childhood and having been placed in an orphanage for the two years prior to her death, had now been placed in the care of childless family friends.

Why Haskell had abrogated his paternal duties was none of our business, particularly when none of us had offered to take the children under our wing; not that this stopped us from expressing an opinion about the matter: about Haskell's drinking, for instance; about his second wife's professional obligations; about the idea one of the children wasn't his. If the children had been better off without him, that's not the way they saw it.

Anyway, putting this aside for the moment, while he was with us I showed Haskell the book.

'How many famous English painters can there be who were also lieutenants in the Great War?' he said. 'Leave it with me and I'll have a dig.'

On his next visit I got the lowdown on a painter who'd been a Second Lieutenant in the Royal Artillery. This bloke had fought at Passchendaele and was a great friend of a Captain Guy Baker: an art fancier who as it happened had purchased a number of the painter's pictures, subsequently bequeathing them to the South Kensington Museum.

'What do you think?' said Haskell.

I knew him well enough to know there would be caveats and there were.

'Practically an invalid: rheumatism. He was on crutches for a year after an injury on the battlefield, some god-awful skin complaint; died the year the war ended. That said, stories change over time: as many as 10 years could have passed before the son heard the story. On the one hand we have a rich captain; on the other, a scrounging lieutenant who gets what he wants and gets out. What does that add up to?'

I shrugged. After a long silence, Haskell went on.

'Someone looking for a scapegoat is one possibility. Or how about this: captain goes over the top with his battalion, wrecks a leg on uneven ground then hobbles through a hail of bullets, remarkably without copping one. Suicide or is that stretching things a bit? I looked into the details of another captain, a bloke by the name of Hart-Davis.

Now his wife did have an affair with our man, but her son would have six years on you and you say this Jacob is younger?

'Anyway, Hart-Davis's son never saw active service in the second war; never got out of England in fact. So why is our man at pains to paint the captain as being ill? So that we'll think the captain's poor health compromised his marriage? Furthermore, when it came to playing the field they were as bad as each other. One final thing: what happened to the paintings? Perhaps they were destroyed in the Blitz? Because all I could find were a few nudes dating back to 1919 of a sturdy woman whose face is either obscured or averted, or which are studies of her back?'

Haskell was convinced he had his man. The painter was well-known for numerous affairs with married and unmarried women, preferring the former presumably because there were fewer strings attached. As for sending his son to boarding school, that was par for the course in those days: it had happened to him and he in turn had had nothing to do with a number of children by different mothers.

And that was where we left it.

For my part, I couldn't help thinking there was something else behind this story and I got the impression from Alfred's book that he thought so too: that Jacob was seeking comfort of a sort we didn't talk about then or not openly.

What struck me the most in Alfred's book and which sticks in my mind still is his heedful acknowledgement of the farmers' and the farm workers' families, who having done their bit by us, were machine-gunned for it in their yards and backyards. I mean the sheer bloody horror of it, of war.

When I got back to Alfred, it was to tell him what I knew about what had happened to the others after we had split up. What I didn't say – which is based on a piece of information that has come my way since, namely that several hundred Allied soldiers were unaccounted for in Italy – is that I prefer now to think of Tomaso as a happily married man living with his large family in a village in the Apennines.

As for Guido's translation, when friends and relatives heard about it they wanted to borrow it, in spite my warnings. Then what I thought might happen, happened: someone lent it to someone else and I never saw it again. *Mahleesh!*

Four

In April, we got word that the government had bought Grasmere. Grasmere was an orchard between Hastings and Havelock North that had been managed as an estate since the death of its owner in the early 1930s; there having been no children. On the 1st of May under the caption 'Ballot Of Grassmere Orchard Blocks To Be Held This Month', the local rag ran the following item.

The well-known Grassmere orchard in St. George's Road South, which has been acquired by the Crown for the settlement of ex-Servicemen, will be balloted for in Napier on Thursday, May 29, and possession of the sections will be given on the following Tuesday, June 3. The 80 acres of orchard will provide for the settlement of six men who have been graded A for fruitgrowing . . . The flat and fertile land on which the orchards are established is described in the soil survey report on the Heretaunga Plains as being first and second class orchard land . . . As there are about 50 men in the Hastings district alone with A gradings for settlement on orchards, keen competition for the sections seems inevitable. Two of the blocks have an advantage over the others in that they already possess houses, but dwellings will be subsequently erected on the other four properties . . . Provision of these six properties will give some relief to the acute situation which exists in the Hasting district in connection with the settlement of the many men interested in fruit-growing – a situation which is stated to have almost reached a stalemate recently. Nevertheless, the settlement of six of the graded men will be like a drop in the ocean.

Queen's Birthday Weekend was four weeks away.

A copy of the Crown Lands Schedule, courtesy of the Young Fruitgrowers' Club, arrived the following week. The six-page document included a sketch of Grasmere with the blocks outlined, descriptions of them, a dozen or so special conditions and a number of instructions or pieces of advice. Applicants were advised to inspect the properties and to make a list of those that interested them in order of preference. Applications were to be in by the 26th. It was tempus fidgits.

The special conditions were that the spray-tank and ramp on Section 28 were to be made available to the other owners for five years; that no trees could be taken out without the written approval of State Advances; that the packing and implement shed were to be owned equally by all the section owners; that the one truck on the property was also to be balloted.

I carted the Schedule round with me till I knew it inside and outside and from back to front: I had to because whoever had written it hadn't made it easy to understand what they were getting at. I pored over the sketch. No map can give you as good an idea of the ground as the ground itself, so at the first opportunity we went to see it with our own eyes.

Section 25, the first section off St. Georges Road, was to the right or south side of the driveway. Half of it was in asparagus; the rest of the 13¼ acres were in pears and apples and walnuts. Thinking the chances of an application being accepted by the Rehabilitation Sub-Committee from someone with no experience of growing asparagus, we didn't linger. There were three further sections on this side of the driveway; the remaining two were to the north of it. Three had a river boundary.

Section 26 was 12½ acres of mostly pears and apples. It was one of the four sections that would have a new house built on them (the others being: 23, 24 and 27); interest payments on the loans to be waived till the houses had been built and the artesian bores installed and operating.

Section 27 at a fraction over 13 acres was mostly pears.

Section 28, according to the Schedule, was either just shy of 14 acres or a tad over. Most of it was in peaches and pears, but there were also good numbers of plums and nectarines and apples. It had the homestead the driveway led to and beyond it the Karamu Stream.

Sections 23 and 24, north of the driveway, also had the Karamu Stream on their boundary. Section 23, a fraction over 12 acres was mostly peaches and pears. In addition, it had its own packing shed and a drying shed for walnuts. Section 24, at a fraction over 11 acres, was mostly apples and peaches and pears.

To make things simple, I listed them according size, reasoning that the largest stood to be the most productive. I'd have been happy with any of them, of course, with or without the house.

The almost four weeks till auction day were a rollercoaster: one day I'd be the proud owner of such and such a section; the next I would have dipped out altogether. On these latter days, the 12 iterations (and that was not counting variations) of the expression 'the successful applicant' would stick in my craw. I'd be reminded of the façades the earthquake had brought down; the revelation that not everyone had done it tough in the Depression. On the days in between, feeling a bit more philosophical, I knew that was the state of the play: some looked after others, some looked after number one and some did a bit of both.

Grasmere's owner, before the government bought it, was Edward Heathcote Williams, a grandson of the bloke whose overnight translation of the Treaty of Waitangi had wrong-footed the signatories enabling the colonists to exploit the land and the people they'd stolen it from.

Williams was a pioneer of commercial fruit growing in the country. As president or vice-president of this or that board, he'd lent his weight to the development of cool storage and exporting. When Thomas Tanner, who'd overextended himself, was caught out by the long depression of the late nineteenth century, Williams got Grasmere for a song. By 1895, 10 acres were in peaches (varieties you don't hear about much these days, fortunately and unfortunately) and walnuts (eight varieties), sheltered by pecans and walnuts; plus five acres of prunes and plums and apples and pears and nectarines and figs and grapes and berry fruits. The nursery that supplied the root-stock is still in business (I'm one of its customers).

If the name was from the lake immortalised by Wordsworth, then you'd have to say Williams had a sense of humour, because the only still water on Grasmere (other than the lakes beneath the pears after a downpour) was in the sump holes he shot duck on. Never having enjoyed the best of health and having lost most of that after the earthquake, he left for the Bay of Plenty where he died the same year.

Tanner, who wound up bankrupt, was gone by this time too. Till it burnt down, his house was just across the river from Grasmere. It's on a map that was made in 1873 (possibly to illustrate the inquiry into the Heretaunga Purchase that had begun that year). It was the first house the settlers came to, after tying up at a landing there, on their way to Havelock North (or Te Hemo a te Atonga, as I believe it was known then), which was mostly grassland then, crisscrossed with tracks leading to places where birds could be caught and eels and flounder and where stock was grazed and kumara cultivated. Extensive native cultivations in the vicinity of Grasmere, if not including Grasmere, can also be seen on this map.

All this was before the Ngaruroro broke its bank behind Roy's Hill and, on finding a less torturous route to Te Matau a Maui or Hawke Bay, left the old riverbed a much-reduced catchment with an increasing burden of effluent from Havelock.

When Tanner and his associates saw the fertile plains and rolling hills of Hawke's Bay their eyes lit up; the lessons of the Clearances and the fencing of the Commons had not been lost on them. They referred to it as wasteland and, frustrated by government cautions, forced the issue by arranging illegal leaseholds and squatting on them. When the government came out with the 10-owner rule, they went after those 10 owners as if they were individual title holders and, with the connivance of publicans and shopkeepers, got them into debt then chased them up with threats of fines and imprisonment and beatings till they got what they wanted. Then if they had to, fought off or shut down any inquiries.

All of which begged the question: how would it sit with me owning land the original owners had been diddled out of, when I knew (or ought to have known) that their descendants were living in houses lacking weather proofing, proper sanitation, running water; that a quarter of their children were dying before their fifth birthday; that access to their traditional sources of food and medicines was now off-limits; that these larders were being cleared and drained and polluted; that the much-touted, much-promised, so-called civilization had turned out to be not only more of the same but on a bigger scale; that Christianity no longer meant what it originally did. And what did I do?

Iris woke with a headache, a sore tummy, nausea. I took her a cup of tea.

'Would you mind if I don't come?' she said.

'Would you like me to stay?'

'No, it's just a headache and in any case you can't.'

'How about I give the doctor a call then?'

'I can do that; what time's your bus?'

'If I leave at twenty past, that should give me plenty of time.'

On my way out, I popped my head in the door: Iris was asleep, the tea was untouched. At the letterbox, I felt a few drops. I paused and looked up, then went back for my coat. Having had bags of time, I found I had left myself short. I wasn't used to running either, so I was out of breath when the bus went by. Bugger, I thought, elbows on knees and breathing heavily. I carried on anyway, thinking there might be a timetable at the corner. When I got to the corner, there it was; somebody must have seen me coming. It wasn't packed either, in fact there were only a few familiar faces; the rest were shoppers. John shifted over and I sat next to him. John and I had gone to the same primary school: different years but we remembered each other.

'That was a mistake,' said John, 'knowing your luck. How did you get on with the form?'

'It was a head-scratcher alright. I couldn't see the point of listing the sections in order of preference when we could have a crack at them all.'

'So what did you do?'

'Listed them according to size; what about you?"

'I think it's in case you get first dibs on more than one section, so you'll know which to go for if you get an option. I can't imagine that happening much though. I went for the ones that were listed as first grade orchard land first.'

'Where did you find out which was which?'

John touched the side of his nose.

'Did you know that Grasmere was part of the Heretaunga Block? They had an inquiry into it in the 1870s; turned up all sorts of shenanigans.'

'There were some dicey goings-on among the Maoris too, you know. I used to see them when the Land Court was in session coming into town to collect their rents. The chiefs would go out and buy a motorcar, someone further down the pecking order might go out and buy a bicycle.'

'Did you go down for a look?'

'I did and I have to say it's changed since my father was there in the 1920s. In the holidays, I used to take him his lunch. He wouldn't talk to me, not a word – I embarrassed him – so I'd go off exploring. There were glasshouses then, a summer house, concrete terraces where the toffs used to drink champagne: you know, the English gentry and their sense of entitlement. The earthquake tipped the lot in the drink.'

Lands and Survey was in the Post Office Building on the corner of Dickens and Hastings Street. Looking round I counted thirty people – nothing like the stiff competition the Herald had predicted – and that was including the Crown Lands Commissioner Frank Burnley, the manager of Grasmere estate Horace Paynter, the current orchard manager Bill Borch, his two assistants and the wife of one of the applicants. As the only woman present, Eric Bixley's wife was asked to do the honours.

The ballot box was mounted on a cradle, was about two feet long by half that in depth and had a sliding door. It had the look and gravity of a miniature coffin and indeed it had been used to conscript men for the First War. It would have to be loaded 12 times: the number of wooden marbles varying according to the diminishing numbers of sections and the interest in them. The Commissioner spun the box, slid back the lid and Mrs Bixley, her eyes closed, reached in, took out a marble and handed it to him.

'Section 25,' said Burnley.

Twenty-five was the asparagus. On Iris's advice, I had decided to leave it to the powers that be to decide if I was up to managing six and a half acres of asparagus and as it happened, they had more faith in me than I had in myself: Fred Blackberry's name was first out, mine was next. Overly generous and, it struck me, somewhat stunned applause followed. Perhaps it was me who was stunned? I might have to get used to my urine smelling of asparagus afterall.

Eleven marbles were loaded for Section 27.

'Ralph Clapham,' said Burnley.

John's was second out; there was more generous-to-a-fault applause. John and I were neck and neck.

Section 23 needed 13 marbles. When Mrs Bixley drew her husband's name, there was a chorus of good-natured allegations of skulduggery. John now had second dibs twice.

Section 28, the largest section at 14 acres, had 14 applicants: a symmetry Burnley duly noted. Bernie Deeley came up trumps and a bloke by the name of Gillespie got second option. I couldn't see anyone passing up on Section 28.

There were two sections left (I was leaving my run late again). Section 24 was second-to-last: fifteen marbles bounced into the box. Len Crawford drew first blood and a bloke called Styles got second option.

It was last chance saloon, last spin of the dice. My heart was in my mouth, I had a tremor in my stomach.

'And the first name is . . . ,' said Burnley, pausing for effect . . . M.

Gunn.'

'Santa Maria!' I breathed.

'The second: Sandy Lowe.'

That left the ballot for the truck and guess whose name came up? Unbelievable! I was now the proud owner of 12 acres, two roods and three perches; of 460 pear trees, 590 apple trees, a row of quinces and a row of walnuts; of a yet-to-be-built two-bedroom house; of an implement shed and a garage; of a yet-to-be-bored artesian well and a flat-deck Ford truck. On top of this, I was part-owner of a packing and implement shed and the 34.3 perches it stood on. A shout at the early-opener was called for.

'I knew we should have left you behind,' said John.

'Your turn will come,' I said.

I got in, somewhat the worse for wear, to find I wasn't the only bearer of good news: Iris had seen the doctor and he had confirmed what she had suspected.

Five

'You'll be wanting to finish up now then?' said the boss. 'Don't worry on my account: I've already got somebody lined up.'

This was the bloke I'd worked for before the war, who'd paid no more than he had to; at least he'd paid. At midday when he told me to bugger off, I shook my head. Things had been awkward before I'd broken one of his trees – this was back in the Depression, yet hardly a week had passed without him finding a way of reminding me what I'd cost him and gone on costing him. I should've gotten off the ladder and shifted it, because when I leaned out the ladder tipped. To avoid doing myself an injury, I'd ridden the leader to the ground, stepping from it as you might from an elevator, several bushels of fruit bouncing on the floor around me. The boss's mouth fell open. Now here he was shaking my hand and wishing me well. Wonders will never cease, I thought, tipping my hat back and returning the compliment.

That afternoon, we signed our lives away. The loan – £4500 –

covered the orchard, two years of living expenses, the wages of an orchard hand and various other contingencies. We would have to manage on a weekly budget of two pounds, 17 shillings and sixpence; quarter the average weekly wage.

Agnes and Hammond arrived. Hammond drove with the window down – left hand on the wheel, right elbow on the windowsill – and tossed his hand like a G.I. liberating the Italian peninsula. Everyone we passed smiled and waved at him. He was a veteran too: his war having required the removal of six ribs with a handsaw without anaesthetics.

The staff had finished up for the day, if not for good, and we had the place to ourselves. We skirted the lakes in the pear block, appraised the bark of the quinces, scanned the crowns of the walnut trees then – the unpromising forecast having been right on the money – settled in the packing shed with our picnic lunch and gave some thought to which orientation of a house was best: morning sun in the kitchen or bedroom or bathroom?

'How's the loan coming along?' said Agnes.

'It was approved on Thursday,' I said, 'our lucky day.'

'Oh?' said Agnes.

'Well the article about the ballot appeared on a Thursday and the results were published on a Thursday.'

'Mumbo-jumbo,' said Hammond.

When the builders turned up the following Thursday, I kept my thoughts to myself.

The section had a kink in its middle and was pointed at one end like a bent arrow or painted road sign. The point was a shallow triangle: the drive ran along one side of it and the plan was to bring our driveway along the other; to put the packing-shed on the base and the house in the middle. That left plenty of space for a lawn and a vegetable garden and for the expansion of the packing shed should that be required. My main concern was the number of trees that would have to make way. The builder waved a piece of paper.

'Approval in principle,' he said.

He rolled out the plan on the deck of his Dodge and we leaned in: the kitchen and master bedroom would get the rising sun, the living room the afternoon sun, the children's bedroom and the other side of our bedroom the late afternoon sun. The bathroom and the laundry would face the southerlies.

'All the mod cons,' said Iris, 'a shower!'

'Monday then?' said the builder.

Our first job was bowling those 100 trees: that done, I got on with the last pick. It would take a couple of weeks and that was with Iris doing the labelling. Then it would be onto the pruning. With over a thousand trees to attend to, it was time I got that orchard hand.

I put it to Chas over a beer in the local. Since leaving home, Chas had been round the province: in Napier he'd worked as an electrician's apprentice, in Waipawa as an assistant in a plumbers' shop; he'd been a boot-maker in Otane, a cobbler on one of the big stations near Porangahau and a gardener-cum-handyman in Maraetotara. A job with the local town board had brought him home. Between-times, he'd chased the Japanese round the Pacific: his reputation must have preceded him though, because the closest he got to the action was a handful of dead bodies. And he'd gotten married. Drink meanwhile had become an all-consuming passion: the passage of it through his body and the passage of his body through it (he pulled out some photos of a river in Vella Lavella with swimming lanes marked in it; servicemen in a waterhole grinning from ear to ear). Of late he had turned his hand to coaching; he would teach me to swim yet. There were things we had in common (a liking for the odd drop for one, an aversion to paperwork for another) but swimming wasn't one of them. He took me up on my offer. I cried off his.

'I was on a boat that was torpedoed,' I said. 'If I'd known how to swim, I wouldn't be here.'

We moved house to be closer to the orchard. Iris was flat out: she was doing the paperwork, she was making curtains for the new house and she was getting ready for the bairn. She and Agnes were on their way to filling a packing case full of hand-knitted booties, mittens, hats, blankets, shawls, cardigans, you name it.

The migraines meanwhile had persisted and she had high blood pressure. Like me, when she had a break, she had a smoke. Perhaps that had something to do with it? As soon as the cigarette was out, she was back into it. If there was nothing pressing to be done in the house, she was down at the orchard, bringing us smoko or lunch and stopping to help. I'd see her coming down the row and my heart would skip a beat.

'Is it me or the smoko?'

'Neck and neck,' I'd say.

'Keep the middle open like a chalice,' said Chas, mimicking me with his hand, tipping his fingertips toward his lips and grinning broadly.

After the pruning, it was the thinning; after the thinning, the picking. A year had passed since our holiday. It was as well we'd taken a break then, because there was no time for one now. I showed Chas how to lift the fruit against the stalk, how you empty your apron to minimize bruising. On the rainy days, he showed me how to take the straps from worn aprons and sew them onto new canvas; how to replace broken and missing steps on the wooden ladders; how to service the truck. We built a mountain of packing cases.

It wasn't all work and no play. Every second Friday, a group of us returned servicemen who worked on orchards round the village would meet up in the local. Eddy was the ringmaster or the ringleader; for the most part, he held the floor.

Eddy and Henry had been wounded in the withdrawal from Greece. When the Germans caught up with them on Mt Olympus, Henry was bayoneted. They were both wounded; they were both sitting on the ground with their hands clasped behind their heads. Eddy never forgave the Germans for this.

Before we left on the *Mauretania*, the three of us had gone home for a brief visit. There were the usual photos: you can see we didn't have a clue (Eddy less so perhaps; he had a wry take on most things). Babes in the woods we were, allowing ourselves to be flattered by those who had more sense than to go themselves. If I'd known what it was going to be like I wouldn't have gone; because if you were lucky enough to get back, you were on your own: you couldn't tell yourself what you'd been through.

Eddy was working in an iron ore mine on the border with Yugoslavia for three years. On a work party one day, he and the Yugoslavs captured their guards, then marched them over the border and shot them so they couldn't be followed. Eddy got flown out to England and came home on furlough. When he saw all the fit and healthy men here, he refused to go back. He wasn't alone in this: others had had a gutsful too of being treated as cannon fodder, of having to go where they were told, of empire jingoism, complaints about not being able to buy this, that or the other thing by people who had a roof over their head, a bed to sleep in, good food to eat; of the Prime Minister blathering about none of them wanting to come back till the job was done, of the promises of furlough that didn't eventuate, of the ignorant talk about the war, of the wharfies going on strike when they were getting 20 quid a week plus danger money for loading shells (let them try loading shells on a battlefield), of the miners strikes, the coal shortages that meant old people couldn't heat their homes, of getting back and finding they'd lost their jobs or their place on the promotion ladder, by those who'd been in support roles getting the same treatment as those who'd served at the sharp end or spent years in captivity, of the housing shortage, of people getting more than their fair share; of strikes by freezing workers, dairy workers, railway workers and the rest of it. We'd been risking our necks to safeguard a way of life that was being sabotaged by selfishness! The press wasn't entirely blameless either with its fixation on soldiers' leisure activities, their rest camps while turning a blind eye to the atrocities, the carnage, not to mention the orphans. Where was the Vassily Grossman of the NZPA?

While some men had second thoughts about going back, others joined the Returned Servicemen's Association, which formerly they'd dismissed as a home for the bewildered. Now it was society that was out of touch. It was a novel way of putting it and one I had some sympathy with.

Having missed out at Grasmere, John was picking asparagus for £12 a week (he was doing better than we were). A Stuka bomb on Mount Olympus knocked him out. He woke on the *Hellas*, the Greek Royal Family ship, it had ferried them from Egypt and now that the tables had been turned, was taking them back.

And all would have gone swimmingly, had some British engineers not forced their way aboard, because as soon as the Germans' reconnaissance planes picked this up, irrespective of the red crosses painted on the deck, the ship was dive-bombed; one of the bombs went down the funnel. He thought he was in a bad way, John (he had malaria and dysentery and concussion), but when the Stukas turned up he jumped over the side in his underpants and swam ashore. It took longer than he thought it would, but eventually he was fished out by some Aussies who removed the clothes from one of their dead mates and put them on him. Six hundred men died in the attack; 800 if you include deaths from injuries.

John went south with these Aussies looking for his unit or a beach with a ship offshore, whichever came first. Along the way, they blew up a bridge over the Corinth Canal (it didn't stop the paratroopers of course). They would hear about this or that ship, such and such a beach, but by the time they got there it would have gone, or threat of being bombed had deterred it from coming in.

At last they got to a beach with a destroyer in the roadstead and joined the queue, but it was stretchers first and John could stand. He'd get his chance the following evening, according to the bloke in charge, but there was no ship the following evening; it had been sunk.

He was rounded up and marched up and down Greece for three months. For 10 days he was in a six-acre camp in Corinth with 10,000 others and little or no food or water and what there was as often as not bad. He never did catch up with his unit; it had been taken off to Crete.

He ended up in a magnesite mine near Graz (magnesite was used to harden steel). They were on 1800 calories a day, morale was low: it changed how he thought. The guards rubbed it in, telling them they'd be working for them on their farms in the Ukraine after the war. After two years of this he became sick and was sent back to the main camp at Wolfsburg: there he saw how the Russians were treated. Six weeks of starvation and ill-treatment reduced 1500 men to 750. He saw photographs of what had been done to them; no attempt had been made to conceal what was being done: *Untermensch* was how the Russians were seen.

From Wolfsburg John went to Klagenfurt to make room in the old graves for fresh bodies. Most of the bodies were from Yugoslavia; they could hear the battles across the border. Allied bombers flew up the valley on a daily basis: anything between 17 and 3000 planes. If the leading plane dropped a flare, they were the target: from the air, the camp looked like a military base. Sometimes they'd hear radio reports through the open windows of the local houses about which way the bombers were headed. There was never any other news; the stations cut straight to music.

As the war drew to a close, the broadcasts were about generals defending strongholds to the last man; preparing the people to follow their example. Had Hitler not been at the helm, Germany would have capitulated a year or two earlier. One day they woke to find the guards gone. It was the day after Hitler died and the townspeople – very subdued – were taking down their Nazi flags and putting up red, white

213

and blue ones.

There was a rumble of trucks on the road: a British column was trying to get to Vienna before the Russians – the race was on to divide Europe. The whole of Europe was on the move, but not them: the NCOs were uncertain how to act. Eventually a truck stopped and someone asked them who they were (though they must have known, because they'd have seen others like us in other places). One soldier offered them bread, another offered them toothpaste: John spread the toothpaste on the bread. They were told then to return to the camp. Not John: because he could speak a bit of German, he was given a truck to drive to the Yugoslav border to look for other camps; when a Serb opened fire with a machine gun, when the bullets were hitting the cab, he gave up on that idea.

They were back-loaded to Bari on Dakotas. From there they went to Taranto then Naples then back to Bari then back to Naples again. Eventually they got on a ship to England.

Six

Before they came out in support of the Vietnam War and we parted company, I used to pop into the RSA for a spot of Dutch courage. After the parade, I'd be in there again, drowning my sorrows. On one of these occasions, I got talking to a couple of blokes from Petrol Company.

'We had this Sergeant Major,' said Quentin, 'as sharp as a tack and with a wicked wit to go with it. From reveille to lights-out, we'd be scared shitless he was about to wipe the floor with us. Okay if it was the other bloke; pink little hedgehogs if it was us. It wasn't just us either: the officers would sooner skirt round the parade ground than risk having the mickey taken out of them in front of us.

'We had a mate, Frank Armstrong, who was dead set on getting married before we embarked, had everything organised except his leave, he was just waiting for the application to be approved. When routine orders were posted and only his best man had been granted it, Frank didn't know whether to laugh or cry.'

'Dave,' said Cyril, 'Frank's best man, told him to go and see the S.M.
It's an oversight, he said, he'll sort it out.'

'Frank couldn't do it,' said Quentin. 'As far as he was concerned, the
SM had it in for him. He pleaded with Dave. You're a sergeant, he said,
the S.M. will listen to you. Know what the S.M. said to Dave?'

'I think I've heard this before,' I said. 'Go on.'

'If you had any balls, you'd be in like Flynn.'

'Not quite the version I heard,' I said.

'What did you hear?'

'Something along those lines, it was just a bit more polite.'

'Who told you?'

'Actually, I got it from the horse's mouth.'

'Frank?'

'His missus.'

'Copped it on the second day, the poor bugger,' said Cyril, 'and that
was a quiet day after the first.'

'Too much going on for my liking all the same,' said Quentin,
flicking the bottom of the packet and offering it around.

I leaned back and exhaled. The late afternoon sun was streaming
in through the clerestory windows: clouds of smoke were going the
other way.

'Refill?' said Cyril.

'Here, let me,' I said.

'You can get the next one.'

'Didn't happen to cross paths with him, by any chance?' said
Quentin.

'You were stationed in El Daba for a while, weren't you? I thought I
might run into him there.'

'Last few months of '40; first few of '41.'

'We were there till about mid-December, so we could've been in
the same bar at the same time.'

'Frank was a teetotaller.'

'Actually, I think you might be right.'

'I met Irene once; I think that was her name.'

'Iris.'

'Iris? Frank dragged me along to one of those dry dos they used to
have up there: waste of good drinking time, as far as I was concerned. I
think he thought he could convert me. The way he went on about her,

you'd have thought he was the only bloke who'd ever fallen in love. We used to have him on about it. No rhyme or reason the way things turn out, is there?'

'He was dead stiff alright.'

'I heard she was having a fling with another bloke?'

'Would that be before the war or after?'

'Before and after.'

'Sounds like somebody's got their wires crossed. Her best friend had taken a shine to my best friend and needed a chaperone, so I got roped in to make up the numbers. Not that I was complaining, of course.'

We fell silent. Cyril reappeared with a fistful of jugs.

'To Frank,' he said.

'Frank!'

'I heard the bodies had all been moved to Suda Bay?'

'That was where we got in,' said Quentin. ' Jaws of bloody hell, it was: full of crippled ships with palls of black smoke like barrage balloons hanging over them.'

'It was a delicate matter,' said Cyril. 'Jerry's dead all ended up in a new cemetery above Maleme, despite the opposition to them being on the island at all. It was tough, it was tough all round: tough on us, tough on Jerry, but most of all tough on the Cretans.'

'I'd open my eyes,' said Quentin, 'and straightaway the old ticker would be going like the clappers. I thought I'd just closed them, but I can't have because I'd missed the fireworks out at sea. We were up and away in the dark, heard grenades going off below and to our right: one of our patrols had run into one of theirs. We kept going, but Jerry must have taken off.

'It was getting light when we got back. I had a poke around in my trench with my bayonet, just to make sure it hadn't been booby-trapped and found a bar of chocolate. The Luftwaffe wasn't due for a bit, so I checked my gear then ate the chocolate: not bad chocolate either, as I recall.'

'We could hear the odd stifled cough from the prison,' said Cyril, 'other than that it was eerie as hell: that was when we realised all the birds had buggered off to the mountains. If we'd had any sense, we'd have done the same.'

'When the drone reached my ears,' said Quentin, 'I'd break into a cold sweat: same as every other morning since they started coming. I'd clench my eyes and then when I opened them, the horizon would be black with Junkers, Messerschmitts, Heinkels, Dorniers, Stukas like swarms of flies and I'd be a kid all over again, waking from a nightmare, wanting my mother, having to clean up after myself again.

'By the time I'd hitched up my belt, they were on us: Daimler Benz engines vibrating, cannons pounding away like sewing machines. The Messerschmitts had four machineguns above the cannons and a fifth out the back; the cockpit looked like a greenhouse. I'd be chucking myself around in the trench, trying to make myself scarce.

'It wasn't long before the trees were as bare as oaks in winter: big old stumps with spindly new growth sticking out. I reckon if they x-rayed those trees, they'd find they were half metal. The ground would be crisscrossed with furrows and covered in leaves; a fair sprinkling of them in the trench as well.'

'Jerry meanwhile,' said Cyril, 'would have opened up from the prison and from Cemetery Hill above and to our left. We had shrapnel, bullets coming at us from all directions. Around midday, the hill got shut down: 19 platoon, D Company had cleared it with the help of a couple of tanks and some mortars – cleared our hill too.'

'The great counter attack?' I said.

'Don't get me started!' said Quentin. 'Shellshock: that's my guess. The bosses were all veterans of the first war. I reckon they went into their shells as soon as the bombs started coming; the old injury had come back to haunt them. Even Jerry thought we'd have won if it hadn't been for our bosses.'

'Kippenberger was a veteran and he was the one who called for a counterattack at midday,' said Cyril. 'The trouble was the RT lines kept going down: Jerry was shooting them up along with the runners. Lucky I wasn't any good at harriers.

'Puttick was dead set on hanging onto the reserve in case Jerry got past our Navy; he didn't change his tune till Kippenberger sent him a report about how they were planning to build an airstrip in the valley. Something he'd got out of one of the prisoners.'

'Two companies and three light tanks!' said Quentin. 'It was supposed to be two battalions – though one of them had already been spoken for. It wouldn't have been enough anyway. When word finally got back to Kippenberger about a counter attack having set off and what it consisted of, he sent runners out to call it off. It was dawn before the runners caught up with them: by which time they'd killed 20 Jerries, wrecked some mortars and machineguns and were getting ready for another crack. That was why Pink Hill was deserted. Heidrich thought it was the counterattack and he was on the point of skedaddling.'

'It would have been the sound of the tanks that put the wind up him,' said Cyril. 'Freyberg only let Puttick have the reserve because he thought, being Johnny of the spot, Puttick would have a better idea of how to use it. Everybody knew that a counterattack was critical. Which makes me wonder if this report about Jerry wanting to build an airstrip in the valley was a ploy, because anyone with half a brain could see those olives would take some moving?'

'I heard there was some heavy machinery on the flotilla that got sunk?' I said.

'We thought it was tanks,' said Quentin. 'It all ended up on the sea floor anyway, whatever it was; which is the point I'm trying to make: the Navy did their job; we should have trusted them to do it and gotten on with ours.'

'So what was the hold-up?'

'What it always was. Another reason Puttick wanted to hang onto on the reserve, was in case it was needed at Maleme. Maleme got away on us because Hargest was reluctant to bring up the reserve he was in charge of.'

'Shellshock?'

'Hard to see what else it could have been,' said Cyril. 'Keeping Jerry pinned down was as much as Puttick could manage at the time. Once Maleme was sorted out, they would give us a hand; that was what the thinking was. You could put the holdup down to trying to cover all the bases, but it was trying to cover all the bases that cost us all the bases.

'Monte would have insisted on decent communication from the outset. We had everything going for us, apart from decent radio equipment and air presence. We had the Greek Army, the locals; we had the Maori Battalion, blokes like Charlie Upham . . .'

'And like us,' said Quentin.

'And blokes like us. The Aussies cleaned up down the road at Rethimnon. The Poms did their job at Heraklion. It was four to one. We didn't need those 16,000 Cretan soldiers who were fighting up in

Albania. Inglis, who was in charge, wanted to take the reserve up the valley, clean up there then swing round through the hills back out to the coast at Maleme and finish the job there. But Puttick wouldn't let him and Freyberg backed him up because they'd lost their bottle: Jerry's command of the air had them rattled. They didn't want their glorious careers ending up on Crete, that's my view.'

'To his credit though,' said Quentin, 'Freyberg had doubts about the operation from the word go. Maybe he thought he was being asked to fall on his sword after the failure on the mainland? Bear in mind too that Hitler's only defeat till then was in the Battle of Britain. It would be six months before he was stopped again: this time by the Russians and the Russian winter.

'He didn't know about Barbarossa. He didn't know Student had already used up most of his paratroopers. He thought Jerry would keep on coming till the job was done. And that's what it felt like to us too: 130 drivers and technicians with Lee Enfields against the might of the 12th Army! Not to mention being short of bayonets and four rifles short – we had them ripped out of our hands at Marathon and chucked into the sea because some silly prick thought the ban on heavy equipment included rifles!'

'When it looked like we'd lived to fight another day,' said Cyril, 'we breathed a sigh of relief and put our feet up – when we should have been putting the acid on Jerry. We did our bit; no one can take that away from us. And the Greeks honoured us for it. Only I can't help feeling we let them down and they were just too bloody decent to say as much. Either that or because it was the first time anyone had helped them: the kind of generosity that is born of great suffering.

'How would we have felt if our families had been left to fend for themselves? And would they have got stuck in with their bare hands and rocks and pitchforks and axes and breadknives tied to muskets? We should have known that's what they'd do; we should have given them Home Guard status and armed them. I'm not saying it was us alone who were at fault: their government disarmed them in the first place.

'They had AA guns in Piraeus and Athens that could have been shipped over. There were caches of arms in a warehouse in Canea. We lived to fight another day: they were left holding the baby. Hitler had a fit when he learned the flower of German youth had been lost; he then ordered the occupying force to execute an equivalent number of villagers. Yes, there was the odd show of magnanimity: the German soldier who tried to warn the villagers of what was about to happen; the father and son who were spared for arguing about which of them should be executed, each arguing it should be him. Otherwise Jerry did what we knew he was capable of: 8,000 Cretans died or were captured, leaving 12,000 orphans behind and an equivalent number of houses destroyed.'

'And then in the end the evacuation was slow,' said Quentin. 'The Greek military were excluded from the process, so Jerry went on burning and executing and plundering. Then the civil war began and even heroes of the resistance weren't spared.'

'All that partying in Cairo!' said Cyril. 'We should have known it would end up on Crete. We should never have gone to Greece. We should have been preparing to hold Crete.'

'I'll leave you with this,' said Quentin, 'for what it's worth. It's a story I heard about some Kiwis who ran into a German patrol near the prison; they were getting the better of them, till another patrol turned up and they decided to make themselves scarce. One of these Kiwis got a bullet in the leg and was dragging himself along the ground, desperately trying to catch up with his mates, till he came across an abandoned Spandau pit. So he turned the Spandau on the Germans – to protect himself of course as well as to cover his mates; doing his best to ensure they all got home, trying to spare the people who cared about them the agony of loss.'

When I got in and told Iris who I'd bumped into, she didn't say anything, then was quiet for some days. The reason, I suspect, was not as I had originally supposed it to be. The Ministry of Defence had forwarded some letters and cards that had been found among the loot confiscated from the Germans on their departure from Crete. Of course it's possible there had been an intention to forward them, I don't know. This was what had knocked the stuffing out of her. I didn't read them then, nor did I give them another thought till ten or a dozen years ago, when we got a call from the owners of the house we had lived in before Grasmere. While having batts installed, a shoebox had been discovered in the ceiling.

Seven

Air Letter Card

Dear sweetheart,

There's been so much happening I've hardly had time to think of you. Then when I do I get a big grin on my face. Knowing that you love me makes me feel like the luckiest man alive.

Your everloving Frank

Letter 62

Dearest Iris,

I am allowed to tell you where we are now, it's Greece. Ted's here too more's the pity because it's a beautiful place, like home. Last week we got our tropical uniforms but we didn't know where we were going to be wearing them. The Sergeant-Major said he didn't know either but as usual we didn't believe him. Some of the boys took French leave and went on the bash in Cairo. We are the advance guard. The others are coming later. The sooner they get here the better because Ted is pretty determined. We can only hope the Yugoslavs know what they're doing. We have been welcomed like heroes. The children run so close to the trucks I'm afraid of running them over. When we are walking along the street the people come out of the shops and hug us and shake our hands and kiss us, the men too, on both our cheeks. They force presents on us like flowers and oranges and bottles of drink, which I give to my friends. The old people cry. I only hope we don't let them down. Today in a cafe I had baby squid fried in olive oil and salad. The salad had little squares of cheese in it made from goats' milk and vegetables I have never seen before let alone eaten. Afterwards I had black coffee with lots of sugar. At the bottom of the cup was an inch of coffee grounds like mud. They have a saying here that if you have an accident with your cup it means you are going to be rich, unfortunately none of us did. When I get back I want to take you to one of the Greek restaurants. Our camp is on the outskirts of Athens. We can see the Parthenon. It is humid here but it beats being caught in a sand storm. It is just as cold at night though and that is when I miss you the most. Well my darling, time to get my beauty sleep. Καληνύχτα. That means goodnight. The way you say it is kalineektar.

Your loving husband,
Frank

Air Letter Card

Dear sweetheart,
Just to let you know I am still in the land of the living and still in one piece. We got out of Greece by the skin of our teeth. Ted drove us out like a herd of animals, biting at our heels. Fortunately we were able to keep one step ahead of him all the way. Perhaps he thought we would be trapped on the beaches and cliffs and his planes would do the rest. He might have the upper hand in the sky but we must have the upper hand at sea because we got off safely. We had to leave our trucks behind. We had to put them out of action so he couldn't use them against us. That was a terrible blow after nursing them up hill and down dale. It was like having to put down a pet.

All my love,
Frank

Letter 63

Morning
Dearest Iris,
We got here two mornings ago. It didn't look good with all the smoke coming out of the ships. Some just had their masts sticking out of the water. We had to get off pretty quick in case the Luftwaffe turned up. The Stukas wings are bent like gulls wings. They have sirens on the landing gear which scream when they are diving. The noise is supposed to frighten us and it does but at least we know they are coming. The fighters are different. They come over the crests of the hills without warning, their machine guns making furrows straight for you. I feel

lost without my truck. I started talking to it when we had a difficult stretch of road to get over or a bridge that had been damaged. Some of the roads were just goat tracks. But I expect I am safer without it. Last night we camped in an olive grove by the beach. We made bivouacs out of brushwood and slept on piles of grass. It's quite cold because we have only one blanket each. Tonight I will get enough grass to go over me as well. This morning the owners came to prune their vines. The vines grow between the olive trees. The men wear leather boots that go up to their knees and baggy trousers and wide bands of cloth round their waists. They look like pirates. They had eggs and wine and honey and oranges for us to buy. The women, especially the young women, cross the road when they see us coming. I never used to like honey but here it smells and tastes like the herbs we can smell in the air. We pour it over creamy, sour milk called yowti. I could eat a whole mixing bowl full at one sitting. The skins on the oranges are thick but the fruit is sweet. The wine is not so good I am told. This morning we went down to the beach for a wash and a swim. I still haven't gotten used to where the sun comes up or goes down. The local dogs follow us when we go on patrols hoping we will give them something to eat. They have the run of the villages. The map of Crete looks like a dog rolling on its back.

Evening

I feel at home here. It's a bit like Kaikoura with the mountains so close to the sea. The waves are like chorus girls waving their frilly petticoats as they come in. The water is clear so you can see the shells on the bottom. I am collecting the small pink ones to make a bracelet with or a necklace for you. It might have to be a bracelet as the talk is we will be moving inland soon. The shells are flat and frilly round the edges and as fine as bone china. The cord I will make from cotton using a cotton reel the way we used to at school. On Tuesday I found a coin with a picture of an owl on it perched on a jug. Quentin tells me it is the sacred owl of Athena. I would like to know more about it. I also found something that could be from Vesuvius. It is light like pumice and looks like a sea sponge. Here are some more Greek words for you: ΠαραΚαλώ means please, it sounds like paracarlo. Ευχαριστώ means thank you, it sounds like effcaristo. Εντάξεl means alright or okay, it sounds like endarksy. You can also shorten it to darksy or darks. It was pretty bad on the mainland and I am still getting my breath back. We were taking men and supplies up north to the front then going back to get them and take them to another place. The front line was 15 miles long. In the end we picked them up and everything else we could and turned tail and ran. The Luftwaffe was on our tail all the way. All our planes had been blown up on the ground. Their planes outnumbered ours anyway. Half the time we didn't know where we were, we were just following the truck in front of us. Once I found myself on my own. I must have taken a wrong turning and turning the truck round was a nightmare because it was pitch black. I had to keep getting out to feel where the edge of the road was. Then when I caught up with the convoy there was a lot of driving through swamps and fords. I was dog tired. I had to pour water from my canteen over my head to stay awake. Some of the Greeks we brought out were so terrified they refused to get off the trucks. I think they were scared they would get left behind. We expect Ted to turn up in numbers any day now. He wants control of the Suez Canal and it's no good us being here in case we attack him from behind. Also the oil fields he has captured in Romania are in range. I think the bosses knew that Greece was a hopeless cause. Thank goodness they called it a day when they did, for now anyway. Actually it wasn't them who called it a day, it was the Greeks. We lost a lot of good men and are just lucky not to have lost a lot more.

Your loving husband,
Frank

Letter 64

My dearest Iris

It means a lot to me to get your letters even though they were written months ago. Some of the boys have had letters from their girlfriends saying they have met someone else and won't be writing again and telling them not to feel hard done by because it wasn't as if they were engaged or anything. As if we didn't have enough to worry about already. Now we have to watch out for them as well as ourselves in case they lose heart and put all of us in danger. What browns me off is these girls think they're doing the right thing by being honest and coming clean when really it is only themselves they are thinking about.

Things are heating up here. Ted is becoming a regular nuisance again. All seven planes of our air force have been knocked out. The three he didn't get buzzed off back to Egypt. The RAF is a joke. I won't tell you what it stands for in our book. The first thing he does every day is comes over and strafes and bombs the airfield not far from here. Then the fighters turn up spraying everything that moves. We have moved to a new spot and are digging in. We have to use our helmets to dig in with because we are short of entrenching tools. We are short of bayonets too, which hasn't stopped us having bayonet practise. We had to cut down some pine trees for a road block. The owners weren't too happy about that. It is so hot here that by the middle of the morning we are exhausted. We have become like fishermen or farmers always watching the sea or sky to see what the weather is about to do. The sky is radiant and the air is fizzy. Mostly now we swim in a reservoir not far from here. It saves us from having to go down to the beach which is a lot further away. But we don't stay in long in case Ted turns up. It's hard to believe that war is coming here. While I am drying myself in the sun I listen to the insects and the birds and the bells tied round the sheep's and the goats' necks. There aren't as many sheep here as there were. I think they have been moved inland. Our village is a maze of tiny roads and tracks and paths. I asked someone if there was a map of it when I was in the cafe and the locals had a great laugh at my expense. If there was a map of it, someone said, it would look like the map of Athens. I would like to come back when the war is over because the people are friendly and very generous and dignified. I would like to learn Greek. There would be no shortage of work either with all the houses that have to be rebuilt. I think you would love it here too, the food, the heat, the fresh air, the sea. I had a dried fig today and it tasted like honey. It tasted like the honey does of the flowers and wild herbs.

Your loving husband,
Frank

Letter 65

Dear Iris,
This might be more for me than for you. Ted turned up yesterday and we were at each other's throats all day. If I slept last night it wasn't

anywhere near enough because I am still tuckered out. Now we have to do it all over again and I am afraid it will be just as tough as it was yesterday and that it will keep getting tougher and tougher till Ted gets his way because he seems to have an endless supply of men and ordnance. I am back in my trench. The sun has just come up and the ground is already clammy. I write a sentence then stick my head up and have a look around. It's like driving and looking at your map at the same time. The trench is my cabin now. You could say the opening is my front door. We are back at the bottom of the hill where we were all day yesterday except for when Ted got the better of us. He is only a few hundred yards away and probably doing the same thing as we are, getting ready for another torrid battle. We are waiting for each other to attack. It should be us doing the attacking but I don't think we are strong enough. We would be if our reserve was here instead of standing by a few miles away in case it's needed there. If they gave us a hand we could wipe the floor with Ted and the longer we leave it the harder it will be. He is probably expecting reinforcements as well. The difference is he will probably get them. I got the shock of my life when I heard that most of our company didn't do much yesterday and now I wonder if the reason we have been sent back is because we know the ropes. I am shaking like a leaf, not because I am afraid of dying, well I am afraid of dying but because I am afraid of not being brave enough to do something like carry a wounded mate to safety under fire. I don't think I would be able to live with myself if I didn't so I probably will manage it. I am afraid of leaving you to pick up the pieces. I know you would manage and I know you wouldn't have to do it on your own. All the things I dreamed of doing only became possible when you married me. I might not set the world alight with my piano playing and I might not make a picture but I'm going to do my best to build a house and raise a family. If I don't come back though I want you to be happy with someone else and only remember that I loved you. Now I know why other men were smart enough not to join up. It's like we are doing their dirty work for them. I did my bit yesterday, we all did. We killed a lot of men, which is nothing to be proud of. It was like the opening day of the duck shooting season. The only thing I think that excuses me is that they were trying to do the same to us. At least we weren't going to be caught out like Brightnoth at Maldon. If I had known what taking another man's life was like I would have been a conscientious objector. They came while we were having breakfast and we had to drop everything. Some men carried their tin of tea back to their dugouts. Mine was too hot. We should have known what was coming because the bombing started earlier than usual and went on for longer and the bombs were bigger. They dropped a string of 1 ton bombs on the ridge that comes up from the coast to just behind us. It was like a shroud had been drawn over us. Then the Junkers flew in at about two or three hundred feet above us. The Junkers have a funny nose like the head of a fly only painted yellow. There were gliders too. We were shooting as soon as we got to our trenches. There were tiny black darts coming out of the side of the Junkers like spent cartridge cases that would suddenly blossom and then it would be like the sky was full of jellyfish. The gliders came in even lower. We could hear the sound of the air rushing past their wings and fuselages. Lots of bullets were fired at them so I don't think many of the men inside them would have survived, also because they were crashing into the big old olive trees and the rocks. Thinking about that now makes me a bit more hopeful because I realise Ted isn't that well organised after all because if he was he wouldn't have used gliders or not here anyway. Today we have to make every shot count as we don't have much ammunition left. It's hard to avoid wasting ammunition though because we have only about 30 seconds. Some of the parachutes didn't open and the men fell to the ground kicking and screaming. That was a terrible sound. There were others shouting encouragement. Some pretended to be dead but you know when someone is hit because they relax and what they are holding falls from their hands. And Ted helps us by hitting his own men. The planes fly in formations of three. We see planes banking to fly back to the mainland with parachutes caught on their wings and tails. Well here they come now again Pet so I better leave off for now

Eight

We were at the top of our ladders, up in the pink winter twilight, up on the tablelands of the canopy; Te Mata o Rongokako dilating in the afterglow, other points of the compass dropping their grey roller doors and every now and again out of the corner of my eye a glimmer of Iris flitting up and down the rows, gathering the prunings. In her mitts and coats and Cossack Hat, she was the spitting image of Katya. I was about to say something of the short to Chas when there was a short sharp cry.

'Heron?' said Chas.

'Possibly; close whatever it was.'

'It's going to be a stiff one.'

'It's going to be a stiff one, alright.'

While Chas was packing up, I had a look up and down the rows then crouched and looked under the canopies, thinking I might see the bird; which was laughable because the grass was long overdue for a cut. At the same time, I felt an odd twinge of guilt at having thought about Katya when Iris was about. There was no sign of Iris; she must've gone back to the house to get dinner on. We shouldered our ladders and set off through the wet grass. The house was in darkness. I opened the door and sang out.

'See you tomorrow,' said Chas.

'Hang on a minute, will you, Chas?'

I slipped off my boots and padded round the house: nothing but creaks and echoes.

'Maybe she's gone over to Fred's to use the phone?'

'Do you want me to check?'

'Would you and I'll go and check the orchard?'

I found her in the long grass. She was on her side, her back arched, arms and legs pushing away from her, her teeth grinding, eyes staring. I'd seen it often enough to know the first thing to do was get her mouth open and make sure she hadn't swallowed her tongue. I took my jersey off and draped it over her hip. I stroked her brow, told her how much I loved her over and over and when the fit had run its course, lifted her as gently as I could and set off for Fred's. I met them coming back through the trees.

'We'll need an ambulance,' I said and Fred turned on his heel.

'Anything I can do?' said Chas.

'Take the torch.'

Rose, Fred's wife, was waiting in the porch light. 'She's bleeding,' she said, 'bring her inside. Don't worry about the blood. A little blood won't hurt anything.'

There was a bit more than a little. I could feel it. I was thinking the worst.

'I'll give Agnes a call,' said Chas.

Fred went out to the road to wait for the ambulance. It wasn't long before we heard the siren. I told the officers what I knew, which wasn't much. Chas followed us to the hospital.

Agnes and Hammond must've called in at the house to get some clothes. Hammond didn't know where to look, Agnes looked truly miserable. As a rule, in a waiting room you don't have to look far to see someone worse off than you. That night that someone was us. An hour or two must have gone by before the nurse returned to tell me the doctor was ready to see me.

'How is she?' I said.

'Not good, I'm afraid. She's had a stroke.'

'Hell's bells! The bairn?'

'And a miscarriage.'

'What are her chances?'

'She'll have to come out of the coma first then we'll see.'

'How long do you think that will take?'

'That's up to her. If she recovers, she may need long-term nursing care. The chances of her dying are greater than the chances of her living. She may not last the night. On the other hand, she could hang on for days, weeks; a month at the outside. All we can do is look after her as well as we can. The only good news is she's survived the stroke for now.'

Iris's parents, Ron and Shirley, and her brother had driven through the night. I let the Duty Sister bring them up to date.

Day was breaking when we got to the house. Ron and Shirley

wouldn't hear of having our bed, so we made up a bed for them on the living-room floor; Luke slept on the couch. He went back the following day; he had to for work. While they were there, Ron and Shirley visited Iris in the afternoons; if there was a bit of rain around, I went with them, otherwise I visited in the evenings.

Sister suggested I talk to her. I was already doing that but I stepped it up. I reminded her of all the things we'd done together. I told her how much I needed her. When I ran out of things to say, I read aloud from the books we'd both liked. I told myself that despite appearances she was fighting tooth and nail. I dreamt I was underwater, swimming into a cave, looking for somewhere to come up for air.

Former colleagues from the hospital came all the way from Wellington: family – hers, mine, and Frank's – childhood friends.

This was in the days before they had tube feeding, of course: patients could be hydrated but not fed, which meant that with nothing to come and go on her body was shutting down. After five weeks her breathing and blood circulation systems collapsed and she died. It was Thursday the fourth of September. I didn't find out whether the foetus was male or female.

Going through her things, I found the will she had made after Frank's death; it included a request that his remains be buried with her. We had talked a bit about that, but with everything else that was going on, hadn't made any progress. Even supposing it was possible, I had my doubts as to whether I was up to it. The best I could do was to keep the option open and accordingly I purchased a three-berth plot.

The graves in the row we buried her in faced the graves in the row where my parents were. I was a little unsteady on my feet and happening to glimpse the adzed walls and a tiny shingle slide spilling out of one corner, I very nearly joined her.

Chas meanwhile had gotten on with the pruning: our roles had been reversed; it was me giving him a hand now, albeit going through the motions and sometimes not even that. Levi, my neighbour from across the road had taken to popping in from time to time, never overstaying his welcome or having much to say; needless to say, the gesture was much appreciated.

Levi, as you're probably aware, had something of a reputation in the village. His three-quarter draught, having been hitched to a post from opening till closing time, could often be seen carrying him home; the barman having helped him into the saddle. The horse knew where it was going, but without Levi's finer promptings, didn't always distinguish between the road and the roundabout. So from time to time, the villagers woke to divots the size of dinner plates, like the stages of a skipping stone's progress across a pond, splashed across its pride and joy. The Mayor didn't see the funny side, however, and Levi was read the riot act.

Not everyone looked down their nose at Levi. Because he always raised his hat and bowed deeply in their presence, women thought he was a true gentleman. Nor did Chas have a bad word to say about him: when they worked on the council together, Levi had saved his life. A blockage had developed in the outfall over the old Ngaruroro and Chas and Levi had been tasked with rectifying the problem. While prising the planks from the chute, Chas had slipped and been sucked in, which may very well have been the end of him had Levi not been on hand to pull him out.

Ron and Shirley had not long gone back when Agnes and Hammond moved in, as much to keep an eye on me I suspect as to keep me company. Things didn't improve. Finally I roused myself sufficiently to put the orchard on the market and book a passage to Sydney. Chas stayed on to work for the new owner, my old schoolmate John Silver. When Eddy heard I was selling, with the blessings of the family, he passed the news onto John and John made a beeline for State Advances. Agnes and Hammond stayed on in the house till they had somewhere to go. Accommodation was hard to come by in those days and while it was his place, as John said, you waited your turn. In the two years it took me to get to Melbourne and home again, rarely staying longer than a fortnight anywhere and rarely without company (because while I had money, I had mates, the best a bloke could have: when the money ran out so did they), John went on paying the rent on a flat in the village.

It was Haskell who rescued me. It was time to come home, he said; I've got a job lined up for you at the hospital. Had it not been for the examinations, I might still be there. It wasn't the reading that was the problem, it was the putting down on paper of what I thought about what I'd read. So I transferred to the ground staff.

To cut a long story short, a mate and I were on the roof of one of the villas, cleaning out the guttering, when a couple of nurses wheeling a tea trolley crossed the courtyard below, one of them I hadn't seen before: tall, brunette, not half bad looking.

'What about a cup of tea for the workers, Nurse?' I called out.

'I thought he was very cheeky,' said Liz, 'and not very handsome either with his freckles and red hair. He was shorter than me too. But my girlfriend said he'd had a hard time as a P.O.W., so I should be kind to him. So (more fool me) the next day when they wanted a cup of tea, I took them one again and he asked me out.'

'And that's where you came into the picture,' said Max.

A Game of Two Halves/
Cook Ting's visit

Zongnan Retreat

In middle age I inclined to the True Way
and retired to the edge of the southern mountains.

Going alone is always a joy,
pleasant things known only by oneself,

walking to the water's end,
sitting and watching the rising clouds,

meeting by chance an old man in the woods,
talking and laughing without thought of return.

One

Les Bleus drift into the half they will defend at the restart and drop to the ground. A bag of orange segments does the rounds, Lagisquet is the only taker. Berbizier guzzles from a bottle. Mesnel gets his head seen to. Meanwhile, in the half they have deserted, J.K. – a gate ajar in a palisade of shadows – probes a hamstring, Fitzy and Jonesy jog on the spot.

The sound system picks up the wobbly drone of a single-engine aeroplane. The hills lean back like old men on a park bench and joke about conditions changing so that the team that was disadvantaged in the first half will be disadvantaged again.

The spectators in the East Stand, shading their eyes with their programmes, catcall and wolf whistle two old boys in All Black strip flexing their stuff while waving a placard that reads 'Just Say the Word Mr Wyllie'. The linesmen stroll self-consciously back and forth across the hallowed yellow turf, the ball boys in tow. More All Blacks are jogging now, *Les Bleus* are in position, Blanco places the ball, a spectator yells "Hurry up!" and the linesmen and ball boys get theirs A's into G.

Blood wicking through his bandage, Buck raises his arm. Pierce takes the ball, crouches and backs into the opposition forwards. The All Blacks put a drive on and the ball squirts out of play.

Foxy takes out his mouth guard and shields his mouth so only his backline can read the call.

'The French will have to chance their arm and spin it wide,' says Kirton. 'It's interesting to see Blanco up in the line.'

The French win the throw-in: Berbizier to Rouge-Thomas, Rouge-Thomas to Sella, Sella to Blanco, try!

'Tous les caprices des stars!' says the French commentator.

The crowd is stunned.

'Did you say something?'

'Eh?' says Max.

'Do you want me?'

'No! The French just scored!'

'Good for them. What's the score now?'

'Eighteen/four.'

In the replay he sees Jones hanging off (half an eye on a potential intercept) while Rouge-Thomas goes past him, ball in hand, arms revolving like a ferris wheel. It's the transparency of the move that mesmerizes and unpicks the All Black defence. And that's not the only trick up the French sleeve: Mesnel swerving out brings Sella into his position, which really puts the cat among the pigeons because now their opposite numbers are unsure who they're marking. So he sees Schuster (covering Sella) looking round as Rouge-Thomas goes inside him to see why he hasn't passed. He sees Stanley checking Mesnel, while Rouge-Thomas, still outrageously swinging his arms round and round, keeps on going; he sees Jones (and Foxy too now) still waiting for the pass, still holding off.

Finally Jones wakes to the ruse and lunges at Rouge-Thomas. Foxy meanwhile, following a split-second after, gets caught in the traffic and that leaves the gate wide open for Rouge-Thomas (going down in Jones' tackle) to pop a line ball to Sella; for Sella (passing Schuster) to bolt into open pasture (Wrighty chasing back hard) and veer out to link up with Blanco where, losing his footing at Gallagher's feet (his limbs entangling Gallagher) he pops the move's second line-ball to Blanco. Blanco leaps inside Wright who, thinking Gallagher had Blanco covered, had turned to keep tabs on Berot. Blanco hurdles J.K.'s last-gasp attempt at an ankle-tap and, swinging round in the in-goal area and losing his footing, grounds the ball; bringing his legs together so they don't cross the dead ball line.

'Well . . .' says Kirton, 'that's exactly what I said they had to do. Fullback used to be a defensive position. Blanco has reinvented the role.'

Berot misses the conversion.

At the restart, Jones angrily flings Rodriguez to the ground. The French win the ruck, Blanco languidly punts up the touchline; the ball bounces into touch and he claps his hands to encourage his teammates. The French win the lineout but lose the maul and a scrum is set. The scrum screws and is reset. Deans box-kicks: Lagisquet collects and runs it up but is run down by J.K.; the All Blacks are penalised. Berot converts: eighteen/seven. Cut to the coaches Wylie and Hart shading their eyes like tank commanders or is it rabbits caught in headlights?

'All Blacks . . . All Blacks . . . All Blacks,' chants the crowd.

For the second time in as many minutes, Foxy restarts. McDowell collects the tap-back; Cécillon wrests the ball from him. Sella cuts inside Schuster and Foxy and, heading for the outfield, going past Pierce hands the ball onto Lagisquet. Lagisquet pins back his ears for the corner, Schuster giving chase; Wrighty and Gallagher and Deans attempting to cut him off. Running out of room Lagisquet puts up a centre-kick and the ball drops toward the All Black try-line. Blanco and Rodriguez go up for it together, but the ball goes through their hands and bounces off Rodriguez's shoulder; Jones lines it up, but the bounce favours Cécillon who, coming through like a locomotive, dives over the tangled heap of Rodriguez and Blanco and dots down.

'C'est formidable!'

'Did they score again?'

'Hang on a minute.'

Rodriguez is down: a stretcher is called for, his team mates plead with him to get up.

'Maybe he's the French Colin Meads?' says Kirton.

Berot converts: eighteen/thirteen.

'What's the score?'

'Eighteen/thirteen!'

'To the All Blacks?'

'Who else?'

The All Blacks knock on at the restart, Rodriguez takes the ball up; Rouge-Thomas grubber-kicks. Gallagher gathers, sidesteps, sets off; chip-kicks. Berbizier gathers and clears. Buck collects from the ensuing lineout and passes to Deans. Deans has a dab then passes to Pierce; Pierce loses the ball in the tackle. The referee plays the advantage. Blanco clears and the negligible advantage is deemed over, Blanco swallows hard.

Fitzy throws in, the ball goes wide; Wrighty is hit hard by Sella. From the ruck, Berbizier looks to pass one way then u-turns and feeds Rouge-Thomas. Before Deans can get to him Rouge-Thomas feeds Blanco. Before Whetton (Gary) can get to Blanco, Blanco feeds Sella who passes back to the long-striding Blanco before Gallagher can get there. Stanley misses the ankle-tap, Blanco goes over in Wrighty's tackle.

'The French have staged one of the most remarkable come-backs in test match history,' says Nisbett, a tremor in his voice.

'It's leaving me absolutely speechless,' says Quinny.

Berot misses the conversion: eighteen/seventeen. The crowd is buzzing.

The restart fails to make the ten yard line; Buck concedes a penalty: Berot misses again.

The French help themselves to another All Black lineout. Cécillon is penalised for arguing with the referee, when it looks like Buck should have been penalised for going over the ball. The camera zooms in on a full moon rising over Banks Peninsula, then out till it's pea-sized again.

'I wonder what the man in the moon thinks of all this?' says Quinny.

Jones bursts onto Schuster's pass and feeds Gallagher, Gallagher passes to Pierce who takes it into a ruck. Rouge-Thomas, stopping the ball from coming back, concedes a penalty.

'Good curl, Earle Kirton?' says Quinny.

Foxy licks his lips, eyes the sticks, scratches the air and makes it twenty-one/seventeen. Rodriguez departs with a sore neck. A.J. is penalised for talking. Fitzy is penalised for stomping: the close-up shows rake marks on Mesnel's thigh. Berot misses again.

'It's desperate times,' says Quinny.

Foxy puts up an up-and-under. Blanco loses it forward. J.K. to Jones, Jones to A.J: try! Now it's Foxy's turn to miss: twenty-five/seventeen.

J.K. hauls Lagisquet, without the ball, over the sideline. Lagisquet gets to his feet and slaps the backs of several All Blacks then argues with the touch judge who holds out his flag and Lagisquet is penalised. Foxy kicks the ball out and the crowd invades the field.

Two

Tin bums – that's what he'd say if he and the young bloke next door happened to be out picking up their papers at the same time or if he bumped into someone in the village and it came up or if Ned called –

the All Blacks were tinny, the French were dead stiff.

It was a pity they weren't a bit closer: Liz would've been in her element having the kids around. What's more, Ned would've known what to do about the gaps in the hedge, how to hang a gate and the rest of it, otherwise they'd have to keep the pup on a leash till things were sorted out. Ned could've done the mowing; it was getting beyond him even with Liz doing a third of it. They could've taken turns with the digging then taken a top off a bottle and watched the game together. On second thoughts – given it was going straight through him now – he might have to leave it to Sean. Good bloke Sean: always had something for them if he'd been out hunting; they had venison steaks every night one week.

He glanced out the window. Across the road, the yellow streetlight on the shrubs (hydrangeas, hebes, camellias, rhododendrons: you wouldn't know where you were) was eerie. The road had settled down (the traffic had got to where it was going; albeit in a few hours it would be going in the other way) and aside from the few birds still battling it out for the last word, things were quiet.

The French had done their homework alright: that Rouge-Thomas should have been called Legerdemain. Foxy didn't have a bad game either; he was the difference between the two sides. Turning to pick up the glass, he caught a flicker out the corner of his eye, heard a low growl get up over the house then something shot out of the shrubbery – the window flexed and the curtains trembled – and biffed him in the bread basket.

It was Cook Ting come to pay him a visit: zip went the knife between the intima and the media, zoop – zip zap zoop – and straight away he didn't feel so good; perspiration prickled his brow. The shadow like a shockwave swept on, it was in the next town before he got a word out.

In the kitchen, Liz paused and turned her head and noticing a mark above the sliding door crossed the cork tiles for a closer view then with a flick of the tea towel removed a skein of cobweb.

'Well I'll be damned,' she said. 'Max, look at this.'

His hands were on the arms of the armchair, his elbows were raised, but that was as far as he'd got. She glanced at the coffee table, at the solitary bubble rising up the side of the glass; at the tobacco pouch, rarely out of his hand of late, belly up, flap open beside the untouched beer.

'Look,' she said again.

He was turning his head slowly from side to side.

'What is it?'

'Me bloody back!' he said, his eyes squeezed shut tight.

'Do you want to go and have a lie down?'

He nodded.

'Do you need a hand up?'

She got her arms under his shoulder.

'On the count of three,' she said.

He was white as a ghost.

'Oh you poor thing, you're not too good are you?'

She got him into the bedroom and into the bed and covered him up.

'Can I get you anything?' she said and getting no reply went straight to the phone.

There were bits of paper all round the house with the number on them (in case of just such an emergency) but none looked like the one she wanted and in any case she would have to find her glasses first and they weren't anywhere to be seen either. She fumbled through the directory, tears collecting on her eyelashes and running into her eyes and making them sting. She blinked and a tear fell on the glass. She wiped the lens with the hem of her apron and dabbed her cheek and dialled the number. She thought she must have misdialled and tried again. In between checking on Max, she eventually got through.

'Doctor Ross is busy,' said the receptionist, 'however he does have appointments in the area and might be able to drop in between them, would that suit? Otherwise, he could call in on his way home?'

'What time would that be?'

'Let me check. He has an appointment in Guthrie Road at 7.00 and another in Breadalbane Road at 8.00. Otherwise it would have to be after 9.00.'

'Oh,' said Liz.

'Is it Mr Gunn?'

'Yes.'

'Is he alright?'

'It's his back, it's playing up.'

'How is he at the moment?'

'Asleep, I think . . . Just a minute, I'll go and check.'

'Yes, he's asleep.'

'Has he been complaining of a sore back?'

'Yes.'

'How long for?'

'Since the game finished.'

'The rugby?'

'Yes.'

'And what time was that?'

'About half past four I think.'

'Well, I'll let the doctor know when he gets in or if he calls. You'll call again if Mr Gunn gets worse, won't you?'

'Yes.'

She returned to the bedroom and stood at the foot of the bed, rocking from her heels to the balls of her feet and back again, clasping, unclasping her hands. Then she went back to the kitchen and stood before the windows at the back of the house. The sky beyond the garage was lit by lightning, in the distance thunder rolled. She thought about their first house, how she had to do the washing in the basement, about the time she couldn't get the copper going because the newspaper was so damp it had yellowed and the heads of all the matches had crumbled on the igniter strip because the basement door had been left open and the rain had gotten in making puddles on the floor and swelling the door so it couldn't be closed; how all her neighbours had washing machines with variable speed agitators and wringers and laundries off their back porch and so they didn't need husbands who could split kindling into three different gauges; how it had occurred to her then that he would probably predecease her; how it was just a matter of getting through till then before she could get on with her own life, do what it had occurred to her she had it in her to do. Then she thought she heard a noise and returning to the bedroom found it empty.

'Are you in there, Max!' she said, and getting no reply looked round the edge of the door.

His chin was on his chest, his forearms were on his thighs, his hands were clasped – the fingers bluish like spiders' legs – he was breathing in short shallow gasps. She had read in an article in a magazine that the toilet was one of the most common places where people died: they thought they needed to use the lavatory, but it was their hearts that were giving out. She got him off the seat and checked his bottom and helped him back to bed, but he wasn't comfortable; he had to sit on the edge and whimper and pant while his head lolled and he got colder. She got a blanket and draped it over his shoulders and back.

'Can I get you a drink?'

He shook his head.

'You haven't had anything since lunchtime, what about a cup of tea?'

He groaned.

She went to put the kettle on and instead brought him a glass of water and put it to his lips: he gulped. She refilled the glass and looked at the clock: it was nearly 7.00, time for the news. She turned on the radio then thinking she better do a quick tidy up, cleaned the toilet and washed her hands. Looking at her face in the mirror reminded her of a photo she'd seen of a face imprinted in the soot on the front of a train. She wondered if she should ring Agnes then thought she would leave it till after the doctor had been, partly because she wanted Agnes to know she could be as strong as Agnes had been. She looked in on Max and found him on his side on the pillows panting. She got him sorted out and went back to the kitchen.

The dishes done (her cup and his glass), she swept the kitchen and dusted the dresser and folded the clothes and was putting them away when she heard the crunch of footsteps on gravel and went to the door.

'How's the patient?' said Doctor Ross.

'Not so good.'

She followed him into the room. He was Ned's height, he had a short plaited ponytail at the nape of his neck.

'How are you feeling, Max? It's Dean.'

Max stirred and groaned.

'Can you lie on your front for me? I want to have a look at your back.'

The doctor drew back the quilt.

'How long has he been breathing like this?'

'Since the game finished.'

'How long ago was that?'

'I don't know; it finished at half-past four.'

'He's better off resting for now, I'll pop back on my way home.'

Three

He came to, blinking. It was up his nose, it was in his eyes, his ears, his hair; it was under his foreskin, up his urethra, in his digestive tract. He blinked. All the noise had drained from the landscape, everything was white, the heavy mechanical thundering had come to a stop, the racket from the wadi had ground to a halt and for the moment it appeared he would not after all become saltbush fertilizer, not today anyway, but the sand had drunk him dry.

'Hang on; this might hurt a bit,' said a voice.'

Hullo, he thought, someone's got a sense of humour. A vulture swooped down, flapping its wings, landed on his back and gripped him with its claws: the blossoming pain took his breath away. Something warm ran under his cheek and into the sand. He'd been gored. He opened an eye. Liz was in the doorway with a cup and a saucer, the cup rocking on the saucer.

'He's bleeding again!' she said.

'What do you mean he's bleeding again; you didn't tell me he was bleeding? When did this start?'

'After you left before.'

'Why didn't you tell me?'

'I thought he'd bitten his tongue.'

The doctor straightened. 'I'll see myself out,' he said.

Max's lips were bluish now too. She tried cleaning them with the flannel but the blue wouldn't come off. His breathing was frightful. He looked like death warmed up. She considered getting into bed with him, but didn't want to fall asleep in case he needed her, so sat on the armless chair with the quilt draped over her, watching the lights of the passing cars crossing the ceiling in the opposite direction to the noise they made.

Sometime in the middle of the night, she woke to him trying to get up. His eyes were half-closed as he bumped against the wall and again as they lurched through the door and along the passageway to the bathroom.

The phone was ringing. Ned threw back the covers and strode through the house in his underpants and singlet. Only the foyer was warm: that was where the night-store heater was. The rest of the house was freezing.

'Hullo . . . Hullo Mum, what do you want?'

'It's your father, he's not too good.'

'What do you mean?'

'He's had a bad night.'

'And?'

'I think you better come home.'

'I can't come home, I'm in the middle of a section; you know that!'

'Hang on a minute. I think he's gotten up again, I have to go.'

He went back to bed. He had stopped thinking about the call when the phone rang again.

'Hullo . . .'

'I'm afraid I've got some bad news. Your father's dead.'

'Are you sure?'

'Yes; quite certain.'

'Have you phoned the doctor?'

'No.'

'Don't you think you better?'

'He can't do anything for him now.'

'Well, ring anyway and let him know. I think you'll have to call the police as well. I'll come as soon as I can.'

'When do you think you'll be here?'

'I don't know, it depends on the airlines; maybe today.'

He put the phone down, got halfway to the kitchen door and paused. It felt as if his mind had popped out, as in popped out to the dairy to get the paper or something; had come adrift anyway and was hovering a few feet away in the vicinity of the chip-heater; which was a matter of some concern because he was going to need it to tell people what had happened and to organise things; besides which if he didn't get it back sooner rather than later it could take longer and be harder. In the first instance, he would have to tell Jette. So he went and did what he usually did when he woke: sat on a cushion on the floor with his legs crossed and his hands cupped together, the thumb tips barely touching, back straight and felt his breathing coming into his body and going out. And after a few minutes his mind came back and resumed service. Then he got up and went through to the bedroom and told Jette and she turned over and searched his eyes.

'I'm sorry,' she said.

'Sorry' is mostly used to apologise, so in this context it seemed out of place (what's there to apologise for?) It seemed like a very small word was taking on a very big job. But it was a loss for Jette too. They turned to the business side of things.

At the stopover, Ned ran into his tutor, who was returning from a conference. She excused herself for not offering her sympathies; her relationship with her father had not been a good one, she said.

On the second hop, some of the passengers who were already seated could have been kids he'd gone to school with. The driver of the shuttle was someone he had gone to school with.

'They go away and they come back,' said Tony. 'They get married and they have kids: same as the parents they rebelled against. Not you and me though, eh, we're going to make something of ourselves?'

Liz came out.

'Hi, Mum, this is Tony. We went to school together.'

'Hullo, Tony,' said Liz, discretely, smiling warmly.

'Pleased to meet you,' said Tony.

Tony got Ned's bag from the trailer and Ned got out a note. Tony waved it away.

When they got inside, Ned kissed his mother on the lips and she leant back, a look of surprise on her face.

'He got up to go to the bathroom while I was on the phone. He was just sitting there, so I got him back into bed. I was about to go and phone you again when he asked me not to leave. While I was holding him in my arms, he relaxed. I looked at him and the light in his eyes was sinking, fading, departing then his eyes rolled back and I knew he was gone.

'That's when I called you the second time. Then I called the doctor and I called Agnes. Agnes came over straight away and washed him. She wanted to do it by herself; it would be her way of saying goodbye to him. She said there was hardly anything to him, that it looked like he'd aged twenty years overnight.'

The funeral parlour could have been the venue for a private concert. There were five chairs at an angle to the room: three in the front, two at the back. Their frames were black, the upholstery was aqua. Behind Ned, the sun shone whitely on full-length lace curtains. Before him, sliding doors opened onto an enclosed garden with miniature roses and casts of figurines from classical antiquity. It could equally have been a lobby in a rest home or a hotel, were it not for the turquoise carpet's lack of underlay.

The undertaker wore the blackest suit Ned had ever seen. He had fat lips and ruddy cheeks and the refreshing lack of confidence of someone who was new to the business. The refrigerated drawers of the embalming room had battered fronts. The assistant drew the gurney like a man-sized hāpuku from the sea and there he was, there Max was all dressed up with nowhere to go in his dark-blue wedding suit, pale blue shirt and dark-blue crested tie hooped between neck and vest.

On the end of the peg that kept his mouth shut (it was hardly as if he ever talked too much) there was a little blob of makeup. The fingertips of one flipper-thin hand had been super-glued to the nails of the other. The crowning glory was the thin-lipped supercilious smirk. It reminded Ned of the photo taken before Cheops: hubris-cum-hangover with a touch of gippy tummy thrown in for good measure. The backs of his orangey-brown hands were mottled with white spots like fat globules on soup stock. The saving graces: his eyebrows hadn't been trimmed; recent gardening injuries to his hands hadn't been made-up. Ned ran his hand through Max's hair and lifted an eyelid (all there was to see was a plastic shield with spurs on it to keep the lid shut). It was sideshow in a showroom.

He made an appointment to see the doctor. He was late – by a good two hours – and the surgery was full, yet he was called straight in.

Wanting to put him at his ease, Ned thanked the doctor for all he'd done for Max and the doctor at last met his eye.

'He wouldn't have wanted to have been put on a respirator; he knew he was living on borrowed time.'

Still the doctor said nothing.

'He liked you,' said Ned then, thinking the doctor was busy, extended his hand again and departed.

Next on his list was the breeder: he rang to cancel the pup.

'No, she doesn't want it. It was his idea.'

Four

The coffin was well down on the pile: it was a causeway over a carpet of blue moss, a stepping stone in a temple pond, a pontoon in a river with only one shore; a ship in a roadstead awaiting the convoy, its upper deck massed with flowers. The coffin, the altar, the communion table, the pillars, the door frames, the pews – in their hi-gloss varnish, gleamed wetly in the natural lighting – everything stood proud of the sea-blue carpet as blue as a theatre with the evening sky for its ceiling.

Liz and Ned had the front row to themselves. Agnes (as close as anyone to Max) by her own choice sat in the row behind.

'No, this is your day,' said Agnes and Liz beamed.

Chas's daughter, Nina, and her husband Burt and an old friend of Max's and the old friend's wife, joined Agnes. Hammond, given to moping about the hand he'd been dealt (of whom, Max, after a skinful, by way of explaining one or two things for Ned's benefit, had compared to a dying tree in flower), his heart having succumbed three months short of his sixtieth birthday (bang on the money by the doctor's prediction) was long gone. Agnes (who hadn't attended her husband's funeral) had now outlived her siblings: Chas, after turning up on Max's doorstep in the winter of '58 to say goodbye; Hugh likewise (on his way to the hospital, his bones infiltrated by the cancer, shaking his head at the devilry of it); and Haskell, another great legend consigned to the blaze of ignominious alcoholic glory. The others had simply left their hats on the seats of their chairs and not returned to claim them.

In ones and twos the mourners entered, dithered, retired then returned to sit in the shadows in the back row. It was beginning to look like a service to match the fag end of Max's life when, just as proceedings were about to get under way, the whole beaming shipwrecked tribe, almost unrecognisable in their glad-rags, washed up the aisles – who was the woman in the peach-coloured dress, white belt and matching handbag, with the air hostess smile? Angus worked his way into the second pew, ruddy face aghast, bared teeth blazing in his skull.

At the sight of the coffin, there were sharp intakes of breath: here was a mate who on the same day in the same river and the same boat had been lost overboard and swept out to sea. The Reverend cleared his throat.

'Today we give thanks for the life of Maxwell Gunn . . . .'

Ned looked out the window at the huge bluegum that having towered over his childhood now towered over his early middle age. A tiny whirlwind danced across the clay, picked up a leaf, held it like a flame then set some gum nuts spinning like tops. In the few spare moments he'd had, he'd realised he'd need more than a few spare moments to prepare a eulogy that would do his father's life justice. So he settled instead on reading aloud the two poems written out in longhand that had fallen out of the book that had been on Max's bedside cabinet for the past two decades. The dust jacket had long since parted company with the cloth-covered hardback. In its place was a picture of a white horse on its hind legs (centred on the cover's sky blue cloth with dark blue biro markings). The two poems weren't in the book and were better than anything in it. They had been copied from unattributed sources onto a sheet of an unlined newsprint pad that had been folded in half and in half again. One of them was by Han Yu, it was called 'Mountain Stones'; the other was by Wang Wei, it was called 'Zongnan Retreat'. Poems are best recited from memory and he wasn't able to do that either.

Max wasn't a big man and as Agnes had said, there was nothing to him. That being the case, they had opted for four handles. It was like picking up a sarcophagus. In a sequence that would not have been out of place in a Charlie Chaplin flick, they staggered up the aisle.

'Phew!' said Angus, setting his corner on the hearse. 'I thought we were going to drop him for a moment there.'

'Me too,' said Ned.

'Not me,' said Troy.

'Who was the soldier?' said Ned.

'What soldier?'

'The one you just walked past.'

'Must've been the Unknown Soldier.'

'Not Oldman?'

'Oldman, no; he died a couple of years ago.'

The undertaker got behind the wheel. The minister got in beside him and laid his arm along the top of the bench seat. They looked for all the world like a couple of lads out for a spin in the old man's car. Pedestrians coming towards them paused, removed their hats and bowed to the hearse like grass to a zephyr. A young woman in sunglasses, her arms full of gifts, stepped out onto the crossing and as one the minister and the undertaker ducked their heads for an eye-full.

The slope was all but full. Grass grew up to the stones and moss and lichen took over from there. A korowai of artificial grass cloaked a barrow of earth. The hole had been double-dug with a front-end digger: the walls were chiselled.

Iris would have to go on going it alone. You could say all three had missed out, but would lying next to each other have made them any less alone?

There had been more tears when they buried Kari (named after the dog that lost its life in saving his; the one other time Ned had seen tears on his father's cheeks). The weather then as now had ramped up the ambience with a fine mist; the street lights and the day's last light a duet of oranges and blues. Digging through the loam had been a piece of cake: they had lowered her on a sack, discussed what tree to plant over her. Max had wondered about saying something, before leaving it to the few spots condensing out of the mist.

'Not on your life,' said Liz – her back to the hearth: gracious, solicitous; having risen to the occasion, doing what he would have done – 'when he died, I knew his body was the last place I'd find him.'

Cousins, meeting for the first time, spoke of hearing about each other all their lives; others hadn't seen each other since childhood.

'Since the picnics we used to have at the river that smelt of sex,' said Trish.

'He meant the world to me when I was young,' said Lynn. 'He said I was his favourite niece. Do you remember me coming to stay with you when I was in trouble at home and him and me sitting out on the back step, smoking and talking and looking at the sunset? I used to wish I was older and that we weren't related and that I'd met him before your mother did; just being with him made me feel worthwhile because in his eyes I was always okay.'

'How come your family never visited when we were kids?'

'You shouldn't have asked that question because the answer's not very worthy. Oh well, what the hell, if you can't be honest at funerals when can you be? Dad always felt inferior to your dad. He's not a reader, see? And he's got this huge chip on his shoulder because of it. It's not that he can't read; it's that he doesn't. Nor does he do anything about it, like enrol in an adult learning course or anything. So when he meets people and they start talking about books and ideas and stuff, he just freezes, goes into a tailspin.'

'We wouldn't have come, if it wasn't for your old man,' said Marvin, 'he gave us the time of day, he had time for us. We used to look forward to coming to visit you so we could play with you, you were our hero, we idolized you; but you were never there, you'd gone off to play with your friends – I can understand that – so we played with your toys instead; grouse toys, man.'

'It was the same for me,' said Ned, 'when we visited my older cousins. They'd always either gone to the beach in their two-door sedans or shut themselves up in their rooms with their electronic gizmos.'

'Wanna know why Dickie's not here?' said Marvin. 'It's because he thinks you think he's shit because of when you met outside a picture theatre and he said he was a Sunday dad and you laughed.'

'I wasn't laughing at Dickie. It was the song I was laughing at. And besides, for what it's worth, that's what I was then; so give him my regards.'

It was shaping up to be the best chat Ned had had with his Uncle Adam, but no sooner had they started than Adam was on his feet.

'Got a long drive ahead,' he said. 'Even if we get going now, it'll be after midnight before we get in.'

'Stay here for the night?'

Adam shook his head.

'Stay in a motel then.'

'Too expensive.'

'Can I give you anything then: something of Max's?'

Adam shook his head.

'Are you sure?'

'What have you got?'

'Gardening tools, clothes?'

'No.'

'Come and have a look in the garage then, there might be something that takes your eye.'

'I'll take this,' said Adam. 'Not the plant, I don't want the plant.'

'It's a bonsai.'

'I know what it is.'

'I know what you mean: it should have been a microphylla. Trouble is the pot was from me and the bonsai was from him: sentimental value. Is there something else perhaps?'

'No.'

'When your dad got home from the war,' said Andy, 'my father and Uncle Haskell took him aside to have a word with him about his politics: he was full of it, how the Reds were just up the road, how things would be different when they got here.'

'Last time I saw your dad,' said Ned, 'he was on his way to the hospital, Uncle Haskell was taking him; they stopped in on the way. We went out to the car to see him because he was too ill to come in. He was in the back on the passenger side, a doubled blanket wrapped round his waist and legs like a lava-lava; he couldn't keep his eyes open, let alone say anything.'

'I stayed at your place for a week then,' said Andy. 'I think it was your place: your mum and dad moved the daybed into the living room for me. I went to the hospital to see the old man every day. He wanted to know what I'd been up to, so I told him I'd just swapped my huntaway for a horse; it was the best dog I'd ever had but it was getting old, it was going round and round in smaller and smaller circles till it dropped. The horse was one of those horses from the Kaimanawas; I had to break it in. I was wheeling it round and round when my foot slipped out of the stirrup and I came off and put my hip out. I had to do my belt up tight to hold the hip in place. It was because I was wearing gumboots, you see, that the accident happened; they didn't have a proper tread. The first thing Dad said was: what was I wearing on my feet? And when I told him I was wearing gumboots, he blew up. Because that was what he was always telling me: wear proper boots with a tread on them when you're on a horse.'

'You couldn't do anything right, eh?' said Ned.

'That was about the size of it. But he could draft sheep: he could draft sheep from three pens and keep each tally in his head. The shepherds and the shearers would be counting too but when their numbers were checked it was always Dad's they matched. He could draw too; did a fair sketch of a horse's head once. I wished I'd told him about the time when I was nineteen and the boss took crook and I had to sort the two-tooths from the hoggets and the wethers, how when the boss checked my work he said he couldn't have done a better job.'

When all the guests had gone, Ned stuck his head round the bedroom door and found Liz sleeping on Max's side. He took off her shoes and spread the rug over her. She opened her eyes and smiled.

'You did Dad proud,' he said and she smiled and closed her eyes.

Quotes

P. 7 Śāntideva, *The Bodhicaryāvatāra*, 'The Perfection of Forbearance'

P. 12 Han Yu (my reworking of a translation from an unknown source); Walter J. Willis, 24ᵗʰ Battalion, quoted in *Myth and Reality* by John McLeod

P. 30 Ryokan, 'The moon in the window' (my reworking of the translation by John Stevens in *Dewdrops on a Lotus Leaf*)

P. 35 Ryokan, 'Pine needles on my doorstep' (my reworking of the translation by John Stevens in *Dewdrops on a Lotus Leaf*)

P. 48 Walter J. Willis, from a letter to Alwyn Hewitt, quoted in Susan Jacobs, *In Love and War*

P. 52 XI *Rubáiyát of Omar Khayyám*, trans. Edward Fitzgerald

P. 82 G. Theotokas, diary entry for 6 January 1943, quoted in Mark Mazower, *Inside Hitler's Greece*

P. 97 from *The Iliad of Homer*, translated by Richmond Lattimore; XLVII *Rubáiyát of Omar Khayyám*, trans. Edward Fitzgerald

Pp. 110-11 'Tell me the old, old story', Katherine Hankey

P. 114 from Alfredo Bordin, *Sette Uomini Sotto le Stelle* (my translation)

P. 131 from John Donne, 'The Hill of Truth'

P. 132 from Phil Baxter, 'Piccolo Pete'

P. 152 from Viktor E. Frankl, *Man's Search for Meaning*

P. 182 from Giancarlo Vianello, an email to the author (my translation based on a google translation); from Rose Mannering, *100 Harvests*

P. 202 from *Hawke's Bay Herald Tribune*, 1 May 1947

P. 234 Wang Wei (my reworking of a translation from an unknown source)

Postscript

When Giancarlo Vianello posted a page from his father's book *Sette Uomini Sotto Le Stelle* to a Facebook thread in March 2021, I found out that the dialogue had been printed in red. I explained to him that while I'd been aware of the existence of the book in the late 1950s I had no recollection of having seen it: the translation or the original.

I had made notes of a few of the stories in the 1970s. In 1989, I began to make drafts of them, but it wasn't till 2007 that I got on with it in earnest. I rang my aunt: she didn't know what had happened to the book, either the original or the translation. I translated the several words of the title I could recall, googled them and found there were copies in several Italian libraries. For the cost of photocopying and postage, the Biblioteca Nazionale Centrale in Roma kindly sent me a black and white photocopy of the 1970 edition (the 1945 edition was considered too fragile).

Anyway, Giancarlo said he would send me a copy . . . purtroppo ne ho poche copie, ma sara mia premura recuperarne una e spedirla ad Auckland. Visto che tua padre e fra i protagonisti del libro, chi dovrebbe possederne una copia? Certamente tu! In fact he sent me two copies: one of each edition.

Appendix

This letter, found among his father's papers, also comes courtesy of Giancarlo Vianello:

508 Alexandra St.
Hastings
Hawke's Bay
New Zealand
9-3-47

Dear Alfred,

I do not understand your language well enough to be able to use it in writing to you but I feel sure you will find someone who can translate this for you.

You must excuse me for not writing to you much sooner, but, as we say, better late than never. Perhaps you will be interested to know something of what happened to the six 'uomini sotto le stelle' to whom you, your wife and friends were so very kind.

When the three of us who remained at Conchi [Conche] were captured we were taken to the casermo near the church of Sant' Antonio and were there for a week. Then by train to Mantova where we spent a night and the following day were put on a train to Germany. We attempted to escape by cutting a hole in the bottom of the wagon but unfortunately were discovered and two guards with machine guns stayed in the wagon with [sic] for the rest of the journey which was most uncomfortable as we were so crowded it was impossible to sit down and had to stand for three nights and two and a half days. When we had been in Germany for some months two of the three men that went to Piove di Sacco came to the camp. They had been caught attempting to reach Switzerland. (Roberto e Jacimo)

From that camp in Germany we each went to different working

camps and (Roberto vecchio) was the only one I saw until the war was over and I got to England.

We were in England for two months before returning home.

Unfortunately Tomaso must have been discovered as a prisoner of war while in Italy for our authorities have been unable to trace him so he is presumed to have been killed there.

Roberto (giovane), Jacimo and myself are now married and although we live too far apart to visit one another Roberto and I write to each [sic]. I have not seen or had news of the other two since returning home.

When I have received an answer from you and know your address definitely I will send you some illustrated papers & photographs.

Do not be concerned about answering in Italian as there are several Italians living in this town and I know one of them. He would translate your letter for me.

Do you remember the watch I gave you which you were going to have repaired for me? My mother and father gave it to me before I went to the war. If it were not for this fact I would not be concerned about it, but if you still have it could you send it to me. If through il fortuna di guerra you have lost it do not worry about it. I hope that you will write soon, that you, your wife son and brother are well and happy. Please convey my regards to your friend – my friend who always came with you to see us. I do not know his name.

If you are ever in Conchi will you tell the people who were kind to us that I often think of them and remember their kindness with gratitude.

Your sincere friend
William Lindsay.
(Rosso)

Acknowledgments

Max Gunn's Pay Book is based on stories and references my father, William Lindsay, made to his experiences in the 1940s and on research.

Many people have supported this project in various ways: David Barry, David Birch, Hannalore Daniger, Catherine Day, Brenda Hayes, Rowan Ingram and Christine Apel, Phil Knott, Daniel Lubecki, Konstantina Miskioti, Vassilios Miskiotis, Gaylene Preston, Chris Pugsley, Colin Read, Glyn Strange, Don Trask, Ken Wright.

I am indebted to Susan Jacobs particularly for putting me in touch with Adolfo Zamboni; to Adolfo Zamboni for his considerable research assistance and for putting me in touch with Gianni Pozzato (an historian of the Conche area) and Alfredo Bordin's son, Giancarlo Vianello; to Giancarlo Vianello for sharing his memories of his parents and his grandmother Carolina Emilio Donà; to the proprietors of the Hotel Achilles in Methoni for information about the warehouse where the POWs were held after disembarking from the wreck of the *Jason* and for translating the comments made by the grandfather of one of them who as a boy had been taken by his mother to see the wreck; to my cousins Janice Cooke and her husband Lawrence for information about my uncle Alex; to my cousin Robert Frame for his recollections of Larkhall; to Edwin and Russell Gallagher for making available the unpublished diary of their father Eric Gallagher; to Jean McIver for assistance in tracking down the 'miniature' train that carried the POWs up the Peloponnese; to Tracy Pilet for her generous provision of information about her great uncle, Earle Pickering, who died on Crete; to John Sunley for his incisive recollections of Grasmere orchard and fellow veterans; to Delyth Sunley for copies of her father's photographs of Grasmere; to Karen White for sharing her research on Grasmere; to Patsy and Reg White for showing me around the Grasmere orchard and the house that had been my father's for a short time; to my brother Robert for his advice and recollections; to my partner Roslyn Norrie for making possible our visits to various locations in Europe for the purposes of 'ocular research' and for her support and advice.

I would also like to thank the following institutions for their assistance: Alexander Turnbull Library, Aotearoa NZ Centre Christchurch City Library, Bergbaumuseum in Lugau (Dagmar Borchert), Defence Library HQ NZDF, Hastings Library (Veronika Hogan), IWM (Sally Richards), John Kinder Theological Library (Nick Wotton), Kew National Archives, Museum Moosburg (Bernhardt Kersher), National Army Museum (Dolores Ho), New Zealand Defence Force Personnel Archives (Pete Connor), Old Town Hall and Margate Museum, Spitfire and Hurricane Memorial Museum at Manston, WordReference Forums.

Acknowledgements are also due to Michele Leggott and nzepc for the publication of an earlier draft of one of the chapters in Six Pack Sound # 6 and to the English Department of the University of Canterbury and Creative New Zealand for the award of the Ursula Bethell Residency in Creative Writing for 2004. And lastly, to the team at Lasavia Publishing (Rowan, Daniela, Mike and Innes) for their hospitality, foresight and expertise.

Selected sources

A Strange Alliance, Roger Absalom; 'Te Rauparaha', Robert Richie Alexander, 1966 Encyclopedia of New Zealand; *Get Rommel*, Michael Asher; *Hitler's Digger Slaves*, Alex Barnett; *Sette Uomini Sotto le Stelle*, Alfredo Bordin; *City of the Plains*, M B Boyd; *A Tale of Two Battles*, Geoffrey Cox; *No Honour No Glory*, Spence Edge and Jim Henderson; *The Sharp End*, John Ellis; Stalag VIIA 1939-1945, Moosburg on the Isar River, ed. Herbert Franz; *POW*, Adrian Gilbert; *The Barbed-Wire University*, Midge Gillies; *Farewell Campo 12*, James Hargest; *Fernleaf Cairo*, Alex Hedley; *The Quest for Origins*, K R Howe; *Last Line of Defence, The Desert Road, Inside Stories*, edited by Megan Hutching; *Fighting with the Enemy*, Susan Jacobs; *Haka*, Timoti Kāretu; *POW*, David Kidd; *Petrol Company*, A L Kidson; *All Blacks Don't Cry*, John Kirwan; *Blasting and Bombardiering*, Wyndham Lewis; *Hitler's British Slaves*, Sean Longden; *100 Harvests: A History of Fruitgrowing in Hawke's Bay*, Rose Mannering; *Inside Hitler's Greece*, Mark Mazower; *The Lost Battle*, Callum MacDonald; *Death Raft*, Alexander McKee; *Myth and Reality*, John McLeod; *The Relief of Tobruk*, W E Murphy; *Documents from the Battle and the Resistance of Crete*, George I Panagiotakis; *Pylos – Pylia: A journey through Space and Time*, George and Thanos Papathanassopoulos; *25 Battalion*, Edward Puttick; *In the Bag*, Peter Ogilvie and Newman Robinson; *The Master: J.D.Ormond of Wallingford: A Family Portrait*, Rosamond Rolleston; *Two Worlds*, Anne Salmond; *Expendable*, Peter Winter.

Websites, archives, films: AIF POW Free men in Europe – B. PG57 – Udine/Gruppignano; *Lion of the Desert*, Moustapha Akkad (film); 238th All Black Test, Allblacks.com; Rebecca Anderson 'Shell Shock' (*Molecular Interventions* Vol 8 issue 5); Anzac POW freemen in Europe (www.anzacpow.com); *Ka Mate*, John Archer (draft version, 2009, PDF online); unpublished diary of Eric Gallagher; The Haka, It's Meaning and origin (www.kawhia.maori.nz); Deed of settlement of Historical Claims – Heretaunga Tamatea and Trustees of the Heretaunga Tamatea Settlement Trust and The Crown; Hawke's Bay. Native Lands

Alienation Commission – Report of Inquiry into the Heretaunga Purchase| NZETC; Letters to family, Ian Thomas Young Johnston, 1912 – (MS-papers-7852-01, Alexander Turnbull Library); (Private Papers, IWM) of Reverend R G McDowall; (periodical) *New Zealand Farmer*, March 1896; New Zealand Military Forces History Sheet for William Lindsay; (www.ngatitoa.iwi.nz) Te Rauparaha, Steven Oliver; Papers Past (www.paperspast.natlib.govt.nz); *Home by Christmas*, Gaylene Preston (film); (NZETC) *War Surgery and Medicine*, Thomas D.M. Stout; Television New Zealand's Television Archive (video) *NZ vs France 1st Test 1989*; articles on Te Rauparaha at www.ngatitoa.iwi.nz, www.kawhia. maori.nz; (unpublished ms) 'My Interesting Four Years 1940-1944', L. J. Read; 'Muted violence: Italian war crimes in occupied Greece', Lidia Santarelli, *Journal of Modern Italian Studies* Vol 9 Issue 3 2004; 'The One That Didn't Get Away', J.H. Witte (unpublished m.s., IWM); WO 2/113 concerning casualties from Allied Air attacks; WO 204/Y05 'NZ Field Censorship Section'; WO224/136 PG 85; WO 311/346 and other references at MD/JAG/FS/42/110 'Conche di Codevigo, Padua, Italy: killing of New Zealand POW'; WO311/1286 'General Charge – Ill Treatment of POW at Arachia (Phonetic) Camp nr Patras'; WO 361/133 'Casualties at Sea: Middle East; Italian vessels carrying British Prisoners of War ...'; 'Report of Inspection of Prisoners of War Camp No. 65' (Gravina), Leonardo Trippi.

Context: You Can't Get Much Closer Than This, Andrew Z Adkins, Jr and Andrew Z. Adkins, 111; *A Woman in Berlin*, Anonymous; *Captain Corelli's Mandolin*, Louis de Bernières; *Poor People Poor Us*, John Evelyn Broad; *Crete*, Dan Davin; *The Diary of Anne Frank*, Anne Frank; *Life and Fate*, Vassily Grossman; *Defying Hitler*, Sebastian Haffner; *Passage to Tobruk*, Francis Jackson; *The Trial*, Franz Kafka; *A Crowd is not a Company*, Robert Kee; Diary of Gilbert M H Knott (CD); *The Strategic Bombing of Germany*, Alan J Levine; *If this is a Man* and *The Truce*, Primo Levy; *The Cross and the Arrow*, Albert Maltz; *The 'Signor Kiwi' Saga*, Florence N. Millar; *And when did you last see your father?*, Blake Morrison; *Report on Experience*, John Mulgan; *Love and War in the Appenines*, Eric Newby; *The Road to Wigan Pier*, George Orwell; *The Reader*, Bernhardt Schlink; *Dewdrops on a Lotus Leaf*, John Stevens; James Steel Diary (http:// kiwisoldier); *The Pianist*, Wladyslaw Szpilman; *"The Good War"*, Studs Terkel; *Das Lugau-Oelsnitzer Steinkohlenrevier*, Rolf Vogel; *The Camomile Lawn*, Mary Wesley.

Also by the Author

Poetry
Thousand-Eyed Eel
Public
Big Boy
Return to Earth
The Subject
Legend of the Cool Secret
Lazy Wind Poems

Edited
Morepork 1-3

Graham is the author of seven poetry books and the one-time editor and publisher of a literary periodical. He has a degree in English, a diploma in teaching, and was the Ursula Bethell Resident in Creative Writing in 2004. Max Gunn's Pay Book is his first novel. He enjoys reading, brisk walks, and designing gardens. Of English and Scottish descent, he grew up in the lower half of the North Island, but now lives in Northland on an acre of native trees and tropical fruits. He has lived in all of New Zealand's major cities, as well as in Essex for a decade, from where he travelled throughout Europe and the Mediterranean, visiting sites that feature in this novel.

Printed in Australia
Ingram Content Group Australia Pty Ltd
AUHW021630140224
390404AU00002B/4

9 781991 083098